Wakening
THE
Crow

Stephen Gregory

SOLARIS

First published 2014 by Solaris
an imprint of Rebellion Publishing Ltd,
Riverside House, Osney Mead,
Oxford, OX2 0ES, UK

www.solarisbooks.com

US ISBN: 978 1 78108 242 3
UK ISBN: 978 1 78108 241 6

Designed & typeset by
Rebellion Publishing

REBELLION

Printed in the US

for Tony and Rauni, with love

Prologue

CHLOE HAD HER tongue stuck onto Robin Hood's thigh.

She'd run off as soon as we turned the corner and she saw the statue ahead of us. Before I could call out to stop her, she'd leaned up to lick the smooth green bronze, and her tongue had stuck.

January 11th, one of the coldest days in memory. In the shade of the castle gatehouse, it was minus five or six. The cobbles were gleaming black ice. The ivy on the castle wall was frosted hard, as though cast in the same bronze as the statue, and the pansies in the municipal flower beds had collapsed into lifelessness.

Why do children want to lick everything? Why do they need to explore their strange new universe by licking? And Chloe, not an inquisitive toddler anymore but a bonny seven-year-old, why was she still wanting to stick out her tongue and...?

I ran up to her, a bit out of breath because the air was so sharp in my throat, a bit wary on the treacherous cobbles and nicely fuddled by the beer I'd had in the Ye Olde Trip to Jerusalem. She was moaning, half afraid and half laughing. She had her tongue pressed on the outlaw's bare, muscular thigh, it had stuck because of the cold and she didn't dare move. But with my arms wrapped around her, my face in her hair and her funny red bobble-hat, we both started giggling and I was muttering for heaven's sake Chloe what on earth are you doing, and my beery breath was close to her bluey-chapped lips and her mouth which smelled of the chips we'd had in the pub...

Together we thawed the air enough to unfasten her kiss from the freezing metal.

We sat on the edge of the flower bed and we giggled and snuggled. She pushed out her tongue at me, and it was raw where the ice had burned her. She stared into my face, she smiled her blank, angelic smile, and she said nothing.

Chloe, a perfect, silent angel. She hadn't said anything for nearly a year.

This was one of her favourite places. Our little day out together: a morning on the boat, then a walk from the canal to the pub for lunch, and afterwards up the hill to the castle gatehouse and hugging the legs of the Robin Hood statue. Down to Broadmarsh and the bus station and a bus back home. Oh, and I might drop in to see what odd and occult treasures Mr. Heap might have saved for me.

Heaps. I said Heaps, she seemed to recognise the word and she tugged me away from the derelict flowers and the looming shadows of the gatehouse; an old corner of Nottingham, where the cobbled streets were narrow and winding against the massy boulder on which the castle was built, by the offices of solicitors and architects with their leaded windows and peculiar turrets... and when I said Heaps again, she pulled me into the shop doorway.

It was dark and warm inside. Only a tiny ground-floor, it was a chaotic jumble of books and pictures and engravings and curios. There was a fire glowing in the hearth, and as we tumbled inside and I quickly pushed the door shut, the coals collapsed into a shower of sparks, brightened into flames and breathed a cloud of soot into the room.

The man I called Mr. Heap appeared from behind his desk in the corner. He was very small and thin and wrinkly-ancient, as though he'd been huddling in his shop for decades or centuries and become mummified inside it, smoked and desiccated like the maps and manuscripts he'd accumulated around him. In faded gold letters on the shop window it said Heaps, and I'd never been sure if it referred to this man or the clutter of stuff in his shop. So when he emerged from the darkness and I said, as always, 'Good afternoon, Mr. Heap,' and he just nodded, I reckoned, as always, that that was his name.

I poked around. The warmth and the dust seemed to fold around my head and neck, pleasant at first after the sub-zero temperature outside, but then it was too hot and oddly suffocating. I was looking for books, but there was nothing different since our last visit. The buzz of beer in my head, which had been comfortably numbing in the frozen shadows of the castle, was more of a fug, the beginning of an afternoon hangover. I straightened up, from an avalanche of mildewed tomes and tatty paperbacks. Chloe was standing by the fire and staring into it, utterly silent, her eyes gleaming and her mouth fixed into its permanent, lovely smile... lost in thought, lost somewhere, lost in the locked-away memories she'd inhabited for the last nine months.

'She doesn't say much,' Mr. Heap said.

'She doesn't say anything,' I said. 'She just smiles.'

The man angled his head towards the little girl, frowned and then squeezed his eyes shut as though he was trying to remember something he'd heard or read a long long time ago. And then, reading my own thoughts and echoing them almost exactly, he murmured, 'She seems lost... and yet, even with the utterly lost, to whom life and death are equally jests, there are...' and he paused, opened his eyes and blinked at me and muttered, 'I can't remember, it's a quote from somewhere or someone.'

To lighten the moment, because on several of our previous visits to his shop the old man had commented on Chloe's silence, I ventured to tell him how she'd stuck her tongue onto Robin Hood's thigh and maybe that was why, today, she was so quiet. He smiled, disbelieving. He made a dry chuckling noise in his throat, and for the first time I saw that, among the reptilian wrinkles of his skin, there was a flicker of mischief in his eyes and on his lizard lips. Chloe heard him. She swivelled her head and held him with her gaze for a few seconds, before turning back to her communion with the fire.

'Come on then, Chloe,' I said at last, putting my hands on her shoulders. 'Let's not get too cosy in Mr. Heap's shop. It's

going to get dark outside and even colder, and we've got to hurry and catch our bus home.'

Indeed, as I pulled the door open, the fierce air of a January afternoon seemed to pounce into the room. The cold, or another puther of smoke from the fire, provoked the old man into a flurry of movement.

'Got it...' he was saying, 'it reminded me, yes, the utterly lost and all that, I was trying to remember where I'd seen the little girl before. Here, let me give you something...'

He'd rummaged behind his counter and come out with something in his hand. He pressed it towards me, saying, 'Here, take it, I'd forgotten all about it, but I've been keeping it for you and for your little girl and waiting for you to come back again...'

I took it from him. It was a little box covered in black velvet, a jeweller's box for a ring or a brooch or some other kind of trinket.

'Go on, take a look,' he was saying, 'and hurry up, you're letting the cold in... it may be something or nothing, but it's got a story and who knows if it's true or just a bit of nonsense or...'

I opened the box. Nestling on a bed of silver satin, there was a yellowing fragment of something. Something like bone or horn. A relic? I peered closer, held it to my face, squinted and sniffed, and for a moment, almost put out my tongue to touch it.

'What is it?' I said. 'What's the story?'

But by then he'd manoeuvred us outside and closed the door. Through the darkened window, I saw him cross to the fire and stand over it, a dim, wizened figure in the glow of the flames, in a swirl of soot.

I snapped the jewel box shut, pushed it deep into the pocket of my coat. I reached for Chloe and squeezed her hand. The ice seemed to nibble at our faces as we hurried down the narrow street and into the brightness of the big city.

Chapter One

Nine months? A year? To be exact, it was last April 3rd, a beautiful springtime afternoon, when Chloe had last spoken... before she'd been touched with a strange, random and rather brutal magic wand which had shocked her into a secret world of silence and smiles.

The last thing she'd said? My wife, Rosie, asked me many times to recount how it happened: what Chloe was doing, what I was doing, what I'd said to her and what Chloe had said. I never told her the exact words, Chloe's parting pithy words before she was touched by fate and switched off.

April 3rd. It must have been a Saturday because I was looking after Chloe, otherwise she would've been at school. A Saturday, yes, and Rosie was at work, her bustling busy-body work as a dental assistant at Dowling & McCorrister, one of the biggest, smartest practices in Nottingham. So I had Chloe. No, not sweet, angelic, utterly amenable Chloe. I had rude, petulant and defiantly uncooperative Chloe. And I was manning, as far as I ever manned anything, Erewash borough council's mobile library. That was my job of work. Six days a week I drove the library, a creaking, swaying old Commer van weighed down with hundreds of books on their sagging shelves, from one corner of the county to the other, stopping in village car parks and schoolyards, in town centres and leafy lay-bys, parking and waiting and serving the public.

My last words to Chloe, on that April afternoon? 'Chloe, don't do that... do you have to do that? Why are you torturing the poor thing? It's...'

I didn't mind the job. Five days a week I enjoyed the trundling around and the scenic stops and the odd enthusiasms of my customers. I had time, my own time. I could sit in my travelling room-full of books and brew a coffee or a mug of soup... on breezy bright days and gloomy dark days, on sparkling mornings with the door thrown open or torrential thundering afternoons with the door pulled shut and the van all cosy and steamed up... and I could read. I could fire my own enthusiasms, even if the fire was short-lived and fizzled and smouldered and went out. A dead-end, poorly-paid job, but it was alright, it was a world of my own, for five days a week.

But on Saturdays I had Chloe.

Saturday, 3rd April, and I'd parked in the middle of Breaston, a village about ten or twelve miles east of Nottingham, on the old Derby road. Breaston, with a modest, perfectly unassuming church in its own close, the Bull's Head across the way, a Co-op and a fish 'n' chip shop, a primary school and a community centre... just the neatest and nicest of English villages which never a tourist would need to visit.

'What's so great about saxophones anyway?' She'd been niggling at me, with a whining, wheedling edge on her voice. 'You got your head stuck in that book and you'll never learn to play a saxophone anyway. What is a saxophone anyway?'

So yes, I'd been ignoring her. I wouldn't say neglecting her. In fact I'd already sent her across to the pub with a five-pound note and she'd come back with a huge bottle of lemonade and an assortment of crisps and nasty cheesy crackers.

And then a wasp flew into the van. We'd been parked an hour, and not a single person had come to the library although we were there at my scheduled time on my scheduled day. But then a wasp came in.

Chloe flapped at it, screaming horribly and hysterically as though she were a surfer in the jaws of a great white shark. Her bottle fizzled into her lap. Crisps and cheeselets, a bag burst open. Only a wasp, but Chloe was screaming. I shouldn't

have laughed, but I did. To escape her swiping and yelling, the wasp dived into the top of her shirt and burrowed down, to find a bit of peace and quiet from her unnecessary violence. And then it stung her, in what it must have thought was the safety of her armpit.

She peeled off her shirt. Though I say it myself, she was a pudgy, rather horrid little girl. She was squeaking and snivelling as if the puncture wound she'd received from the wasp would actually kill her, she might pop and go whizzing around the inside of the library and out of the door and die in the car park, wrinkled up like the rubbery remains of a party balloon. I couldn't help laughing at her. Fatherly, I fumbled at her pants, which were drenched and sticky with lemonade, and she recoiled with a sneer of disgust. So when she caught the wasp and extracted its poor crumpled frame from under her arm, she grabbed the book from under my nose and pressed the insect onto it... and there, on top of a diagram of the saxophone I was daydreaming of learning to play one day, she started to pull off the wings of her attacker and flick them one by one out of the open door.

At which point I asked her what she was doing, and why. She answered, 'Fuck off, Dad, you can see what I'm doing. Because it fucking stung me, that's why.'

And then she flung the remains of the wasp out of the door, flung the book onto the floor, and flung herself outside as well. 'Fuck you, Dad, and keep your hands out of my pants... I'll tell Mum, I'll tell her...'

Best to ignore her, I thought. She was a spoilt, fatty kid, grazing and gorging and whingeing when she had hundreds of nice books to choose from.

I retrieved the saxophone book, wiped off the crumbs and dabbed at the ooze of fluid she'd squeezed from the body of the wasp. Just as I ducked to the floor to try and grab her bottle before all of the liquid spilled out, I heard an engine revving loudly and I sat up and looked out of the window.

It all happened in a second or two.

There was Chloe, smearing at her tears of anger and frustration and huffing away from my van in the direction of the Co-op... oddly half-nude, a cherub with baby tits. A car came out of the pub's back-yard, a neat little Triumph, dark blue with wire wheels and the soft-top folded down, and a good-looking young couple in it. Squabbling... I could see in an instant, they'd had a few drinks and a row in the Bull's Head and hustled out into the sunshine, still snarling and spitting at each other.

The woman was driving. She was turning to the man to say something and then squirming away from a hurtful retort. And there was Chloe, as the woman accelerated so sharply the tyres squealed, Chloe, squatting down and rubbing at her eyes with one hand, holding her wounded armpit with the other.

No, the car didn't hit her. Not exactly.

Just in time, the woman saw Chloe and swerved to miss her. Didn't quite miss. The wing mirror, protruding from the car on a chromium-plated stalk, slapped the little girl smartly and very hard, flat on the back of her head.

That was all. The impact made a sharp metallic ping. Chloe wobbled for a moment and fell very slowly forwards, onto both her knees and even more slowly face down into the ground. There she lay, very still.

The car stopped. Only for a second or two. There was another snarling moment, the man and the woman literally at each other's throat. With a crunch of gears, she floored the throttle and the car went snaking around the corner and roared into the distance.

Chapter Two

IT WAS VERY warm on the bus back home. When we'd first clambered on, at the Broadmarsh bus station in the middle of Nottingham, we'd been so cold we'd huddled together on a cosy seat at the back and felt a lovely thawing in our hands and faces. By the time we were passing the castle, its enormous cave-riddled boulder glowing in yellow floodlights, Chloe had pulled off her bobble-hat and I was undoing the buttons on my coat. Her blonde hair smelled of the cold and the smoke of the city. I kissed her nose, pretended to grimace at the iciness of it, and she smiled and suddenly sneezed. Through Beeston and Chilwell, past the golf course and the army depot, past Attenborough and Toton, we were almost too warm, basking in the hot air blowing from the vents beneath the seat.

And it got dark. January, deep mid-winter, and freezing dark by five o'clock in the afternoon.

I watched Chloe. She sat beside me and she just stared and smiled into her own reflection in the window. And my thoughts returned to that day in April, when she'd been so changed.

As always, since that time and every moment of her new life and my new life since it had happened, I felt a stabbing of guilt. No, a gnawing, as if the blame I'd attached to myself was eating me, like a cancer deep inside my belly. So yes, I'd deliberately ignored my daughter, when she'd tumbled tearfully out of the library van. But then – PTO 725G, and 3.17 – something chemical in my brain, when I witnessed the accident through my window, had made me imprint the car's registration number on my memory, made me glance for a millisecond at the clock and log the exact time... some extraordinary instinct

for self-preservation which made me think that, by noting these details, I'd be accounted responsible and cool-headed and my momentary negligence might be overlooked.

I'd run outside. People were running out of the Co-op. The landlord hurried out of his pub. I knelt next to Chloe and turned her gently onto her side. She was unconscious. A little breath bubbled from her mouth. There was a gush of blood from her right nostril.

An ambulance was there in no time, and the paramedics had Chloe and me inside it and racing out of the village minutes later. They were reassuring, I'd described what had happened: no, she hadn't been knocked down by a car, she'd been struck by the wing-mirror of a car going no more than ten or maybe twenty miles per hour... and they said she might be alright, she'd had a bang on the back of the head and no other injuries. We sped out of Breaston village. With the siren wailing and the blue lights flashing, we barely paused for any other traffic, only a momentary hold-up in Long Eaton, for a back-up of cars and police and some kind of incident outside the gates of Derwent College. I'd called ahead to Rosie. She was waiting at the Queen's Medical Centre in Nottingham when we arrived at the entrance to A & E.

'Oh god... where's her shirt?' Rosie's first question as we marched down the corridors of the hospital on either side of the child's trolley.

'In the library van,' I answered.

'Where's the library van?'

'In Breaston. That's where it happened. She got stung by a wasp and she...'

'A wasp? She got stung by a wasp? Oh god...'

It didn't take long for a nice Indian doctor to examine Chloe and get her into X-ray. He too was reassuring, suggesting she was concussed, she was young and strong and if the X-ray was alright she'd wake up with a cracking headache and in the next few days she'd have the most amazing black eyes we'd ever seen, like a panda. A young policeman took me into an interview

room. I recounted everything in the most meticulous detail and he wrote it all down in his note-books. Rosie was there too, interjecting, her interrogation more fierce and accusing than his.

A wasp? So if Chloe took off her shirt and she was upset, why did I let her just run out of the van? Didn't I try to comfort her, take a look at the sting, put something on it? Why didn't I take her across to the Co-op and get some kind of ointment or cream to put on the sting? Why did I let her just run out of the van, without her shirt on, into the road, by the pub carpark, with a couple of drunks coming out and not even stopping, the bastard hit-and-run drunk drivers...?

The policeman put his hand on her arm. He made shushing noises. He'd noted how vigilant I must have been, he was impressed by the exactness of my statement, he was sure her husband had been perfectly attentive. Yes, there'd been an accident, but fortunately the impact had been relatively slight and...

She swatted his hand off her arm, as defensive as Chloe had been with the wasp. She was asking him if they'd got the car and the hit-and-run drivers I'd described so precisely, when another policeman opened the door. With an upward jerk of his head, a flash of anxious eyes in my direction, he beckoned his young colleague to come outside.

We followed. We pushed past the police, who'd gathered into a tight knot so they could talk into their walkie-talkies, we pressed ourselves to the walls of the corridor as another emergency came in and two more trolleys hurtled by, the dead-or-alive casualties of another momentary carelessness... and we hurried back to the doctor, who, as he'd predicted, had the good news that Chloe had suffered no real damage to her skull, she was badly concussed and would very likely be fine in a matter of days.

So. Overwhelmed by relief, we sat with Chloe in an observation ward and she lay there as though blissfully asleep. The nurses had cleaned the blood from her nose, and Rosie had bathed her daughter's forehead with a cool cloth and brushed

her lovely blonde hair. Outside our room, where the three of us were swaddled in a cotton-wool world of thankfulness and exhausted anxiety, the business of A & E went on. There was a flurry of activity, the arrival of yet another ambulance and trolleys rattling past our door, the drama of life and death barely inches from where we were sitting. We didn't really care. We were safe. Chloe was safe.

'Hey, wake up now. We're here.'

Now, nine months later, I was on the bus with Chloe. She'd fallen asleep, all her weight slumped against me, in a fuddle of warmth and weariness after a day out in the bitter January cold. She groaned and wriggled and opened her eyes. When she looked up and straight away her face formed her new Chloe smile, all sweetness and fragile innocence since the day of her accident, for a moment I thought she was going to speak. She opened her lips, she fixed me with her level, penetrating stare, and for an unnerving split-second I braced myself for what she might say. But she didn't speak. I felt a shudder of guilty relief. As the bus slowed and stopped, I helped her to her feet with her bobble-hat stuck on top of her head and we jumped down onto the pavement.

DERWENT COLLEGE, THE massive stone pillars of its gate, on the Derby Road, in Long Eaton. We had a short walk to our new home, to the church at the top of Shakespeare Street.

Chloe was wide-awake again. After the cosiness of the bus, we were both jolted awake by the shock of the cold, still freezing and promising another night of the hardest frost. It was pitchy-dark, and yet only five in the afternoon, and the road was busy with a never-pausing, never-slowing line of traffic coming out of town.

'Hey Chloe, let's go...' I took hold of Chloe's hand and tried to tug her away from the bus-stop, along the slippery pavement. She resisted. 'Hey let's go, we're going to freeze out here... what you got?'

She was bending to the hedgerow, a wiry wall of holly and privet up to the very pillars of the college gate. Darkness and light, the deadliness of January and the orange and yellow and spangling headlamps of the passing cars... the beams of the traffic caught a glitter of reflections, like jewels, in the bottom of the holly hedge.

'Pretty,' I said, 'is it frozen, is it ice?' And to humour her, to allow her one more special, little girl's moment to add to all the special moments of our day-out, we bent together to see the treasure she had discovered.

Broken glass. One of the students, returning to his digs after an illicit evening in town, must've dropped a beer bottle and kicked it into the hedgerow. No, it was clear glass, fragments of a shattered windscreen, crazed into angles and facets and diamond brightness. A council workman, too lazy to sweep it up and into a bin, had shovelled it out of sight, back in the summer when the holly was dense. And the black plastic splinters of a car's number plate. An accident, back in the springtime...

'Careful, Chloe... no...'

But before I could stop her, she reached into the glass and grasped it in her hand. She held the jewels on her open palm, stared at them in wonder, and then squeezed them so hard that prickles of blood stood out on her skin.

I knew what it was. Chloe couldn't have known. She squeezed again, with all her strength, and then opened her palm and shook the bloody jewels out.

Chapter Three

SOME OF THEM must have stuck to her skin, because, a day or two later, I found them in the pocket of her coat when I was putting it into the washing machine.

Seven o'clock on a Monday morning. Rosie was leaving for work.

It was still dark outside. Not snowing. Too cold for snow. It was warm and cosy in our new home, there was toast and marmalade and coffee and Radio 4 and I was going to stay home with Chloe. So Rosie, buttoning herself into her coat, wrapping a scarf around her neck, pulling the flaps of a weird Peruvian hat over her ears and about to set off into the bitterness of a January morning and walk twenty minutes to work... Rosie had the unmistakable aura of martyrdom about her.

'So have a nice day, you two,' she said pointedly. 'What are you going to do, a bit of playing shop, maybe a jolly outing? A bit of writing, I doubt it.'

Rosie. Never a sylph when I'd first met her, now she was more than plump. Was it Titian or Raphael who'd painted women like her? She had a certain fullness of figure, and now, in many layers of clothing and that extraordinary hat, she looked... she looked extraordinary, not so much voluptuous as voluminous. Her pointy, pink mousy face was already flushed before she'd even set off... yes, she was still cute and certainly womanly, but there was a bit of busy-body Beatrix Potter about her. And the woundedness, of course.

'Oliver, I don't know why you're putting a wash on, how do you think it's going to get dry on a day like this? If you put it in

the airing-cupboard you'll steam up the whole place... anyway, up to you. Me, I'm off to work and back about five, I guess.'

She gave me a kiss on the cheek. She smelled of jasmine, a spray I'd bought her for Christmas. And then, leaving me aside, she leaned down to the child.

She gathered Chloe into her body. She seemed to envelop her in the many folds of her clothing and the very being of her motherhood, as though she could go back in time and make her, once again, a physical part of herself – to start again, to protect her with her life, to keep her from all the harms and nonsensical accidents of the outside world.

And she whispered, as always, 'My dear Chloe, where are you?' Every day, she said it every day, like some kind of prayer, a mantra. 'My Chloe, I miss you so much. When will I ever have you back again? Please, please come back to me...'

Then she was gone, dabbing tears from her eyes, down the stairs and out into the midnight darkness of a January morning: Rosie, my wife, longing for the difficult, challenging, combative daughter who'd been taken from her and might never return... leaving me in a turmoil of my own doubts and suspicions.

I heard the door close. I heard Rosie's footsteps, down below on the pavement outside. I tried to silence the mad mutterings in my head, but I couldn't. A notion which had crept into my consciousness over the past months, something mean and unworthy and shameful which I couldn't keep out... I heard it now, ringing like the truth and daring me to deny it. I loved my daughter more, I liked her more, since she'd been changed by the accident.

I looked across the kitchen, where Chloe was silently engrossed in spreading butter and jam on another slice of toast. Even in that, she was smiling. And I saw myself in the mirror. My first ugly instinct was to flinch from my own eyes, but then I made myself look.

You shit, Oliver Gooch. You got it easy now. Chloe gets a smart little whack on the back of the head, and you got it made. Admit it. It's better now, yeah?

'Better for me, is it, Chloe? What do you think?' I didn't expect her to reply. She didn't. She was playing with her mouse.

They'd told me and Rosie to talk to her, to keep on talking and involve her in conversation as though she understood everything we said, and one day, one miraculous moment, she might open her mouth and say something. And of course they enjoined us to engage her with picture books and drawing, with music and stories. Rosie had bought her a mouse. Because, a few weeks or a month after her accident, and she'd recovered marvellously from the blow on her head and was apparently sound in all her limbs, she still hadn't whispered a word. She wasn't the sly, defiant, occasionally foul-mouthed Chloe she'd been before. She couldn't speak. She couldn't read. She just smiled. She blinked and she smiled, in utter, blank, angelic silence. She was lovely, in the same way that a soft and harmless Labrador dog is lovely, but she was altered completely.

And so the doctors, the consultants, the specialists did all their tests on her and pronounced some kind of brain damage, unfortunately, which might be permanent, or she might – one day, with all the energy and stimulus we could apply as parents – she might snap out of it and...

'What do you think, Chloe? Do you think anything? What's going on inside your pretty little head?'

She looked up from her toast and jam. The mouse had run inside her sleeve, I could see the bump of its body snuggling up and up. She smiled and she held a piece of toast towards me, something which the intact Chloe would never have done. I took it from her.

'Thank you, Chloe, that's nice. Yes, better for me.'

Mumbling, my mouth stuffed full, I confronted myself in the mirror, on the opposite wall of the warm, friendly, nice and utterly unchallenging kitchen. I saw Oliver Gooch: hardly an oil-painting, pudgy and unshaven in sloppy pullover and baggy corduroy trousers, a youngish, middle-aged man with receding, thinning dark hair and an odd, questing snout... not

a Titian, not a Raphael, more of a Rembrandt, one of those peasant potato-eaters.

You shit. So what are you going to do today? A bit of writing? I doubt it. Play at shop? Take the angel for another jolly?

I felt again into Chloe's coat pocket. Pieces of glass, like rough-cut diamonds. The windscreen had shattered into hundreds of sparkling gems and some of them were here, on the palm of my hand. I put them onto the kitchen table. Bits of glass with blood. With Radio 4 and toast and marmalade.

She flickered her eyes across them and up to mine.

Then I felt into my coat pocket and took out the little velvet box that Mr. Heap had given me.

'Hey Chloe, it's not even seven-thirty, and we've already got tears and blood and broken glass. I wonder what else we've got here. Let's go and play shop, shall we?'

Chapter Four

WE DIDN'T HAVE to go far. Down the stairs and across the hall, into the front-room. It would've been the vestry. We'd just bought a church.

Oh god, the mouse. Our church mouse, called Mouse. Just as we started down the stairs together, it wriggled out of Chloe's jumper and plopped onto the first step. As it sprang down and down ahead of us, Chloe gave a squeak of surprise and pursued it as fast as she could.

'Hey careful, Chloe, slowly...'

Too late. She'd bundled herself down, hopping on both her feet behind the mouse, and as it reached the bottom and crossed the flagstones of the hallway in a single white flash, she was there too. But she stumbled as she landed two-footed on the final step, she staggered and sprawled forward, face down on the floor.

The mouse was gone. By the time I reached her, Chloe was gathering herself upright again, apparently unhurt, just shaking herself and about to continue her pursuit.

'Hey, clumsy, for heaven's sake take your time... what's up?'

She turned her face up towards mine, smiling through the blood which was welling in her mouth. 'Oh lord, what on earth have you done? Let me see...'

She was fine. She seemed to think it was all rather odd and amusing. She hadn't knocked her mouth on the hard floor, she was just a bit breathless from the impact of landing flat on her tummy. But a loose baby-tooth she'd been wiggling with her tongue for the past few days had popped out, the gasping rough-and-tumble had jarred it out and started a sudden

trickling of blood. By the time I'd swiped at her mouth with a handkerchief, she was wrestling away from my arms and skipping across the hallway and into the vestry.

There she was, amongst all the boxes of books... in and out of the cupboards and cabinets, perfectly entranced by her search for her mouse, just now and then smearing at her face and licking her lips and pressing the tip of her tongue into the tender place where her tooth had been. I'd looked around for the tooth, following a spatter of red spittle which I dabbed into the handkerchief and stuffed back into my pocket, and found it... but it had slipped into a crack into the flagstones too small for my fingers, and I couldn't get it out. I'd come back, I said to myself, I'd come back with something like a pair of pliers and try again. So I followed her into the vestry, where she'd pounced into a dusty corner and was cupping the little creature in her hands.

'You got him. Is he alright, is Mr Mouse alright? And are you alright? What's Mummy going to say when she comes home? Show me...'

We sat on a couple of cardboard boxes and first of all she showed me the mouse. It was an albino. Its fur was strangely translucent, as thought you might see through it and into the myriad workings of its body. Shiny, tinged with a barely visible blush of pink. Red eyes. A pink nose, and such delicate pink ears you could see the tracery of veins. Pink tail and pink feet, altogether it was like a fairyland toy or an expensive, impossibly sweet chocolate. Chloe held it to her lips and kissed it. She left an imprint of her blood on its head. And then, as I put my forefinger on her chin and pressed to open her mouth, I could see the sweet young pinkness of her tongue and the clean, healthy cavity where her tooth had been.

'You'll do. When we go upstairs again we'll give it a good rinse out, and Mummy will be happy...'

I marvelled at her, and what had happened. The new Chloe, all bloody mouth and smiles and giggles and a white mouse with blood on it. So nice and chuckling with an oozy hole in

her gum. What would the old Chloe have been like? A bawling nightmare.

'We could light the fire, hey? On a frosty January morning, just the two of us and a lovely fire...'

We'd bought a church. It was the recently defunct Anglican church at the top of Shakespeare Street, a mile from the town centre. No, not the whole building. As the congregation had dwindled to almost nothing, the commissioners had closed the church and sold it as two parcels. The body of the building was now a furniture warehouse. We'd bought the tower.

It was a new conversion. On the second floor we had our bedrooms and living-room, with views across the town and its leafy suburbs. The first floor was our kitchen-dining-room. And the ground floor...

The doorway of the church opened into a spacious hallway, where the minister used to greet his flock, welcome his Sunday congregations and the weddings and funerals which had taken place in the building for the past hundred years. An entrance hall, where tears of joy and sorrow had been shed, whose stone slabs had been strewn with confetti, puddled with rain and snow, blown with blossom in springtime and autumn leaves...

The vestry was off the hallway. It was small, with a high ceiling, tall clear lancet windows, lovely oak cupboards and shelves where hymnals and prayer books and church music had been stored, and a fireplace. A tiny washroom and toilet. The vestry, where the minister had prepared himself for his services, where he'd lit a fire on chilly mornings and readied himself in front of it.

And it was going to be my bookshop. A specialist outlet of strange and occult and arcane books. The shop I'd daydreamed foolishly about having.

Foolishly daydreaming...

In all my years in the Erewash borough mobile library, I'd been dipping in and out of other people's books, and scribbling my own half-baked ideas and plans and projects and beginnings of poems and stories. I'd spent my time

plucking down other people's pills and capsules of potted knowledge, opening and shutting books and finding their dusty imprint on my fingertips, on my mind, at the end of the day. Of course, sooner or later, I was going to write a book. I was going to write a novel, something so dark and disturbing and demanding of the reader, so odd and unusual and out of the ordinary, so extraordinary that it would carve its own little niche in the genre and be recognised as some kind of minor classic, not necessarily a big-seller, indeed shamefully overlooked, but...

And oh, I was going to have such a dark and dangerous gem of a bookshop that customers would search it out from faraway, for the treasures they might uncover in it.

Two of my daydreams, in the humdrum dreaming-days of the mobile library.

Nice ladies came in and borrowed romantic novels. Out-of-work middle-aged men came in, their clothes smelling of dogs and cigarettes and the cheap alcohol they got from the Co-op. Swotty school-children came in to borrow enormous, brick-sized novels about vampires and wizards. And I was scribbling in my notebook, about the saxophone I'd someday learn to play, the telescope I'd need next winter to explore the frosty night skies, the maps of the coastal walks I'd do next summer, the taxidermy which might be fun. But the two ideas which got fixed and found more and more space in my swarming scribbles were the book I'd write and the bookshop I'd have.

Foolishness. Of course, neither of them would ever happen. How could they? They would need the kind of time and money I could only dream of having.

Until, *ping*.

No, not ping. Harder and heavier than a ping. Not a clang, not a ping, something in-between. How to describe it? I could hear it so clearly in the echoing hollows of my eardrums, in my memory. The impact of the wing-mirror of a Triumph sports-car PTO 725G on the back of Chloe's head, at 3:17 on Saturday 3rd April.

A gift. What had I done to deserve it?

Nothing. Rosie would even say it was my fault. But here I was, Oliver Gooch, on a Monday morning when I used to go to work, with time to play shop. And over there, in another corner of the room, still conveniently hidden by boxes of books I hadn't yet sorted and catalogued and arranged on their shelves, the computer I was going to write my book on.

Yes, the same nice Indian doctor who'd first of all said that Chloe would be alright, who'd declared a month later that she might be brain-damaged for life, had told us we might be eligible for compensation. Tests on the driver of the hit-and-run car had found she'd had a few too many gin and tonics, and we could claim monies for an injury caused by a criminal act. We did claim. There was a substantial pay-out.

Ping. I had money and time. And the sweetest, nicest little daughter to keep me company, to smile agreeably at everything I said and never utter a disparaging word.

'Let's light the fire. Hey, this is going to be nice... what do you think, Chloe? Do you want to help me?

She didn't really help. She couldn't. But she was there and close and warm and smiling, yes, like a Labrador puppy would've been, nuzzling her face towards mine as I arranged a fire-lighter and a few little coals and applied the match. She watched with such a wonder on her face as the flame licked and curled and coaxed the coals alight, and then I added bigger bits of coal and topped it with a log of the silver birch.

Yes, a wonder. The bark sizzled and hissed the perfume of a birchwood faraway in Siberia or Alaska, of deep snow and an ooze of resin and maybe even a tiger or a bear... but actually from a garden-centre in Long Eaton, a smokey suburban town in the midlands of England. Soon the room was warm and fragrant, and me and Chloe, together we could shuffle books and move boxes and open a packet of chocolate biscuits, and, behind the dark-brown voices of Radio 4 drifting down to us from the kitchen, we could hear the traffic going by outside. People going to work. Other people, not me.

'Time for a break, Chloe, we don't want to wear ourselves out, do we?'

I'd opened a box of paperbacks and tipped them out. Nothing really special or unusual, but they would bulk out the shelves and fill up some spaces and sooner or later I'd be going to fairs and car-boot sales and house-clearances and auctions and finding the material which was going to make the shop different. That was what it would need. Or else we'd be just another a funny old bookshop in an old church, and it might take something a bit more different than that to have customers coming in.

And so we sat by our fire. By now it was light outside, a grey glinting metallic light from the black road and the swishing stream of cars and the bare tall trees.

'Let's take a look, Chloe. Remember? Mr. Heap gave me this box. Nice old Mr. Heap, he kept it for us, for me and you and for our shop. Shall I open it, or do you want to?'

We opened it together. The firelight fell on the dark velvet and then the white satin inside, and I picked out the odd little object between the thumb and forefinger of my right hand.

Was it bone? Was it horn? When I held it closer to the flames and we stared at it more closely, I could see that it was a tooth.

Chapter Five

'A RELIC, YES. That's exactly what it is ... and alright, it may be no more real or true than the so-called knuckle-bone of some saint or another, but it's a relic, with a bit of spurious provenance or whatever they call it. And so yes, it's pretty weird and it'll add a nice shiver of excitement to the shop, whenever I open it up and try to get people to come in...'

I'd been looking forward all day to Rosie coming home and showing her the tooth. Later in the afternoon, I'd been out with Chloe to the nearby convenience store and I'd got a bottle of red wine. So that, when Rosie trudged wearily up the stairs and into the kitchen, our dinner was cooking and the bottle was open and breathing, the table was set... and, very thoroughly and carefully, I'd already got Chloe bathed and powdered and into her pyjamas and swaddled in a dressing-gown, her hair glowing golden, her skin fragrant and pink, and, most importantly, her teeth sweetly brushed and we were ready to show off the place from which her wobbly tooth had popped out.

'No, we can't find it,' I'd lied to Rosie. 'It kind of, well, popped out when she was rushing downstairs, chasing the mouse, and when she jumped onto the bottom step she kind of gasped and must've spat the tooth out.'

I didn't say that Chloe had fallen over. I said that I'd looked all over the hallway and couldn't find the tooth and it must have skidded across the floor and slipped into a crack between the flagstones.

We were eating together, the pasta I'd cooked, and we were drinking big glasses of the red wine. Chloe had already eaten

and we'd put her upstairs into bed. The kitchen was very warm. Outside it was freezing harder than before. Rosie had showered and changed after her day at work, and her face was flushed with wine. She was wearing the big soft cotton shirt she wore in bed, or at least which she wore when we first slipped into bed and snuggled up before I helped her to wriggle out of it. I eyed her through my glass and saw that her throat and neck were flushed too and I saw how her breasts lifted and tautened when she raised both hands to her hair and shook it loose. I was relaxed and relieved. I knew she was pleased with the meal and the wine and the care with which I'd cosseted Chloe... and even the loss of a tooth from her precious angel's precious pink gums was alright.

She pushed aside her empty plate, took another swig of wine and licked her lips.

'So what's the protocol? I mean, with the tooth-fairy and all that?' she said, pondering the issue with mock-seriousness. 'The tooth's come out, but we've lost it, so she can't put it under her pillow and expect to find a sixpence in the morning, can she?'

I frowned, assuming the gravity of the situation. 'I don't know, but I remember when one of my baby-teeth came out and I was playing football and I swallowed it... I still found a sixpence under my pillow the next morning. So I guess the tooth-fairy is allowed to use his own discretion in matters like this? Remind me, when we go up, and I'll put a little something there.'

'And so,' she said, 'what is it, this relic you've been dying to show me...'

Not bothering to clear the plates and dishes from the table, we'd just switched off the lights and gone upstairs with our glasses and the rest of the wine. I'd tiptoed into Chloe's room and slipped a newly-minted one-pound coin beneath her sleeping head. And then Rosie and I were tumbling into our own big bed. The heat of it was almost overwhelming, the enfolding warmth of the church tower and our awareness of

the crackling of ice outside our windows, the tumbling heat of our bodies and the buzz of the wine in our heads. We seemed to sink into our deep soft pillows as we lay close and clinked our glasses, and then I opened the black velvet box I'd been waiting to show her.

She reached for her specs from the bedside table. All of a sudden, despite her otherwise nakedness and the tousle of her hair, she assumed her previous authority as a dentist's assistant.

'A tooth, yes, it's a human tooth. Quite old, I would say, from the yellow and brown discoloration. It's from a child, yes, it's what we call a primary or deciduous tooth, what the layman would call a baby tooth.' She angled it this way and that and held it so close to her glasses that it almost touched the lens. 'I would say it's from the upper-left quadrant, I'm remembering Palmer's notation, the chart we use to designate individual teeth. It has two cuspals or points, so it's the tooth just behind the front-left canine. Yes, I'd say it's the upper-left first bicuspid.'

I was bursting to ask her. 'Is it possible to say whether it's from a boy or a girl? I mean, is it possible to tell the difference between a boy's tooth and a girl's?'

'I don't think it is possible, no,' she answered, looking at me quizzically over the top of her glasses. 'Children start losing their baby-teeth anytime around six years old, until they're maybe twelve or thirteen. I seem to remember that girls tend to lose them and replace them with their adult teeth a bit earlier than boys do.'

'And there's this,' I said, my voice hoarse with excitement. 'Hey, I'm not saying that your super-scientific information isn't interesting, because it is and it just helps to confirm this other thing... but look, inside the box, underneath the satin stuff, I found this.'

It was a slip of paper, folded many times. It was yellow with age, freckled and blotched. When I unfolded it, very gently, trying not to let my hands shake too much, the inside of the paper was whiter, as though it had seldom been opened and

exposed to the light, but the lines of the folds were brown. On it, there were a few words of faded copper-plate hand-writing.

'You read it, Rosie. Just read it aloud, whatever you think it says. I've been re-reading it all day. I know what I think it says. Go ahead...'

She squinted at the writing and read it, hesitating, pausing.

'*Dentem puer... ex eapoe... unum denarium... 29th oct 1819... barnsby md... Manor House School.*'

'It's in Latin,' I said, and I teased the piece of paper from her fingers. 'It's in Latin and...' and the words seemed to tumble from me in one breathless rush, 'it says that this is the tooth of a boy, *dentem puer*, and a teacher, a man called Dr Barnsby, *barnsby md*, who was the headmaster of a boarding-school for boys called the Manor House School in the early 1800s, he kept a record of the penny, *unum denarium*, the penny he gave to the boy for the tooth he'd lost... yes, like the tooth-fairy, but keeping an account because... well, I guess because a penny was quite a lot in those days and if he was running a school with fifty or eighty or a hundred little boys he'd want to keep a record for his accounts and...'

She was looking at me sideways. She took off her specs. She swallowed a mouthful of wine from her glass and then held it to my lips for me to drink too. As she reached to the bedside table to put the glass down, her breasts lifted and the warm scent of jasmine rose from her body.

'And Rosie, he was here, in England...' I was saying, although my tongue was loose with the wine and my excitement. 'Edgar Allan Poe, he was here when he was a boy in around 1818 or so, and he went to a school called the Manor House School and the headmaster was a man called Dr Barnsby and he...'

She silenced my mouth with hers. At the same time, she snapped shut the little velvet box with the tooth and the slip of paper inside it and pushed it deep down into the bedclothes.

Chapter Six

Darkness. We both woke very suddenly.

It could have been midnight, not long after we'd made love and fallen into an exhausted sleep. It could have been the small hours: two or three o'clock in the morning and the streets frozen into silence. It could have been seven o'clock, and Rosie's alarm about to rouse her, grumbling and groaning, for another day at work.

A deep darkness. And yet softened by the glow of a golden streetlamp, outside on the corner, near the doorway of the church.

Someone, something, was moving in our room.

'Chloe?' I sat up. Rosie was already sitting up. She was staring into the shadows. I caught the gleam of her eyes and the glisten of her open mouth. 'Chloe, my darling... what are you doing?'

She was standing at the foot of our bed. In her cotton night-dress, her hair tumbling to her shoulders, she seemed to be staring at us, as now, we both sat up and stared at her. She wasn't smiling. She had the puzzled, petulant look on her face of the old Chloe. She had her eyes on us, but no, I realised that she didn't really see. She was asleep. Asleep, and listening. Every wire and fuse in her body and her bewildered little brain was a-buzz with the energy of listening.

'Hey baby...' Rosie slipped out of our bed and moved around to her. 'Hey baby, let's get you back into bed... or do you want to come into bed with Mummy and Daddy?'

But Chloe squirmed away from her. As she did so, the two of us, me and Rosie, we held our breath and listened too, as if

we could tune into the wavelength of the restive child. And we heard it, we seemed to hear what the girl was hearing, and we glanced at each other with a tiny gasp of relief.

'It's only Mouse,' Rosie whispered. 'It's Mr. Mouse, that's all. Let's go and see what he's doing and tell him it's bedtime and he's got to go to bed and go to sleep...'

I followed, as Rosie very gently and slowly walked the child out of our bedroom and back into her own. Indeed, there it was, the mouse was in its cage, on its treadmill. I'd done everything I could to silence the turning of the wheel, with a drop of oil here and a smear of soap there, so that the busy little beast could run as many miles as it liked in the dead of night without keeping Chloe awake. But now, maybe because the world outside was stopped so utterly and locked into an icy stillness, the wheel was just audible. No more than a hiss and a click, but it must have woken the child.

Rosie nodded at me, and I understood her nod, as she manoeuvred Chloe to her own bed. By the time she was tucked into the bedclothes, I'd reached into the mouse's cage, persuaded it off the treadmill with a gentle nudge of my finger, and I'd locked the wheel. 'Sorry, Mr. Mouse, it's bedtime, ok? Some of us have got to go to work in the morning, ok?'

But, then an extraordinary thing... or maybe not so extraordinary, in a building as old and unusual as our church tower. No more than a second after the mouse had been thwarted and stilled, and the two of us had kissed the girl and retreated to the door of her bedroom, she sat up again.

Bolt upright. Eyes wide open. Staring at us but not seeing. Asleep. Listening. And not just listening, but hearing something.

Something was moving, somewhere in the building.

Over our heads, in the roof-space of the belfry, where maybe the pipes were contracting and creaking in the grip of ice? Or some benighted creature, seeking refuge from the certainty of death outside, was fidgeting and fluttering in the hope of staying alive until the dawning of a meagre daylight?

Chloe had heard it. We all listened. Even the mouse seemed to be listening. The child stared up at the ceiling, where the sound seemed to be coming from. And then, all of a sudden it stopped.

In a few moments she'd snuggled herself down and was properly asleep again. The mouse rustled into its woolly bed and was still.

We went back to our own bed and lay there, listening to the silence.

Chapter Seven

'ANOTHER ADVENTURE, CHLOE. Are you ready? It'll be dusty and dirty, but we can get you cleaned up before Mummy comes home, can't we?'

I'd got her bundled into her jeans and an old pullover, and I'd made her put on her red bobble-hat in case it might be cobwebby and spidery up there. She had the mouse somewhere inside her sleeve. I was wearing my oldest pullover too, the one I always wore for going on the boat, so we both looked as though we were about to venture far out into the icy world. We weren't. We were going to see if the boiler and the pipes were alright, in the roof-space above our bedrooms.

We started in Chloe's room. As part of the expert conversion, there was an aluminium ladder stowed high on the ceiling, so unobtrusive that it was almost unnoticeable except for a nylon cord which dangled down the wall.

'Watch out and stand back, Chloe, it's magic...' and she gazed upwards, open-mouthed, so rapt that a tiny bubble of saliva sparkled on her tongue. I pulled gently on the cord and the ladder slid on silent runners away from the ceiling and down towards us and clicked into place in front of our faces. It was new. I think I'd climbed it once before, months ago when the builders were busy and I'd been nosing around to see what they were doing. I set Chloe onto the bottom rung, and as she pulled herself up to the next and the next, I was enfolding her with my arms and climbing with her, my whole body wrapped around her so that she couldn't possibly fall.

At the top, I reached above her head and pushed up a trap-door. All new, all neat, effortless, it swung up and away on a

silent spring. I pushed her bonny bottom and she scrambled up, and I was there, right with her, a moment later.

The belfry? I could've called it that to make it sound old and solemn and oddly gothic. But it had never had bells in it, although the enormous wooden beams of the roof looked mighty enough to have supported them. It was the clock-tower.

A big dark space, perfectly square. Three blank stone walls, and on one of them there remained the inner workings of the clock face which looked south and across the town. A marvellous contraption of great black cogs with interlocking teeth, weights and pulleys and fulcrum, standing silent and still since the church had been closed. I'd meant to find out how it all worked and whether, one day, I might be able to set the clock going again; one day, me and Chloe would drop into the library in Long Eaton and I'd dig out the history of the building we'd bought. But now, the two of us just stood and gaped around us, at the sooty machine and at the shadowy beams over our heads. In one corner, quite incongruous, neat and compact, there was a shiny new water tank and a modern central-heating system.

'Cold... brrrr... hey Chloe?' There were openings in the face of the clock, some of the panes of glass must have broken, so that, as well as the shafts of wintry light which shot the darkness, there were piercing drafts of icy air. 'Brrr, not much warmer in here than outside... are you alright?'

She smiled at me, excited to have clambered into the top of the tower, and she was pottering around and poking into the grubbiest corners. The floor was powdered with a thick layer of dust and strewn with leaves which had blown in; and a jumble of twigs, a debris of dried-up splinters of branches, a curious grey matting of animal fur, wool and feathers, scraps of old newspaper. Unmistakably, nesting material. The child was kneeling to it, picking it up and sniffing, and I had to move quickly to stop her from even touching it with her tongue.

'Hey, no Chloe, that's dirty, I knew we'd get dirty up here. What do you think it is? A bird? Back in the summer, maybe the birds have come in and tried to make a nest...'

I crossed to the central-heating system. I'd come up to check it, to make sure none of the pipes had split with the ferocious freezing in the night. But it all seemed fine, everything was lagged and insulated, all brand-new and guaranteed as part of the conversion. I tapped at the dials on the boiler, although I had no idea what the readings should be. I put my ear to the tank and heard a satisfying burble of hot water.

A sudden scuffle in the dust. The mouse again. As I turned to see what was happening, I saw the creature wriggle out of Chloe's sleeve and plop onto the floor. For a moment it just sat there, as amazed by the strangeness of the room as the girl had been, and then it skittered away from her, sometimes silent in the soft powder, then scratching and wriggling through dry leaves and twigs, scurrying across the room and questing with its little pink snout.

'Hey Mr. Mouse, where are you off to? Leave him, Chloe, he's just exploring, that's all.'

She was springing along beside the mouse, and each step she took raised such a puther of dust that the shafts of freezing daylight were clouded with it. I covered my mouth, the girl was giggling and spluttering at the filthy blizzard she'd raised, and the mouse, so perfectly pristine and unused to such a wintry haboob, was turning round and round in ever decreasing circles. Until at last, it found the courage to break away. It shot across the room and disappeared underneath the water tank.

Chloe was straightway there, on her hands and knees and groping into the darkness. Before I could stop her, she was pulling out handfuls of stuff, the accumulated fluff and fur and feathers which had blown there through the autumn and winter. With one hand over my mouth, I bent to her and encircled her waist with my other arm, and just hoicked her up and away and back into the middle of the room.

'What on earth have you got? Hey come on Chloe... hey what a mess...'

Little angel. She was no trouble. I hugged her close, and her face was a picture of smiles and laughing eyes, the bobble-hat

askew on her cobwebby curls. But she was waving her prize in a tightly clenched fist, and she wouldn't drop it.

Not the mouse. A crow.

She had it by the neck. It was a rag of filthy black feathers. As she swung it around her head, its heavy black beak clacked open and shut. The wings shook out a shower of dust, and the tough plumage bristled and rustled like the wreckage of a broken umbrella. She swung it more wildly, the dangling black claws clattered like castanets. And then she let go. It arced through the air, through a whirlwind of dust, and crash-landed on the floor.

I put her down too. There was a silence, as the daylight cleared and we could see and breathe more easily. As Chloe bent towards the bird, I knelt beside her and held her firmly, gently, so she wouldn't try to pick it up again. I wasn't cross, she wasn't mean or obstreperous like the old Chloe, she was as sweet as ever and merely exercising her unselfconscious childish curiosity... dead bird, pick it up, whirl it around, throw it. No cruelty or malice. And so we eyed the remains of the creature, as a hush gathered around us.

A little sound. Mouse. We turned and saw it nosing timidly from beneath the water tank. Despite the mess in the room and the horridness of the place where it had been hiding, it was as perfect as ever. It seemed to shine with perfection, gleaming impossibly, as it picked its way towards us. It came to the bird. It sniffed and sneezed. Surprising how loudly a mouse can sneeze, in the icy air of an old church tower...

Was it the sneeze? Or was it the movement of the child as she leaned down and let the mouse run onto the palm of her hand?

The bird moved.

My imagination, or the dust in my eyes, or the blurring of the grey light?

Chloe flinched away from the bird and closer into my arms. It moved again. One of its wings straightened and shuddered. A contraction of the muscles, a reaction to the shaking and whirling and the impact onto the floor... a momentary relaxation of rigor mortis?

But then it opened its eyes. It opened its beak and hissed. It exhaled a long hissing breath. And as the two of us edged away and back towards the open trap-door, the crow dragged itself across the floor, trailing one of its wings at first and then shivering and shuffling it back into place... and by the time it reached the wall it was more or less on its feet and with one sudden bound, a bundle of filthy frozen feathers which had been thawed and shocked alive again, it was gone.

Through a broken pane in the face of the clock. A tumble of black feathers, it launched itself out into the air and was gone.

Chapter Eight

THE TOOTH. IT stung me into action. Stung? Maybe not, the word was an uncomfortable reminder of how all this, the change in our lives, had begun. No, the tooth charged me with enthusiasm and excitement, and the following day, downstairs in the vestry, I did more than I would otherwise have done in a month of playing shop, to use Rosie's disparaging expression.

'I'm impressed,' she said, when I took her down to show her, when she'd come home late from work. 'You've done a lot. Did Chloe help you at all? I mean, I hope you've been trying to involve her and not just leaving her on her own in the corner with the mouse...'

I just said yes, as she took a turn around the room to inspect my achievement. I could've groused at her, that she couldn't bestow a bit of praise without adding a note of doubt about my commitment to our daughter, but I let it pass. I'd unpacked all the books and arranged them on their shelves, packed away all the cardboard boxes, arranged myself a desk and chair in the corner with the computer humming, its screen glowing. The fire was lit and crackling, a birch log on a bed of coals. 'Hey, it looks good. It's starting to look like a bookshop, ready to open for business. And this? I guess this is the shrine...'

'Shrine, yes, I suppose so. What do you think? Pretty exciting...'

I'd been down the road to one of the charity shops in Canal Street, and come back with a bedside table, a bit of midnight-purple velveteen material, a lamp on a stalk you could angle this way and that; and in the next-door cyber-cafe I'd photocopied the precious hand-written note and blown it up

to a kind of readable poster size. Now, the first thing you'd see on entering the room was a brightly illuminated display: the lamp bent over the purple velvet, the jewellery box on it... the tooth on its bed of white satin. Beside it, the hand-written note, for customers to read and marvel at.

'Poe's tooth,' I said to Rosie, as she leaned closer to look at it again. 'A tooth from the mouth of the boy Edgar Allan Poe, a baby tooth he lost while he was here in England as a boy, in 1818. He was sent from America by his wealthy step-father, and he attended a boarding-school in Stoke Newington, the Manor House School. The note's written by the headmaster, a Dr Barnsby, and it records the date when the boy's tooth came out or was pulled out, and the one penny that the headmaster conveyed to the boy as some kind of token...'

Rosie had straightened up and was looking at me with a mock-incredulous look on her face.

'Why did the teacher keep the tooth? I get the stuff about a penny being a lot in those days, and I suppose that, if the headmaster was a reasonably genial type he might go through the nonsense of giving pennies to little boys in his charge just to make the school a kind of less scary, more homely kind of place. But why did he keep the tooth, and how did it get to be in that funny old shop in Nottingham, and then why did...?'

'I don't, Rosie, I don't know.' I waved away her questions. 'No one knows. I guess I could go to the trouble of having the tooth analysed for its age, and then getting some expert to analyse the slip of paper and the ink on it. But it doesn't matter. It's as real as any relic, to use that word again... you know, like the fingernail of Santa Maria de Compostela, or a fragment of the Holy Cross, or even a bottle of the Beatles' bathwater. Who cares, if it helps with the bookshop or who knows, it might even help me to start writing a book? It isn't the reality of the thing that matters. It's the belief it inspires.'

She was staring at me, and then a glance at the tooth, her eyes drifting to the flames of the fire and across to the computer where Chloe was blinking absent-mindedly into the screen.

'Rosie,' I went on, to try and keep her attention a moment longer, 'you confirmed that it's a real tooth, from a real child, a something bicuspid or whatever you said. And the note says it's a tooth from a boy called EA Poe, at the Manor House School in 1818, identified by a teacher called Dr Barnsby. I only have to spread the rumour and see if it generates a bit of interest...'

She moved to me and enfolded me in her arms. 'It's all good,' she whispered in my ear. 'You know me, Oliver, you know what I want most and what would make me really happy again. When I come home and find you and Chloe warm and safe together, I don't really care what else you've been up to. I love you. And I love Chloe so much and I yearn for her so much it hurts, it hurts me inside.'

Still holding me, she pulled her head away and looked me in the eyes. Her own eyes were gleaming with tears.

'Belief, yes. Poe's tooth is good, my dear Oliver. It's got you fired up and busy with the shop and everything. So let's all believe in it, the tooth of Edgar Allan Poe, me and you and Chloe, if it's going to make us happy together and give us something to hold onto...'

Time to go upstairs again, back to the kitchen and eat and then get Chloe ready for her bed. I put a fireguard in front of the flames, in case a spark flew out as they died down. I turned off the computer. Rosie took Chloe by the hand and led her out of the warm room, into the bigger, colder space of the church hallway. I switched off the lamp, and for a moment the three of us stood silent and still in the darkness. A draft of the January night air was blowing under the great oak door.

'I was wondering, the other thing I was going to ask...' Rosie's voice was soft and oddly disembodied. It trembled a little, with the cold. 'I was wondering, why did the old guy, Mr. Heap, why did he give the tooth to you?'

Chapter Nine

CHLOE CAME TO us in the night, again.

Not asleep, nothing odd or unnerving. Rosie had put her to bed after her supper and a bath, and I'd followed afterwards to read a page or two of a story to her. As always, she'd stared up at me, all sweetly tucked up, in the same way that any child might stare at her father while he was reading. Except that her eyes never wavered from my mouth. They hardly even fluttered to meet my eyes, but she was watching my lips with a slightly puzzled expression on her face, as if – if she was thinking anything at all – as if she was wondering why on earth this man she dimly recognised was murmuring such a meaningless mumble of sounds.

I read to her, until Rosie came back up with a glass of milk and some biscuits to leave on Chloe's bedside table, and we kissed her goodnight and turned off her light.

Chloe came to us again, later. Nothing odd.

We both woke up to hear her plaintive mewling noises, the noise she made when she'd woken up hot and bothered or restless and she wanted to elicit a response from us. And we dutifully did what we usually did. Rosie went through to her room and soothed her with kisses and caresses, and if she wouldn't settle, she would bring her back to our room. Sure enough, as I waited in a blurry muddle of memories of the dream I'd been having, Rosie was leaning over me, with Chloe, and I could smell their warm and perfumed bodies as Rosie was whispering, 'Come on, my sweetie, come into Mummy's bed, come into bed with Mummy and Daddy, and then maybe Daddy will...'

Not maybe. It was a certainty. After a few minutes cuddling with Mummy and Daddy, Chloe was breathing softly and easily and falling sweetly asleep. And, not a baby or a toddler any more but a bonny seven-year-old, she'd got her knees pressed hard into the small of Daddy's back... so that I muttered, 'Alright, sleep tight, I'll just...' and I slipped out of the bed, trying to dispel a resentful image of cuckoos and nests and so on, and into the next room, into Chloe's still-warm and snuggly bed.

That was what usually happened. The difference this time, I didn't sleep.

I lay there and listened, although I heard nothing, not a flutter of feathers or a skitter of claws. I listened and I thought of the crow and how wretched it had been, how it had come back to life and sculled like a hopeless cripple across the floor before launching itself out of the window. I lay very still and I listened, but there was not a sound. Probably, all but dead, it had fallen to the pavement far below and perished there, frozen to the ground. No matter. In the utter silence I stared at the ceiling, and then I closed my eyes and tried to sleep.

The ladder. The ladder on the ceiling. The shape of it seemed to shine on the inside of my eyelids. It wouldn't go away.

I opened my eyes and sat up. I swigged the milk that Chloe hadn't touched. Reached for the biscuits. Hesitated, with one of them halfway to my mouth. Got out of bed and pulled on the cord, so that the ladder swung silently down and clicked into place.

So cold. At the top of the ladder, when I pushed up the trap-door and eased my head and shoulders up into the clock-tower, the cold seemed to rush at me and pounce and squeeze around me like the jaws of a trap, as if it had been waiting for me. There was a little orange light from the streets of the slumbering town. Nothing was moving in the icy dark room. The workings of the clock were locked into their sleep of obsolescence.

I crumbled the biscuits and tossed the pieces across the floor.

*   *   *

THERE WAS NO sign of the crow, of course, when Chloe and I stepped out of the door of the church. Why would there be?

Cold, again. Cold, still. Minus three or five or six? A flock of grey and black pigeons whirled around the top of our tower. In the bare trees along Derby Road, the old nests of the rooks were exposed, like strange dead fruits still clinging to the branches. Always a magpie churring and chuntering through the blackened twigs of the hawthorn hedges... and gulls, the resourceful inland gulls, a mob of them, tumbling and somersaulting and soaring in the wintry sky, so far from the sea and yet thriving and voicing the triumph of their success with a never-ceasing cackling and laughter. Yes, there were crows, an odd pair across the playing-fields of Derwent College. But the sheen on their wings and the swagger of their gait said that neither of them was the moribund wreck we'd discovered in the church tower.

Rosie was at work. In the weeks following Chloe's accident, of course the two of us had stopped work to look after her and try to settle ourselves in the aftermath of the shock. With the windfall of the compensation pay-out, we'd secured the church tower; but we would still need cash-flow, as Rosie put it, one of us would have to work, or maybe both of us part-time, and we would juggle everything around looking after Chloe. Rosie called Dowling & McCorrister, the dental practice where she'd been a highly-respected stalwart for years, expecting to be welcomed back after her traumatic time off. She wasn't, she'd been replaced. Similarly, my cosy job in the borough council's mobile library had been advertised, there'd been hundreds of applicants and the position was filled.

What to do? Rosie got a job twenty minutes' walk from our new home, as a headmaster's secretary. Brook's Academy was a dismal private day-school in a dismal cul-de-sac, five or six disconsolate teachers cramming sixty-odd pupils for exams they'd already failed once or twice, and so-called Colonel

Brook was, according to Rosie, a crank, a creationist. I would stay at home and look after Chloe. And every morning, as she girded her loins and every other part of her comeliness to set off into the teeth of an arctic winter, Rosie would do two other things. She would whisper her prayer into Chloe's ear, her poignant appeal to the little girl to come back, to come back... and she would issue me with the necessary instructions or suggestions or precautions, entreating me to take every possible care, and I would see in her eyes the shadow of doubt that I was trustworthy, the flicker of fear that I might not be.

No sign of the crow. But I saw Chloe glance up at the tower, to the face of the clock, and then she angled her head slowly down and down and down to the pavement where we were standing, as though measuring the distance and trajectory of something falling. She saw me looking too. She just smiled, made a little chuckling noise, in the same way that she responded to anything, whether it be good or bad or nice or nasty, and together, hand in gloved hand, we set off for our walk across the park.

As instructed, we talked. I talked.

'So we got our packed lunch, our sandwiches and our flask... is it hot chocolate this time? We've got some extra crusts for the ducks, yes the swans too if they're there, and the coots, yes the coots, we like the coots best of all. We're wrapped up warm, gloves and woolly hats and wellington boots... but Chloe, Daddy doesn't want to go out too long today 'cos he's got things to do with the shop, alright? I've got a visitor coming this afternoon, to see the shop and everything...'

I was excited about the shop. I'd tried to do a bit of publicity and had a number of responses to the mention of Edgar Allan Poe's tooth... not all of them encouraging, some of them downright rude, poo-poohing the notion in the most caustic and withering tones. But most of them were from people who were intrigued, curious, for whom the idea was appealingly weird. Nothing wrong with that. And there'd been a phone call from a young fellow at the *Nottingham Evening Post*,

who was coming around at four o'clock to have a chat and take a few shots and maybe do a piece for the paper....

We'd crossed the college playing-fields, I'd clapped my hands and sent up the rooks and the gulls in a cloud of black and white wings. We crossed the brook and onto Long Eaton park.

Not bad, not bad. Indeed, pretty good. For a nondescript, homely midlands town, somewhere between Nottingham and Derby in what was known as the Trent valley, Long Eaton had an unusually big and lovely park. Very flat, no particular features, but expanses of open fields and stands of mature trees, acres of space for runners and dog-lovers and cyclists... and for strollers like me, and Chloe pottering along beside me, the most beautiful of skies, over avenues of poplar and beech and the puthering cooling-towers of Willington power station. No, not exotic or romantic, only the suburbs of a satellite-town in the East Midlands, but somehow, even on the rawest of raw days in January, a place of unusual and ineffable loveliness.

So I said all this to Chloe. I said to her, 'Hey, not bad, Chloe... pretty good,' as we paused at the entrance of the park and took in the cold, bare emptiness of it. The sky was blue: not a cliché, but an expression of purity, perfection. The distant towers were exhaling enormous white clouds of steam. There was a flock of lapwings on the rugby pitch, a shimmer of green. And was that a golden plover, gleaming among them? 'Not bad, eh Chloe? For a funny little town no-one's ever heard of? What do you think? Come on, let's go to the pond and have a nice hot drink and a sandwich and see who wants any of our crusty left-overs...'

The coots did, unassumingly handsome birds, urbane, smug, with their plump grey bodies and elegant legs and their striking white helmets. The swan did, surging towards us, so testy, so irritable. 'Hey, Mr. Swan, why are you hissing and flouncing like that, when you're ten times as big as everyone else and so gorgeous and you know you're going get the biggest bits of bread just because you're so big and gorgeous? Hey, just chill...' And the mallard, the ducks demure and dumpy, like

medieval wenches cowed by the presence of their lordship, the gleaming, iridescent drake.

Chill. For these birds, the chill in the air was death, which might be postponed by swallowing a few mouthfuls of bread. We sat on a bench by the pond. Chloe tossed her crusts into the air and watched them spatter on the surface of the water, or she held on tight and waited for the bravest of the ducks to nibble her fingers and sometimes the swan come snaking and hissing and snap with its big yellow beak. She windmilled her arm and hurled the remains of a sandwich high into the air, and a gull would come... it would make such a daring and brilliant pass that all the air would sparkle around the little girl's golden-blonde head.

And then. And then it all went very quiet.

I hardly noticed how it happened, but we realised that all our friends at the pond, the coot and the duck and the debonair gulls and even the bilious swan, had drifted away. Or rather, they had withdrawn from us. A few pieces of bread floated on the water. It seemed strange that, on such a bitter day, with another long dark afternoon and a freezing night only hours away, the birds would ignore the food which could save their lives and see them survive until tomorrow. A persistent sparrow pecked at the crumbs around our feet, its dun feathers fluffed up to retain a bit of warmth in its scrawny body. But then it fluttered away.

Chloe looked up and around her. I followed her gaze. No hawk, no bully-boy black-back. We looked behind us to see if someone else, a man and his dog, had wandered by. There was no-one.

Under our bench. A wriggle and a writhing flutter.

A crow, but nothing like the swaggering crows I'd seen in the field. A raggedy thing. It was only a second, or two. Chloe squealed and lifted her feet off the ground. I found myself doing the same. A crow, which had skulked under the bench to snatch at the pickings, flapped away and was gone, almost before we'd known it was there. We saw it row into the air

and grapple itself clumsily, like some kind of half-formed prehistoric bird, into the branches of a nearby willow.

There were other crows in the same tree. But they were completely still. Although the tree shook and its branches rattled with the impact of the bird which had just landed there, the others didn't move. They didn't even adjust their weight or their grip to compensate for the movement and keep their balance. We both stared at them. And we saw one of the birds lean a little and stop, and lean a bit more and swing on the branch as though its claws were locked... and then it fell. Without opening its wings at all to stop itself falling, it slipped off the branch and dropped through the snapping cold twigs and landed on the ground with a curious puff of sound... as though it weighed almost nothing.

'Let's go home, Chloe,' I said to her. She was staring at the crows which were still in the willow tree. They were all motionless, their claws locked. Only one of them was moving, the scrag of a rag of a crow which had somehow kindled a spark of life when the others had died in the night. Their withered, empty husks were frozen to the tree.

Chapter Ten

'Very nice, yes. Very cosy. But is that the atmosphere you really want to achieve? Nice and cosy? For a horror bookshop?'

The reporter from the *Nottingham Evening Post*, who'd introduced himself as Joe Blakesley, was probably in his mid-twenties with a degree in journalism from Leicester Polytechnic, but he looked like a schoolboy, a skinny teenager conducting an interview for his social-studies coursework... earnest, with his notepad and camera and duffel-coat and his flopping fashionable hair, and a long red scarf looped casually around his neck. Before I could answer what might've been a criticism of the way I'd organised things, he smiled and went on, 'But no, no it's great, the church tower and coming through the big oak door and into this... the vestry, did you say? Tell me about the books you're going to stock, anything about the history of the church... and the tooth, of course, I'd love to see it. I think it's all great, it'll make a great little piece for me, so please, fire away...'

He'd said, disarmingly, as though he knew that his bookish, journalistic look wasn't entirely convincing, that so far he'd only done a few weddings and funerals... and last week he'd been sent to watch Notts County play Tranmere, but the match was called off because the pitch was frozen. So this was going to be his first feature. He took some shots of me and the room, and me with Chloe, and he browsed around the shelves.

Five o'clock. Outside it was as black as midnight, with the headlamps of the traffic swishing along the Derby Road. Every car that went by, on its weary journey out of town and home after work, shone an orange beam through our tall, narrow

lancet windows and across the ceiling, a steady, unhurried rhythm of light. The vestry door was still open to the hallway, and the door of the church was open too, because I wanted to give the clear impression that it would be a shop, open to the street, open to the public. But the room was warm. I stood in front of the fire, which I'd built especially bright and hot, and I talked... while the young man sat at my desk and scribbled on his pad, while Chloe stood beside him and watched how his hand scurried and scratched like a mouse across his page.

I'd got the shrine ready, but I hadn't switched on the lamp yet. It would be the climax to the interview. And I hadn't told Rosie. Indeed, I'd deliberately arranged it so that she'd be out at work, to make a surprise for her, to reveal the article to her unexpectedly if and when it came out.

Firelight, the flicker of flames. The hiss of the traffic. The play of the headlamps on the ceiling and on the books on their shelves. The reporter writing at my desk. Chloe, so absorbed by the movement of his hand that she seemed to be holding her breath.

I told him about the church. It wasn't very old, it didn't have centuries of legend and spooky lore, a cemetery heaving with graves and lots of mossy headstones and such. No, it was an Anglican church, built in the 1880s, the architects were local worthies called Brevill and Bailey who'd designed many of Nottingham's monuments and grand municipal buildings. Me and my wife Rosie, we'd bought the tower, converted very nicely into comfortable accommodation, and one day I was going to repair the clock in the tower. What else? oh yes, a man called Henry Wass had died during the construction of the church, he'd fallen from the scaffolding and...

At this, the young man glanced up at me, as though he'd found the angle he needed to make something of his story, something gratuitously sensational to bring it alive. For a moment I thought he was going to hurry outside with his camera, to photograph the spot where the skull of the unfortunate man might have smashed on the pavement.

'The books?' I quickly went on. And as I strolled from shelf to shelf, with my eyes half-closed for mysterious effect, I murmured the names like a spell, the names of the immortals, forever and unforgettably enshrined in the pantheon... 'Bram Stoker, Mary Shelley, Conan Doyle, MR James... Wilde, Dickens, de Quincy, Rider Haggard...' and was surprised when I opened my eyes and caught a glimmer of impatience on the young man's face, a surreptitious peek at his watch. 'And of course, the modern masters of the genre, King and Koontz, Barker and Bradbury and Blatty and er...'

He closed his notebook very gently. He screwed his face into a painfully apologetic frown and stood up.

'Sorry, no offence but... but can't I find all of these books in all of the bookshops in town? I mean, I don't even have to go into Nottingham, I can get all of them, the so-called classics, in Long Eaton and Beeston and Ilkeston. I can rummage in any of the charity shops and find a tattered old copy of *Frankenstein* or *Dracula* or *Turn of the Screw* or *Jekyll and Hyde* or whatever. And the newer stuff, in Smiths and Waterstones, the big outlets. Can't I?'

He paused, and his earnest, journalistic face lit into a boyish smile, alive with excitement.

'Poe,' he said. 'Isn't that why I've come to talk to you? Show me the tooth.'

I SWITCHED ON the lamp, bent it over the velveteen table and stood back. There was a gust of wind outside, or else a bus or a truck had just gone by, because all three of us turned at a sudden skittering sound in the hallway and a flurry of leaves blew in.

He bent over the display I'd so carefully set up. Because the room was so dim and the night outside seemed to wrap itself so meanly, so grimly around the church, the velvet box and its bed of white satin shone all the brighter.

And the tooth.

Joe Blakesley, cub-reporter from the Nottingham Evening Post, leaned close and he stared. And he stared. He held his breath and he stared. When he spoke, his voice was so quiet, not even a whisper, hardly a gasp, barely a breath, that it was almost lost in the flutter of the flames and the stirring of autumn leaves across the floor.

'How wonderful. How marvellous. Oh God, *dentem puer*, from the mouth of Edgar Allan Poe...' His voice was lost, in a puff of smoke from the blazing Birchwood, in the holiness of the hiss of resin.

Not wanting to disturb his reverie, but seizing the moment to give him the details he might need for his article, I stood behind him and recited the information I'd gleaned from the precious handwritten slip of paper. He nodded and nodded, hardly looking up from the tooth, as if to indicate he knew already that Poe had spent a few years of his boyhood in England, he knew the names, the facts, he'd done his homework about the Manor House School and Dr Barnsby and... and when I mentioned where the tooth had come from, the name of Mr. Heap seemed to freeze him for a second, he inhaled sharply as if by doing so he would commit the name to his memory.

And what was Chloe doing? Oh lord, heaven forbid I should ignore her or worst of all neglect her for a precious millisecond, she was standing beside him on tip-toe and fixated on the tooth as much as he was... but also, at the same time, she was pushing something towards him on the purple velvet, trying to catch his attention with the glint and the razor-sharp edges of their diamond brilliance, she was nudging her diamonds of shattered windscreen under the focus of the angled lamp.

Too late. He didn't see them. Just as I took two strides forwards, to pull her away from the display and grab the pieces of glass in the palm of my hand, there was another flurry of wind in the hallway.

More than a flurry. More than a whispering commotion of autumn leaves. A soft but sudden explosion of sound.

We all turned to see what it was. 'Hello my love, are you home?' I blurted, and for a moment I thought it was Rosie, home early, and my stomach lurched with dismay. Chloe gave a shout of recognition.

But no, it wasn't her mother. Something, someone or something was in the church hallway. In and out so fast, it was no more than a shadow. A rag of shadow blown in and out by the night.

Me and Chloe, we were framed in the doorway as the reporter whirled round. Some instinct triggered in his investigative brain made him reach for his camera. Pop, pop, pop... he fired off three flashes of dazzle-blue light.

The two of us. And behind us, a rag of shadow, a blur of movement in the darkness. I thought I'd seen it. And Chloe had seen it, with a gurgle of surprise. Then it was gone. Gone with a glimmer of silver it had snaffled from the cold stone slabs.

'Marvellous... it's all I need, more than I need, some great snaps and a great story.' He, Joe Blakesley, was bundling his way out of the vestry, into the hallway and out of the church door. 'Poe...' he was saying to me, although his voice was muffled in the winding and winding of his long red scarf around his face, '... it's all you need... just get Poe, any old books and articles and stuff and the tattiest old paperbacks and stuff you can find... it's all you need...'

Chapter Eleven

JOE BLAKESLEY HAD two pieces in the *Nottingham Evening Post*, in the same edition, a few days later. After nearly a year with the paper, a few weddings and making the editor's coffee in the mornings, he had two pieces in one edition.

Rosie was impressed by the article.

'Poe's Tooth? Is that a good name for a bookshop?' She shrugged and admitted that yes, it might be. She read it all aloud, as we sat side by side in bed, with Chloe snuggled between us. It wasn't long, it was hardly a feature, it was a modest piece on page nineteen, squeezed between a report on the opening of a new dialysis clinic in Beeston and another on the vandalism of a footballer's BMW. But there were a couple of thumbnail photographs of me and Chloe at the fireside, me and the display of books, and, most importantly, a close-up of the relic after which the shop would be named; rather a blurry shot, dazzled by the overhead lamp, so the reporter had transcribed the handwritten note, verbatim, with his own translation.

'"Out of the mouths of babes and sucklings..."' Rosie had laid out the newspaper onto the bedcover, across her lap and mine, with Chloe all but smothered beneath it. With a grimace, affecting a mock-portentous voice, she was re-reading the headline. 'Oh dear, a bit corny, isn't it? But the article's good, I like it, I like it... a new bookshop to be called Poe's Tooth Books is about to open... yes, well done, my darling, I like it.'

She leaned towards me and we kissed. Chloe disappeared completely, under the newsprint and the blankets. There was another photograph, me and Chloe looking utterly startled,

our faces pallid and oddly misshapen, like a couple of victims...
a father and daughter retrieved from the bottom of a canal,
maybe, or rescued from the ruins of a collapsed building.
We were framed in the doorway of the vestry. Behind us, the
blackness of the church hallway was a mouth, agape, leaning
forward to swallow us. 'Scary, look at the two of you. Hey
Chloe, come out of there and take a look, you're famous...'

She emerged, tousled and hot. She pawed clumsily at the
photograph, without any understanding of what it was except
a fragment of material which her Mummy and Daddy had
crumpled on top of her. If she was going to react at all, I thought
without daring to say what I was thinking, she might sneer
and snidely remind us that she was famous already, she'd been
in the paper before, last year, and not on page nineteen but on
the front page with a big photo. 'Hey, be careful, Chloe,' her
mother was saying, 'don't tear it, your Daddy'll want to keep
this and get it framed and put it up in the shop for all of his
customers to read...'

The girl stopped batting at the paper, although the noise of
her fists on it had seemed so crisply percussive. For a moment,
she inclined her face to the photo. She fixed her eyes on it and
she held her breath. And me and Rosie, as we'd done hundreds
of times before, several times a day and every day for nine
months, we held our breath too, in anticipation, in hope, in
a state between joy and fear, that the moment had come...
the moment when Chloe would emerge from her dream-like
silence and speak, and be herself and be with us once more, as
she had been before.

She didn't speak. After a long, literally breathless moment,
we all exhaled. Chloe smiled airily again, as if her head was
full of air, as if her poor little dented brain was nothing but an
airy space.

'No, it isn't the best photo of you I've ever seen,' Rosie said,
disguising her disappointment with a breezy non-sequitur.
'Looks like you've seen a ghost. Is that it, behind you? Spooky...
hey, you can see it, flapping around in the hallway...'

Only a shadow, even darker than the darkness which was gaping around our shoulders. Or a vagrant, an urchin, so desperate to flee the imminent deadliness of the night that it must dare the deeper darkness of an unhallowed church. It had come for something, and gone out again. Unmistakably, in the photo, the shadow of the crow was there.

THE OTHER PIECE? AN obituary. I read it quickly and the following afternoon I went to the crematorium at Bramcote.

Out of curiosity, maybe, wondering at the connection between me and the deceased, wondering what it might be. Rosie had asked why the old man had given me the tooth. No real reason, I supposed, on an impulse he'd handed it to me because it was a curio and I'd expressed an interest in his odd collection of books. Mr. Heap: the obituary referred to him as an antiquarian, a bibliophile, who'd had a business in the oldest part of Nottingham for more than fifty years. Indeed, he'd been active in the campaign to commission and erect the statue of Robin Hood, and he'd been present at its unveiling in 1952. Widowed years ago, he was survived by his sons and grandchildren.

The crematorium stood on an exposed hillside, overlooking the oak woods of Bramcote and the sprawling, comfortable suburbs. It was as cold as ever, but the brightness of the afternoon sunshine cast a silvery loveliness on the frosted grass. Chloe was with me, of course. We were both so bundled up in our coats and hats and scarves that no one could have recognised us, even if they'd wondered who we were. In any case, a family saying their final goodbye to a beloved father or grandfather would hardly notice me and my daughter, as we watched them arrive in a line of enormous black cars, as the coffin was brought off the hearse and wheeled on a trolley into the chapel.

We didn't go inside. The dazzle and glitter of the sunlight was a joy. Despite the snap of ice in the air, I could feel the

warmth of the sun on my shoulders. The sky was a delicate pale blue, without a wisp of cloud, it had the fragile opacity of a starling's egg. The funeral cars kept their engines running, the drivers in their sombre uniforms sitting inside with the heaters on, and a shimmering white fume arose from the exhaust pipes. We heard the music from the chapel – The Lord's my Shepherd – the tremulous voices of grieving women and the growling of bereaved men.

Not long. I could feel Chloe starting to shiver, her hand gripping mine more and more tightly inside her woolly glove. I hugged her close, pulling her body against my legs so she could press her face into my coat, and I inwardly groaned at the prospect of Rosie's interrogation if she came home this evening and found Chloe feverish with a cold... so where did you go today? On the park with the ducks and the swans? No? Did you go into town, to have a look around the nice warm shops and have a nice hot chocolate or something? No? You went where? The crematorium? What do you mean, the crematorium? For heaven's sake Oliver, you took Chloe for a nice afternoon at the crematorium?

Four o'clock. Getting dark. The afternoon was closing around us, the grip of the frost was tighter as the sun dipped away and the evening sky was darker and lower. Darker, so that the glow from inside the chapel and the lights of the cars were suddenly bright. The exhaust smoke was whiter, billowing like steam. And as the music of an organ rose and fell with its pitiless poignancy, the family of Mr. Heap, deceased, started to come outside. Grey smoke plumed from the chimney of the incinerator.

The family processed across the car park, escorted by the minister, who was going to show them where the ashes would eventually be placed. He took them to the garden of remembrance, where the yews and the privet were meticulously cut into deferential, unassuming shapes, where there were already hundreds of crosses and plaques on the grass. We followed at a discreet distance. If anyone had asked me why we

were there or who we were, I was ready to say that I'd been a regular visitor to Mr. Heap's marvellous little shop and wanted to pay my respects. But no one asked me, no one glanced at us. The faces of the middle-aged sons with their wives, the grandchildren in their twenties, were lit only by the last rays of the midwinter sun and the glow from inside the hearse. A few tears, yes, but not of sadness as much as resignation, that a very old man who'd been loved and respected had passed away, after a long and honourable life... tears shining in nostalgic eyes, on cold white cheeks, a tear glistening on the tip of a reddened nose.

They stood and stared at the ground. What else could they do, where else could they look? One by one, they bent and placed a flower or a card, a memento or token.

Not many tears, until...

When one of the middle-aged sons and his wife turned to the next plot, where there was already a plaque in the grass, and they pressed their palms onto it, I could see how their shoulders began shuddering with grief. Not for the old man, whom they'd loved so much and would dearly miss, but for someone else, who'd been untimely and cruelly taken away.

Sobbing, the couple were helped to their feet. It was suddenly terrible. It had been reverent and calm. Now it was terrible. More than sadness: sorrow. More than sorrow: despair. And more than that: pain and anger. The family limped and stumbled back to the cars, they made strange mumbling, mewing noises into their handkerchiefs, and they were driven away.

A long silence. Darkness, and an overwhelming sense of the cold. When the family had gone, the place where we found ourselves standing was devoid of any life or warmth. Only a vacuum, which the bitterness of a January night hurried to fill up.

It was too dark to read the plaques on the lawn. Next to the new plot, the plaque which had provoked such an outburst of grieving was still warm, from the hands which had pressed

on it. Chloe knelt and touched it too. I searched her face for a reaction. She was smiling. She had no inkling, of course. For her, as the old man himself had remarked, life and death were equally jests.

Footsteps behind us.

As we were standing up and about to move away from the frozen grass, there was a crunch of footsteps on the gravel, the flash of a torchlight, and a calm, authoritative, sympathetic voice.

A man, apologetic. Wanting, as discreetly as possible, to tell us it was time to leave the premises. Were we relatives of the deceased, were we family or friends of Mr. Heap? He was so sorry and could he express his condolences?

He angled his torch at the place where we'd been kneeling. Even that, the way he played the beam onto the plaque we'd been touching, was carefully respectful, not wanting to intrude at a time of great sadness. Sad, yes, the passing-away of Mr. Heap, an old gentleman who'd given so much to the community, to the city of Nottingham. And last year, when was it? Last spring... the torch caressed the plaque and illumined the date on it... there'd been a terrible a car accident.

Me and Chloe, we walked away, our feet crunching, our breath pluming in the man's torchlight as he escorted us to the gate of the crematorium. He was asking, were we alright? We could get a bus to Long Eaton, yes the 7B, from the bus-stop on the other side of the road, thank you, good night and take care... he was thanking us for leaving and letting him lock up and go home, his voice was so kind, trained in the business of bereavement.

My mind was a jumble of thoughts, as we waited at the bus-stop and Chloe squeezed my hand with hers. Connections. PTO 725G, diamonds of glass, the tooth of Edgar Allan Poe.

Chapter Twelve

OF COURSE I'D known about the accident. Everyone in the area knew about it. As well as featuring on the front page of the *Nottingham Evening Post*, it was reported on local television news.

'*A seven-year-old girl has been injured in a hit-and-run incident, in Breaston village. A few minutes later, the car involved, travelling very fast along the Derby Road towards the centre of Long Eaton, apparently swerved out of control and struck the pillars at the entrance of Derwent College. The driver, Mrs. Angela Henson, 24, and her husband Mr. Andrew Henson, 29, were rushed to the Queen's Medical Centre, where they both died of their injuries. Chloe Gooch, the child involved in the hit-and-run incident, sustained a head injury from which she is expected to make a full recovery.*'

Of course I'd known about it. All I'd seen in a matter of seconds, like a clip from a movie, was the attractive couple in a nifty sports-car... a pretty blonde woman and a good-looking man, so typically glamorous that they could have been actors playing a part in a TV soap, accelerating past the camera and snarling angrily at each other at the same time. If the director had shouted Cut! at that moment and they'd stopped and got out, everything would've been fine. But it wasn't a soap, it was real life. And in real life they didn't stop. A child was brain-damaged, and five minutes later a young married couple were smashed into the windscreen of their nice little car.

It was like a cancer in my belly. Me, so engrossed in the nonsense about saxophones that I'd sent Chloe to the pub for crisps and fizzy drinks. Me, so exasperated with her and the

wretched wasp that I couldn't help laughing when she pulled off her shirt and ran outside... me, ignoring her when she snapped at me, *you can see what I'm fucking doing, because it fucking stung me that's why*, and I thought it was funny...

She'd been right. I would never learn to play the saxophone. The guilt in my belly, gnawing at me whenever I saw the doubt and fear in Rosie's eyes... the guilt I felt when that shameful, recurring thought came cringeing and fawning and wheedling into my brain, like a craven cur skulking in the shadows... that I liked Chloe more as a simpering angel than I had when she'd been herself. How to atone? How?

And the beautiful couple? Was that my fault too? I had a blurry fantasy that they'd seen Chloe come into the pub and stretch up to the bar and buy her crisps, that they'd said something to her or to the landlord, is she supposed to be buying stuff in here? Where are her parents? And the landlord had said that her Daddy was outside in the mobile library. Worse, in the same blur of wakefulness, in the darkest of fantasies one can only conjure in those deathless, desperate hours in the middle of the night, I heard the couple niggling about the rights or wrongs of the child coming into the pub on her own – and it was the very presence of the girl in the pub, whom I'd sent in there, which had sparked the row and sent them wrangling outside...

Of course I'd known about their accident, the tragedy of their deaths. How many hours of how many nights had I spent thinking about it? But I'd had no idea that the young woman had been Mr. Heap's granddaughter.

A TOOTH FOR a tooth. Chloe's tooth, Poe's tooth.

Rosie, ex-dental assistant, had remarked wryly on it. Coincidences like that only happen in books, she'd said. Was it Thomas Hardy – she was remembering from the lit. she'd done at school – was it Hardy who everyone said was too full of coincidences, unlikely and improbable things happening

to keep his big fat novels rolling along? And I'd said, yes I thought it was Hardy, but he did it because his books were published chapter by chapter, as serials, like the episodes of a soap on the television, so he had to make it all punchy and full of incident. Or was that Dickens?

But that was how it happened. I hadn't made it up. The very same morning when Chloe and I'd been hurrying down to the vestry and I was going to take a good look at the tooth that the old man had given me, she'd stumbled and fallen and jolted out one of her own. Hers, a right lower canine, according to Palmer's notation, had skidded across the flags of the church hallway, I'd followed the trail of bloody spittle as carefully as an aboriginal tracker, and found the tooth lodged so deeply in a crack in the stone that I couldn't get it out.

So there I was, a week or so later, on my hands and knees with a pair of pliers.

Sunday morning. That's why I was on my own, without Chloe hovering around me and staring and smiling, or else wandering into the bookshop to poke her fingers into the fire, or disappearing out of the church door and onto the pavement to be carried away by child-trafficking gypsies, or stepping into the road in front of a bus or...

It was a blessed Sunday morning, and Rosie had gone out somewhere, with Chloe.

The relief I felt was almost overwhelming. It shouldn't have been, because, as I'd acknowledged a hundred times over the last nine or ten months, the burden of care I had with the born-again Chloe was nothing compared with the challenge she'd presented in her earlier incarnation as a rambunctious, insatiable tyke. But still, not having her around, for a delicious Sunday morning, was nice... not having to read the anxiety on Rosie's face as she left for work, not having to memorise her daily instructions. I came down from the kitchen to the hallway, with a mug of coffee in one hand and a pair of pliers in the other, and I threw open the huge oak doors as wide as they would go.

A bitterly freezing morning. It breathed a breath of icy air into the church.

I didn't mind. I didn't mind if a whole thievery of ragged Romanian vagrants came by, or a stampede of buses. I wasn't responsible. As I knelt to the floor with my pliers, I almost hoped, sneakily, that Rosie would come back with a wounded Chloe – nothing serious of course, no more than a grazed knee or a splinter or a nose-bleed – so that I could pull some disapproving faces of my own.

Easier said than done, getting the tooth out. I couldn't find it.

The trail of blood was still there, very faint because, for a week of wintry days and nights, the wind from under the door had scored the flags with dust and frost and a flurry of fallen leaves. I followed the trail, but no tooth. I looked into every crevice, every crack, every cranny, every... whatever, the tooth had been there, I'd seen it, and now it was gone.

Strange. But never mind. I'd already said to Rosie that I hadn't been able to find Chloe's tooth. So I gave up the search and moved into the vestry.

I stood in the chilly grey room and looked around me. Despite the cold, I felt a sudden welling of great joy and excitement in my heart. Tomorrow, Monday morning, me and Chloe – after Mummy had briefed us as rigorously as if we were fighter pilots about to set off on a dangerous mission and she'd gone off to work – we would go down to the vestry with our coffee and chocolate biscuits, we'd put on the lamps and we'd light the sweetest, brightest, crackliest of all fires, we'd put on some music... and then we'd go outside onto the pavement with the sign I'd had made.

Poe's Tooth Bookshop: Open.

Chapter Thirteen

'SLOWLY SLOWLY... HEY don't worry... Rome wasn't built etc etc...'

Midday, and I hadn't had a single customer. Rosie was consoling me. Her wifely way of doing it was to persuade me, against all my instincts, to leave the church door wide open and take me and Chloe across the top of Shakespeare Street, into Azri's for a toasted teacake, and we could watch from there in case anybody came along. So we sat in Azri's tiny, cosy, corner cafe – where Azri, some kind of Kurd, was obviously doing fine, with only six tables but serving customers non-stop morning and afternoon and a little gold-mine – and we peered through his steamed-up windows in case somebody, one person, happened into the church.

No one came.

'Hey, slowly slowly,' Rosie was consoling me, 'did you really think there'd be a mad rush of customers, like the January sales or something? Were you expecting busloads of Japanese tourists, like at Anne Hathaway's Cottage, or the Brontë thing at Haworth, or what-is-it 220B Baker Street? It's a tooth, alright? So it might be the tooth of Edgar Allan Poe, or it might not be. It's your first day, alright?'

Unexpectedly, she had the day off. Colonel Brook had closed the school for his wife's birthday; it seemed that he could run his dismal little school as he liked, he was a creationist, he was God, he could declare a day of rest whenever he felt like it. So Rosie had suddenly reappeared at home and we'd opened the shop together. She'd helped me to light the fire and make everything nice, with the aroma of freshly-brewed coffee and some welcoming music – she'd changed my *Peaches en Regalia* to her *Year of the Cat*

– and by eleven o'clock, when we'd been snuggling by the fire and eating chocolate biscuits and tossing crumbs into the open hallway for the pigeons to eat and not a soul had come in, she'd suggested we adjourn across the road to Azri's.

We watched. A car stopped outside the church. I rubbed excitedly at the steam on the window. No one got out, the driver had pulled over to answer his mobile phone.

Fifteen minutes later, a taxi slowed at the corner of Shakespeare Street. No one got out, the driver only opened his door and spat onto the road and pulled away again.

Great excitement, when a tour bus hissed to a halt, and for a brilliant, fantasy-exploding millisecond I imagined fifty or sixty seriously academic Americans from a university in Kansas or Salt Lake City disgorging onto the pavement. No one got out, only the driver waddled across the road and breathlessly into Azri's, where, at the counter right behind me, he bought a cappuccino in a plastic container and waddled back to his bus, off to Chatsworth, or Matlock, or Alton Towers, with his not-so academic passengers.

Chloe bit into a toasted teacake. Maybe she hit on a dried-up raisin or something, but there was a gush of blood from her mouth and down her chin.

'Oh my lord, poor baby,' Rosie was saying, and she dabbed with the tissues that Azri proffered. Not enough tissue. The blood flowed copiously from the tender place where her tooth had been. It didn't drip, it plopped and splashed onto her teacake and formed a curiously beautiful pool with the butter on her plate.

'Poor baby... hey, keep still...' And while Mummy was trying her best to staunch the blood, applying some of the skills she'd learned in her former employment, Chloe was batting at the steamed-up window of the café and gurgling with excitement. All because... as all of us peered across the road, a mob of pigeons had erupted from the church doorway, where they'd been foraging for the crumbs of our biscuits... a whirling of grey and white feral pigeons, pluming from the wide open door, as though something inside had startled them.

Chapter Fourteen

I AWOKE WITH a terrible suddenness. With a jolt, like in one of those falling dreams, a dream of falling from a high building and being horribly, terminally weightless. A dream of imminent, certain death.

I was dead. For a moment, a moment so empty and cold and black that I had no notion of where I was, I thought that I was dead.

And then myself, my being, came back to me.

The room, our bedroom high in the tower of an old church. The night, a real night in a real January, not yet the oblivion I was dreading. I was warm underneath a thick, soft duvet, and I could feel the radiant, living heat of my wife's body beside me. But, although I should have been reassured and ready to snuggle down and go back to sleep again, I lay still and stared at the darkness of the ceiling and felt a gnawing, an aching in my belly.

It was that time of night. Dire wakefulness and nothing but guilt. I lay still and I stared, and I listened.

A sound. It was Rosie's breathing. We'd drunk a bottle of red wine together, she'd tried to lift my spirits with wine and then with her hot urgent body in our bed, and now she was sleeping a fumey sleep and whistling through her teeth.

Another sound. Something in the roof. A furtive scratching, so dainty and faint it could have been a mouse, pattering in the dust of the clock-tower.

Another sound. It was Chloe. Nothing alarming. In her room, she was making the mewing, mock-pathetic noise she knew would be enough to wake one of us to come and see

if she was alright, and then she would end up snug in bed with her Mummy while her Daddy was nudged out with her bony knees....

Good. I lay for a moment and listened to the three sounds. I was glad they were there. They were real. I had awoken from the forgetfulness of sleep into a night of bitter self-reproach. But now I had something of the everyday world to preoccupy me. Something to do.

I got up and crossed the room. Rosie didn't stir. She was snoring, flat on her back. Naked, I pushed open Chloe's door and blinked into the darkness. I couldn't see her, I could only make out the mound of her bedding, the tumble of her duvet and pillows. I whispered, 'Hey Chloe... what's up? You alright?'

She mewed. And she mewed again, her baby-sound when she needed attention and comfort. I took two steps forward and felt at her bed. She wasn't there.

There was a gleam of silver, it caught the corner of my eye. The ladder. I spun round and there she was, at the very top of it.

'Chloe!' I hissed the word at her. It came out as a puff of sound, no louder than the puff of a dandelion-clock. 'What on earth...? How did you pull the ladder down? Hey, come down from there...'

A gleam of silver, the faintest whiteness of her pyjamas, and the glint of her smile. Yes, she was smiling, and this time there was more in its metallic glimmer than the usual insipid nothingness. Mischief? A challenge? As I moved to the foot of the ladder and reached up for her, she made a tiny gurgle of laughter in her throat and she put up her hands to the trap-door.

'No, Chloe, not a game, not now... I told you, didn't I? I told you not to try and reach the ladder, didn't I? Come on, back to bed...'

She pushed at the trap-door and it yawned open, silent and smooth on its new springs. With another backward glance at me, daring me to follow, she was up the last few rungs of the ladder and disappearing into the darkness.

In a second I was up the ladder. I pulled myself through the trap-door, stood up and narrowed my eyes into the surrounding shadows of the clock-tower. It was freezing up there. I was naked, straight from a hot bed. A shaft of light from the street outside beamed through the broken panes of the clock face. No traffic, no swish of tyres or movement of passing headlamps. In the further corner of the big, black space, there was the outline of the central-heating boiler. Otherwise, nothing. Nothing but dust underfoot, the crunch of a litter of twigs and dried-up leaves... and me, stepping into the middle of the room and turning slowly round and round, stopping, staring, turning again, calling out, playing a children's game in a strange place in the middle of a sub-zero night.

'For heaven's sake, Chloe... come on now, this is silly. Mummy would be really cross, shall I go and tell her? Let's get you back into bed. Or you can go into Mummy's bed, do you want to? Snuggle with Mummy all nice and warm and...'

I saw her movement, just a flicker of shadow on the floor. And another movement, like a puddle of shadow, separate from hers. For a moment the two shadows were one, and I heard the girl's giggle of excitement, a note of triumph in it. But then the smaller shadow freed itself from hers and scuttled across the floor.

Yes, it scuttled; it made a sound of clicking and clattering claws on the dust and twigs, and the flutter of cold, dry wings. Because it was the crow. Chloe had heard it in the room above her head. She had come to find it. And now, as her shadow broke away from the clustered shadows of the wall beside the clock, she was chasing the crow to try and catch it.

'Chloe, what...? Leave it, Chloe, just let it go, it's dirty and nasty and Mummy will be really cross, she'll...'

The bird brushed past my bare legs. I instinctively recoiled from the needle-sharpness of its claws on my bare feet. And then, when I clutched at Chloe as she swerved close to me, she somehow evaded my clumsy grabbing and wriggled past, in chuckling pursuit of the crow. 'Leave it, Chloe...' Her feet

were almost silent, no louder than the whisper of the dead leaves she disturbed, cushioned by years of dust. As my eyes adjusted to the darkness, I saw how the bird was trailing a wing and sculling around the edges of the room, rowing itself along and using all the traction it could achieve with its claws, and even with desperate jabs and tugs with its beak, like a climber making life-or-death use of an ice-axe.

The girl was right behind it. She reached down with both hands and missed. She stomped with one foot to trap the injured wing and she missed. The bird sprang off the floor, managed a moment of frantic flight and lunged for the hole in the clock face, from which it had once before made a plummeting escape. But this time it missed. Dazzled and disorientated by the shaft of light from outside, it struck the edge of the broken glass, beat against it, a grotesque silhouette of wings and claws and beak, and it fell back to the floor. And just as Chloe was right there and reaching for it, just as I reached for her and swept her off her feet and away, the crow made another bid for freedom. It sprang to the trap-door. It fell, like a flutter of old rags, down into Chloe's bedroom.

'Oh great... oh that's great...' I heard myself panting. I squeezed the child's body so hard against mine, almost overwhelmed by a fury of frustration, that she squeaked like a toy. 'Chloe, you silly bad girl... now you're coming down with me, you silly silly girl, and you're going to get into your bed and stay still and I'm going to get the big nasty bird out, alright? Get it out, alright, without waking Mummy, alright?'

She was suddenly compliant, as though I'd squeaked the mischief out of her. I got myself through the trap-door and onto the ladder without daring to let go of one of her wrists, and then I hoicked her unceremoniously down, managed to pull the door shut and then lumped her down to the floor.

'Bed. You, into bed.' I shoved her onto it and into it and she was still. Still, but breathing hard from the madness of the game, and yes, still smiling that infuriatingly angelic smile, as though Daddy had enjoyed the game as much as she had. And

she watched from there, a delighted spectator, as I poked and rummaged under her bed and around her dressing table to try and find where the bird had gone, as I fumbled into her open wardrobe and it burst out of the darkness and scrabbled at my face and neck and chest before hopping out of her bedroom and into ours.

'Oh great, yes that's fucking great...' I hissed again at Chloe. 'Bed, you stay there.'

Oh god, the bird was on our bed, it was a black stain on our duvet, a piece of a nightmare snagging its claws into the soft material and struggling to free itself right next to Rosie's face. Oh god, but thank god for the wine and the fume of sleep in which Rosie was so deeply befuddled, because she just groaned and rolled over and swatted around her head with one lazy bare arm so that the bird was free and off the bed and thank god, oh thank god it was closer and closer to the bedroom door... so that, as I herded it in front of me with my naked legs and instinctively shielded myself with both hands in case the bird sprang up and pecked at my penis with its pick-axe of a beak, when I reached for the door and pulled it open, I could kick the bird out.

At least, down in the kitchen, I felt the panic in my chest subside.

Upstairs, Rosie was asleep. The worst was over. The crow had skittered so close to her wheezily snoring mouth that she must have felt its wings on her face. Now, with the light on in the kitchen, it was easier for me to take a breath, to take my own time and locate the bird...

Trying to calm myself, I put the kettle on. While it was boiling, I sat at the table and waited and listened and saw a bristle of raggedy black feathers jutting from behind the fridge. Uninvited. Before I had time to reach for the brush leaning in the corner and force the bird from its hiding-place, it sidled out. With one beat of its wings, as though they'd been strong and whole all of the time, it was standing right opposite me, on the back of a chair, at the kitchen table.

Carrion crow. Not in gleaming, rude health, but more or less intact. A starveling, a survivor. It had the defiant, dangerous look of an escaped convict. An escapee from deathrow. It looked at me and shuffled its wings and feathers together again. It looked at me and cocked its head, and it snorted through its bristly nostrils. Black bare legs, shiny and scaly like the legs of a lizard, knobby-knuckly feet tipped with ebony claws. Those eyes, blue-black, rimmed with a ripple of black skin, and a sudden blink of a pale, membranous lid. The beak, its means of survival, a tool for a lifetime of thievery and thuggery, a weapon for wounding and killing and eating. For scavenging carrion.

A word whispered in my head. I said it aloud. 'Poe.'

The suddenness of the sound, its plosive force, ruffled the bird into action. It opened its wings like a cloak, wide and black and saturnine, as though mocking the ministers who had hitherto inhabited this hallowed tower. It stepped off the chair and floated to the floor, landing as lightly as a moth.

And then it was easy for me, to open the kitchen door and let it hop down and down the stairs into the darkness of the hallway of the church.

Gone. I would have to sort it out tomorrow. It could stay there, it could huddle in a corner and watch for the daylight beneath the great oak door, and in the morning I could put it out.

I had tea. A naked man, sipping from a steaming mug and inspecting a strange map of weals and welts on my body, inflicted in the middle of a winter's night by a mischievous crow. Mischief... the word made me think, as I sat there and felt the desire for sleep come over me, that Chloe had shown a spirit we hadn't seen since the day of her accident. And I pondered the irony that, although I'd threatened the child back into bed with the ultimate sanction of telling her mother, Rosie might – after the initial shock of seeing the child up in the clock-tower with the bird – she might have been thrilled to see a vital spark in Chloe. After all, didn't Rosie want her back, didn't she want a naughty, rumbustious Chloe?

I didn't know. I wasn't sure. What did I know about anything? And what did I want? All I knew was that, hearing the crow in the room above her head, the child had been enlivened... was that the word?

I dropped my mug into the sink. I switched off the light in the kitchen and went up to the bedroom. Rosie was snoring, in a sweet oblivion. Chloe was lying beside her, a sleeping cherub.

So I went into her room. I returned the ladder, on its silent runners, to the ceiling, and I tied up the cord where I thought she could never reach it.

Into Chloe's bed. Game over.

Chapter Fifteen

'It's time you changed his straw. It smells. There's a funny smell in here and I can even smell it upstairs in the bedroom.'

The mouse, Mouse, was working its wheel with a manic intensity. No prizefighter, training in a remote camp in the weeks before a world championship fight, had ever worked harder. It drove the wheel relentlessly, harder and faster until the whole contraption might fly off and smash into smithereens against the bars of the cage, with the mouse mangled inside it. Rosie was almost ready. Chloe and me, we were doing toast and tea and cosying at the kitchen table. Rosie had been smelling funny things since she'd woken up and showered and dressed, she was crinkling her nose in the bedroom and down into the kitchen and looking curiously around her, and at last, seeing and hearing Mouse hurtling the wheel almost to destruction, she'd found the culprit.

'Can you do that, Chloe? Change his straw? Daddy will help you, if he has a few moments between serving his customers in the shop. I mean, if there's a lull for a minute or two, Daddy can grab a breather between the coach parties from China and Japan and Korea, and the Ph.D. students from America of course, and he'll help you and poor little neglected Mouse will be nice and clean again...'

She said all this, clucking and wittering, a gently sarcastic mother-hen, as she donned her gear for the arctic trudge down Shakespeare Street to Brook's Academy. I let it all go, busying myself with Chloe, in a cuddle of coffee and Radio 4 and relishing my status as one of the unshaven, undressed, unemployed. Yes, there was a smell in the bedroom and in the kitchen, and Chloe and I knew what it was, something animal and oddly fetid, and

wild, as though we'd had rats in the house and one of them might have died behind the fridge. The crow, in its scuttling from top to bottom of the tower, had left a curious, unidentifiable scent... unidentifiable, unless of course you'd been there and knew what it was.

At last Rosie was girt for her expedition. And once again, as she nearly always did, she pecked me on the cheek and set off down and down into the cold dark hallway, and she said, 'I may be some time...'

I waited at the top of the stairs and held my breath. I watched the yawning darkness swallow her up, heard her tugging the church door open and her going out and clanging it shut... expecting any moment her squeal or shriek as she discovered our carrion-bird skulking down there and startling her and...

But she was gone. The door was shut. I heard her booted footsteps fading along the pavement.

OVER THE FOLLOWING days I had customers. No coachloads. But a few people came into the shop.

And they bought a few books. Yes, there were doubters and cynics, there were gainsayers and poo-poohers, there were raggedy Romanians and shuffling vagrants who came in because they smelled the coffee and heard the music and saw the flickering flames of our birchwood fire. But I sold some books.

Chloe and I settled in, that first morning, and she sat by the fire and let Mouse scurry around her shoulders and down the front of her woolly pullover and through her sleeves, let it explore the warm and snuggly labyrinth of her chubby, cherubic body. It emerged from time to time at one of her wrists, sat on the palm of her hand panting, as though exhausted by the suffocating heat of its journey, and then disappeared again into another sleeve.

A man came in. For a bizarre moment, I was so surprised that I was going to ask him what on earth he thought he was doing just wandering in and snooping around... and then the reality of the shop came back to me and I was suffused with such a welling of

warmth through my head and my body that I could almost have fainted. He didn't say much. He didn't need to. He was my first customer. No need to describe him, he was a nondescript guy in a coat and a hat and it didn't matter who he was, I could've hugged him and kissed him, I was so happy to have him in the vestry of my old church, in Poe's Tooth Bookshop. In reality, he was a time-waster, he was listening to the music, he was looking funny at Chloe, he wasn't at all interested in the books or the tooth. But when he'd gone, without speaking a word or buying anything, I picked up Chloe in my arms in a huge Siberian bear-hug and we whirled around the room in a madcap Cossack dance inspired by the fragrance of the fire, because someone had come in... we were open!

There was a tiny, tiny scratting sound. I was changing the music, and in the quietness, in the lull, when the logs had collapsed into a shower of sparks and a billow of blue smoke, both of us heard a sound in the corner of the room. We looked at each other. We knew that the bird had come into the shop. Me and Chloe. We'd smelled it when we'd first come in, when we'd busied ourselves lighting the fire. We'd heard it. Mouse had smelled it and heard it, whenever it had poked out its pink little questing snout from the tunnels of Chloe's clothing, it must have sniffed the smell of the bird. Even a mouse, especially a mouse, even a poor, pale, domesticated albino, it must have scented the danger in the air.

Carrion crow. Death, in a raggedy black cloak. All of that morning, we'd seen not a glimmer of a feather, not a reptilian gleam of beak or claw, but we'd known that the bird was there. In the night, when I'd bundled it down the stairs from the kitchen, it must have sought sanctuary in the vestry... where a century of ministers had shaken the dust from their cloaks and hung them on big brass hooks and warmed their legs in front of the fire. As soon as Rosie had gone out of the door, without a squeal or a shriek, I'd known that the bird must've gone into the vestry.

It emerged, dead on cue.

I think it was Chloe who did it. With Mouse. A man came into the shop in the afternoon. He was very big and fat and he smelled,

his clothes smelled of smoke and beer and of being unwashed – the same clothes he'd worn since before Christmas, when the cold weather had taken a grip on the days and nights and the winter seemed like an ice-age, not just a season which would inevitably pass by and give way to spring. He scanned around the room. He was poor and lonely and unhappy, but he conjured a little smile on his cold, wet lips, as though he hadn't smiled for a long time, because he liked the fire and the room and the sweet little smiling girl. He peered and pondered at the lamplit tooth, and at me. I hadn't shaved for a few days and I was scruffy and huddled in my baggy old pullover and coat and fidgeting at the computer as though I was some kind of tortured and tormented writer toiling on my novel. He seemed to like it all. And just as he was lifting a book from the shelf and turning it over to read the blurb on the back, there was a commotion which made all of us stop and turn and look.

A white mouse. It appeared from the sleeve of a beautiful child beside a crackling fire. It dropped onto the floor and it ran. And as it ran, there was a clattering of something big and clumsy in a corner of the room, which knocked over a pile of books and scattered them... and it was a bird, a big black bird with a jabbing beak which was after the mouse.

Big black bird. Tiny white mouse. Giggling golden-haired girl. A scriptwriter couldn't have done it better.

Chloe, by a miracle of dexterity or sleight of hand, snatched the mouse off the floor and vanished it into her clothing. The bird sprang at her hands and then fell backwards, awkward and defeated, like a pantomime villain the audience would love to hiss... and when it shuffled itself together again and limped away, when it made a shameful exit and disappeared among the boxes of tattered and slightly foxed, remaindered paperbacks, the unhappy man gave a funny chortling laugh and pulled a five-pound note from his pungent pocket.

I gave him his change and he went out chuckling, with a paperback Poe, a collection of stories or poems or whatever it was. My first sale.

Chapter Sixteen

'BUT DON'T YOU get it, Rosie? It's perfect... alright, so it's another of those ridiculous coincidences you get in Hardy or Dickens or whoever, but who cares? It happened and I can use it to help the shop. Edgar Allan Poe and his raven, or his scruffy old crow in this case...'

I'd been lying to my wife. She'd come home, sniffing at the air in the tower as soon as she'd stepped through the front door, and I'd given her the good news first, that I'd had some browsers in the shop and sold a book. My hurried version of the story – I wanted to tell her quickly and get some of the truth out before flannelling around the rest of it – was that, just as a man was poking around and looking at the books, some of those pesky pigeons had blown into the hallway, pecking around for the biscuit crumbs we'd left there... and just as I was shooing them out, a raggedy old crow had tried its luck too, except that, just as the pigeons had gone fluttering out, the crow had hopped into the vestry. Not a big deal – I was saying in a deliberately off-hand way – in fact it kind of added to the atmosphere and you should've seen how Chloe's face had lit up. Anyway, the upshot was that the customer had thought it was quaint and he'd bought a book, you know, Poe and the crow and all that. Oh, and by the way – I was adding as Rosie started heading up the stairs towards the kitchen – that must be the whiffy smell throughout the tower, not Mouse after all, but maybe the birds or specifically the bird in the vestry.

At which point, she'd turned round, at the top of the stairs and frowned down at me. 'What do you mean, in the vestry?

You got it out, didn't you? Or is it still in there? What are you saying, is it still in there or what?'

She started downwards again, and I blocked her way, at least for a moment. 'Well yes, no, I'm not sure,' I was blustering. 'I mean, I think it might've been in there yesterday, and maybe even overnight, my fault for leaving crumbs around by the open door. And so the smell must've drifted up the stairs, even as far as our bedroom...' She brushed past me and into the vestry, where Chloe was sitting as meekly as her mouse in the diminishing firelight. I put in, 'Alright, so it might be still in here, I don't know, but don't you get it? It's perfect, it's...'

She bundled the girl into her arms, hugged her close, at the same time staring into the sooty shadows of the room and inhaling long, disapproving breaths through her nose. She didn't say much more, but I could almost hear her brain whirring in a fury of disgruntlement and... and something else, something had piqued her brain when I'd said that Chloe had reacted to the presence of the bird. The notion was snagging in her mind, pricking her like the tiniest splinter of a thought. She was looking oddly at me, a curious mixture of emotions moving across her face as softly as the firelit shadows, so that I couldn't tell if she was going to react by accusing me of further negligence in the care of her daughter or respond to the half-baked idea that having a crow in the shop could be good for business. I'd lied, by omission: she had no idea that the bird had been in the clock-tower, that Chloe and I had been up there, that the bird had been flapping around on her duvet in the middle of the night on its way down through the kitchen and into the hallway... and now she was searching my eyes for the truth I'd withheld.

At last, as she turned and hurried up the stairs with Chloe, she said, 'Well, get it outside, Oliver. It stinks. And you too, you stink, you look a mess, you need a shave and a shower. Or is that supposed to be perfect as well?'

*   *   *

I DIDN'T REALLY stink. It was the baggy pullover and the greatcoat I'd been wearing to keep warm in and out of the church doorway and in the shop. Underneath it, I was my fragrant, manly self, showered and deodorised. But yes, I could sense how people recoiled from me in the charity shops in Long Eaton High Street, even the veteran volunteers who were used to the smokey, beery smell of their unemployed customers. I hadn't shaved, I knew I needed a haircut but I wasn't going to have one, and I'd got my bookshop outfit on, the pullover and greatcoat. Chloe was wrapped in many layers and topped off with the bobble-hat, so that she looked like one of Santa's elves who'd been left behind after Christmas. We'd had a brisk, frosty walk downtown, and I had a list of things I needed.

Photocopies. I got a big blow-up of the *Nottingham Evening Post* article and its photos of the tooth and the old handwritten document of authenticity, as I liked to imagine it to be, and a hundred small copies of the document, postcard size. While we had a coffee and cake on the market square, an elderly gent in his old-fashioned cobbler's and key-cutting shop (the only business which had survived the coming of the supermarkets on the edge of town) was making a rubber stamp for me. And in the animal welfare shop, where I'd been rummaging for any kind of magnifying glass, I'd found, even better, a kind of plastic lens designed to help short-sighted geriatrics to read books and magazines.

An even brisker walk home – because the morning was so bitter but also because I was so boyishly excited to get back and get open – and soon we were kneeling at the hearth, crackling up the fire, boiling the kettle and putting out the sign.

And the crow?

We both knew, from the smell and from the way the white mouse wiggled its whiskers out of Chloe's sleeve and disappeared again, that the crow was somewhere in the vestry. I sprinkled a few crumbs. And the bird came out. It ate up the crumbs, it sprang onto my desk and admired itself in the reflection of the computer screen. It shook out its wings and

splattered a green-white mute onto the floor. As though to announce, we were ready and waiting for customers.

A few gainsayers and poo-poohers, yes.

A very old gentleman came in, shrunken like a mummy inside his dark suit and oversized shirt, so quivery that a puff of smoke from the chimney might have blown him over. Fortunately, the bird made itself scarce, as he looked around the hallway and started snivelling into a white handkerchief. He tried to resist me, screwing up his face and spitting feebly at the smell of my clothes, but then he allowed me to sit him down in the vestry. Screwing up all his indignation, he told me he'd been a Sunday school teacher at the church when he was in his twenties, been married in it, had his children baptized in it and played the organ at decades of harvest festivals and carol services, and last year his wife's funeral service had been held there. He dabbed at the tears in his eyes and gazed into the hallway, as though he could, by a tremendous feat of mind over matter, conjure his memories back into reality: himself and his wife, young and beautiful on their wedding day and those very stone flags strewn with confetti; babies, decades of Easter and Christmas celebrations and a lifetime of Sundays; more recently, his wife's funeral, her coffin being wheeled on a trolley across the same stone flags.

At last he twisted his face at me. His mouth writhed and was ugly. 'And now, this...' he hissed through his teeth, 'in my church. What is it? Some kind of shop, selling dirty books. It isn't right. It isn't right. It's wrong.'

He stood up, pushing away my attempts to steady him, and teetered out of the church.

A man with a briefcase came to ask if I had a licence, said I'd have to get one, running a small business, something something. Depressingly, I supposed because of the economic climate of unemployment and hard times, there were odd bods who came in to sneer. At the tooth. To say it wasn't even a tooth, it was a bit of bone or even melamine, or it was the tooth of a dog, in any case it was a fake and no more real than King Arthur's footprints at

Tintagel or the shroud of Turin or whatever... and one very scary middle-aged man, literally broiling with hatred for all the world and the injustices which had been dealt him, who told me in a voice trembling with anger that he'd been to The Who's so-called last-ever concert in Southampton way back in the 80s and bought a commemorative programme which was going to be priceless, and then of course they'd been touring ever since and were still doing concerts nearly thirty years later and his programme was worthless... like the tooth, a hoax, a trick, a crock of shit, just a fucking scam... he went out of the church and into the outside world, on fire with anger, looking for somewhere else to vent it.

Glory be, for the believers, for whom, as I'd said to Rosie, it wasn't the reality of the tooth which was important, but the belief it inspired.

Like my Beatles bathwater. I'd bought a bottle and it had been precious to me, it was my bit of George, my favourite. And when he died, I searched and searched everywhere and found it, strangely half-gone, mysteriously evaporated although the lid was still tightly screwed on, and no more than a swill of grey scum. The day he died, I held the bottle in my hand and felt the warmth in it still, as though George had just got out of his bath and pulled the plug and here it was, a few drops of his bathwater. And I'd cried.

Belief. Believe. There were people coming into the shop who believed, or at least they wanted to believe. Not many, but a few, they bent over the tooth in its satin-lined, purple velvet box, on its presentation table, under the lamp, and they peered at it through the magnifying lens. They held their breath. Their eyes glistened. And so, when they bought a book, I stamped the inside page with my new rubber stamp, Poe's Tooth Books, and slipped in a bookmark with the very words which Dr Barnsby had written to record that he'd kept a tooth from the mouth of Edgar Allan Poe and slipped a penny under the little boy's pillow... and the customer, the believer, went out into the cold simply glowing with the heat of inspiration.

And the crow helped. I helped. Chloe helped. We were a team.

The bird had an easy job. Whenever anyone came in, it flapped to the highest bookshelf and peered down from it, as though judging from the demeanour of the person how appropriate it might be to make a dramatic entrance. And then it would snort through its bristly carrion-crow nostrils, just enough to make the customer look around and up to see where the sound was coming from, and before he or she could even gasp with surprise it would leap away from the shelf and, with a couple of beats of its shabby, dusty black wings, it would settle on the back of a chair, or even more picturesquely on top of the computer screen.

Me, I was unkempt. Rather smelly. And I would sit at the computer, a distracted, glowering, troubled figure, especially if the crow was perched nearby and ducking and bobbing like a demented Richard III or a bedraggled Rasputin. For extra effect, I could be either rattling furiously at the keyboard in an outpouring of genius or stabbing with two fingers in terrible literary constipation, whichever came over me as I grew into the role.

And Chloe? Having sat by the fire, off and on throughout the day, her face was mottled and blotchy, her eyes were reddened and her cheeks were smutty. Her tousled blonde hair gleamed in the light of the flames. She ran a tiny white mouse from one hand to the other. She smiled, and a smear of blood was on her teeth. Perfect. She was an urchin, a silent, sooty angel.

Chapter Seventeen

'AND YOU'VE STARTED writing? Well, wonders never cease. Soon you'll be telling me you're learning to play the saxophone or peering through a telescope at the night sky or, what was the other thing? oh yes you're setting off to do the coast-to-coast walk from St. Bees to Robin Hood's Bay...'

I aped a smile at her. 'And taxidermy, my dearest Rosie, don't forget taxidermy. Yes, I'm going to do all of those things. Hey, don't be mean, there's nothing wrong with having a few plans and ambitions. Don't knock my little schemes and daydreams.'

We weren't rowing or wrangling, it was just our usual exchange of snidey banter. Oddly, her asides were a bit more frequent, now that the shop was running and I'd done a bit of business. Perhaps it was because I'd stopped shaving for a while, or it rankled because I was making a paltry contribution to the family economy and threatening her status as sole bread-winner. So I parried clumsily, 'Hey, I know you used to work for those fancy dentists in town, Dowling & McCorrister, charging their rich clients extortionate fees to do their kids' braces and veneers and all that stuff... and now you're strolling the groves of academe with Colonel Brook, and God said let there be light and so on... and me, I'm just a dabbler, a dilettante. But yes, I've started to write.'

She bethought herself. 'I'm sorry, my darling, I'm really happy that the shop's actually happening and it's fun. What are you writing? Go on, tell me about it...' And she kissed me full on the lips, stretching up so that her weight was on me and I had to step backwards to avoid overbalancing. So the kiss was very short, and she misunderstood my movement. She turned

away, with a tiny shrug of disdain, as though I'd deliberately recoiled from her. 'Alright, well tell me about it when I get back. I may be a bit later than usual. Colonel Brook's holding a meeting after school this afternoon and he's asked me to take the minutes.' She went out.

Another lie. Well, it was partly true, about the writing. I'd been sending e-mails to a few old colleagues from my days with the borough council, not exactly blogging but spreading the word about the shop and the tooth and forwarding the newspaper article to anyone who might have missed it. Writing a book? Well no, although, in a flurry of hammering at the keyboard whenever a customer came in, I'd suddenly found I could rattle a few thoughts for a story, just by looking around the shop and at the bird and Chloe and catching a glimpse of my own eccentric reflection. No need to look any further for a story, even if I only kept a journal of the weirdness of the past nine or ten months, of the changes in our lives and where we lived and what we were doing. So yes, I'd been writing, not on paper, but into the mysterious workings of the computer. And sometimes, if I was stuck for the next sentence or a link or a dying phrase, I only had to reach for a book from the nearest heap and it was stuffed with the things, every shelf was groaning with other people's hare-brained ideas. Fuck, if I couldn't find something to write now, in this place, after all that was happening to me and surrounded by hundreds of thousands or even millions of superbly-crafted words, then whenever would I?

Well, not today.

Something about the room was wrong. Even the crow, as soon as we opened up and put out the sign and started to light the fire, even the crow didn't like it. It had been huddling in the vestry all night, but now it sprang into the hallway and out of the front door and was gone. It took off, effortlessly, as though all this time it had been pretending to be a pitiful wretch, and beat across the playing fields of Derwent College. I watched it, me and Chloe watched it, we saw how it swerved through

a flock of gulls and spooked them into a panic-stricken mob, and then swerved away again. Chloe too, back in the vestry, although her smile was as constantly bland as ever, had a different, bilious look in her eyes.

It was a glorious morning. Cold, yes, freezing hard although the sun was so bright. And it was the steely brightness of the sun which made the shop seem oddly unwelcoming. It glinted through the lancet windows, yet the glint was harshly metallic. The fire, although it tried its best to look cheery with its friendly puffs of blue smoke, although it sounded merry with its crackle and wheeze and pop, it looked pale. It couldn't compete with the sunlight. The whole room, at its best in a swaddle of dark shadows, with the fire aglow and the books snuggling on their shelves, was kind of shabby.

I looked around it and at Chloe. I knew I was making excuses, about the sunlight and the firelight and all. Yes yes, I'd used the words myself, I was a dabbler and a dilettante and I'd always procrastinate if there was an easier option. Now I blurted, 'Hey Chloe, let's go out, shall we? It's too nice to be festering in here with all these musty old books and this poor little fire. Hey, don't look at me like that, like your Mummy... yes I know I was going to start writing, but what do you think? A morning on the boat, and then some chips in the Trip? Robin Hood and the shops and back on the bus? And we'll be back before Mummy's finished her meeting with the god-squad. She'll never know. We can tell her we were here all day. Alright?'

The boat was on Sawley Marina. The water was a sheet of grey ice, crazed and fluted where it had thawed and re-frozen a thousand times over the past few weeks. But when I started the engine and the propeller churned, I could swing the bow away from its moorings and we broke free. The ice was a crust. We sliced easily through it and the still, black waters of the canal.

The Gay Lady – it was only a little cruiser, twelve-foot or something, wooden on top with a fibreglass hull, a tiny cabin at the front with a couple of bunks in it, a puny two-horse-

power outboard motor slung on the back. At the front, on the back... alright, so boating was something else I'd been dabbling in and I didn't use the correct terminology. But the three of us had had fun on *The Gay Lady* on long hot summer afternoons and long, balmy evenings, chugging along the Trent & Mersey through Shardlow, past the breweries of Burton-on-Trent and drinking in Branston, almost as far as Lichfield. We were hopeless, we butted and bashed at other boats and scraped every bridge we came to. But it was idyllic... coot and moorhen, the stately heron, me and Rosie struggling with the locks while onlookers at the riverside pubs jeered and hooted and shouted ribald, deliberately unhelpful advice. We'd seen a kingfisher, and an otter, and in the twilight we'd seen fox and badger. In the remains of the summer since the accident, we'd seized every moment of joy together with an eagerness bordering on desperation. And our fumbling mishaps on board the silly little boat had been an escape from our anxieties.

This time, I swung the boat into the city... into a mysterious, dripping world which only a handful of people would ever see.

While hundreds of commuters swept overhead in their neat, warm cars, on the bridges and flyovers into the centre of Nottingham, we saw an underworld they didn't know existed. The canals beneath a modern city – secret tunnels and echoing caverns, a tumble of frozen undergrowth, the derelict forests of nettle and wort and fireweed; stone archways, groins and quoins and other architectural curios; odd little doors, locked and never opened since Victorian times.

Chloe sat on the front of the boat. And there was the tiniest change in her, I could almost detect a hint of her old defiance, as she dangled her feet precariously close to the slimy walls of the chasms we entered, as she glanced at me, as though challenging me to reprimand her, and then lowered her eyes. We coasted through dark green shadows, where I stilled the engine and we waited and listened as the real world of business and commerce and work hurried over our heads.

Her old self, she would never have sat and listened like that. Now she was rapt. She listened to the silence.

Not quite a silence. A rat plopped into the water. Pigeons fluttered in their secret, fetid places. A man, in a huddle of old newspapers, drunk perhaps and probably dying, groaned and muttered and lay still. *Drip, drip, drip.* A million, a billion drips, each one a second in the life of the city, hidden away and yet only a few yards from its blinkered, oblivious inhabitants.

'Chips? And beer for me...' We were in Ye Olde Trip to Jerusalem, the oldest pub in England.

From here, as long ago as the 12th century, rag-tag parties of foot-soldiers and so-called knights swaggering on their horses would set off for the Crusades. Chloe ate chips from a basket. She dipped them in salt and tomato sauce and nibbled them with her front teeth, like a rodent, like the vole we'd seen shivering in the tumbledown thistles on the canal-side or the mouse she'd secreted somewhere about her person. I drank a pint of dark, sweet ale from a brewery in Kegworth, only a few miles away. We both peered out of the window, at the beetling cliff of the castle, into which the pub had been built eight hundred years ago, and at the frosty cobbles on which the hooves of the Crusaders' horses had rung before they'd set off to a distant land of disease and death and never come home.

'Chips for you, beer for me... cheers, Chloe. Right now Mummy will be toiling away and thinking we're toiling as well. So cheers, here's to us and our little secret.'

She looked at me sideways, and again, unnervingly I saw her mother's look in her eyes. Worse – no I shouldn't use that word or allow the idea into my shallow, callow, lightweight excuse for a brain – I thought for a terrifying millisecond that she was going to speak. Oh god, I gulped on my beer, which Chloe had paid for with the clang on her head. I flinched from the sudden directness of her, and looked out of the window at the sunlit day of my not-having-to-work that she'd paid for.

Please don't speak, I inwardly begged of her, *please don't speak, not now. Don't spoil a perfect day by opening your*

mouth and saying something, by saying anything. Please, not now.

She didn't speak. She smiled like an angel and ate another chip. I took another swig at my beer and pondered the... what was it? The dichotomy, the conundrum, the enigma? Whatever it was. I pondered the paradox that Rosie prayed every waking moment for Chloe to come back, and yet I was dreading her return.

It would start to get dark. An afternoon in January. The temperatures hadn't risen more than a degree or two above freezing for three weeks or more, even in the brightest of winter mornings, and at night, every night for nearly a month, they'd plummeted to minus eight or ten. So now, only three o'clock and a fug of smokey, warm bodies in the pub, I could see how the light was dulling outside. The very moment the sun was off the castle wall and the cobbled yard, you could sense them, feel them and smell them, the creeping grey fingers of ice and the cloak of darkness they were tugging with them.

Chloe made an odd little sound. She stood up suddenly and did it again. I held my breath. It was almost a word. It was the closest to a word she'd said since last April.

'What is it, Chloe? Is it Mouse? Where is he?' She was feeling around her tummy and up and down her arms for the creature, which eventually emerged at her wrist and she caught it very gently. Alright, so the sound she'd made, which had paralysed me for a moment with my glass a few inches from my lips, had been just a squeak, a tiny eek or eeeh. A mouse-like expletive she'd made to echo the fidgeting of the mouse inside her clothes. As I swallowed the last of my beer, she did it again, the almost-word, and she was wandering away from our table in the direction of the doorway. I put down my glass and followed her.

The dark. It seemed to ooze from the caverns of the castle-boulder and from the cracks between the cobbles. Four o'clock, or was it later? Had we stayed longer in the pub than I'd meant to, because of the coddling cosiness of it and

the sweet, strong beer? As I hurried along, fumbling with my coat buttons and scarf and huffing on the steep climb towards the gatehouse, I saw Chloe ahead of me. She was unusually agile on the slippery stones, she'd been a pawky kid and yet now she was swifter than before. She turned and glanced at me, a teasing gleam in her eye. The dark, she was burrowing into it... the shadows lowered around her where the sun had never touched all day, as she swerved into the alley to Robin Hood's statue.

There, I expected her to pause, as she always did, to hug his stout bronze legs or even tingle her tongue on his thigh. It would give me time to catch up with her. But this time, she didn't stop. Flinging me another glance, as though challenging me to keep up, she was off again and disappearing into a further alley, on our usual route through the old part of the town and back to the bus station.

Lost her. Oh god. 'Chloe! Wait! Let me catch up!' I stumbled through the gloom, where the only light was from the upstairs windows of the solicitors and accountants in their oak-panelled offices. So dark... darker than usual in this alley, empty and forbidding, where before there'd always been at least a glimmer of light and even the welcoming glow of a fire. I stopped, to catch my breath and orientate myself, because the place seemed different, something was missing, there was a black hole where there'd always been a...

I heard Chloe. She made that sound again. 'Chloe! Where are you? I can't see you. Stay where you are, don't move, Daddy's here.'

Through the wheeze of my own breathing, I heard her tiny eeeh – the mouse-vowel, not quite a word. I moved towards it and then I could hear her breathing too and smell the warmth of her mouth and her body. 'Hey you naughty girl, don't go running off, especially here in the dark. I was worried, and Mummy would be really cross. Hey!'

She was gone again. I'd been close enough to touch her. But she spun away. Not far this time. My eyes had adjusted to the

gloom of the narrow alleyway, of course I knew where we were, and when I saw her slip into the yawning black mouth of a doorway and vanish, I understood where she'd been heading.

Closed. The door was closed and there was a notice on it. The golden lettering of the name on the window was tarnished, not by age, because it had already been there for decades, but sadly by the lack of light from inside the shop. Heaps. No longer trading. Leaving a hole, a darkness, in this corner of the city.

Eeeeh. Chloe said it again. No, she didn't say it. She made the sound. I whispered to her, 'Yes, Heaps,' as though that was what she'd said. 'Do you remember Mr Heap? What a pity we won't see him anymore. He was a funny old man, wasn't he? And he had some funny old things in his shop, didn't he?'

I made to hold her in my arms. Something in the poignancy of the moment and the sad emptiness of the place made me move to her and put my arms around her. Why had she run so determinedly to this doorway? Not even pausing at the statue, not even waiting for me to catch up, but leading me inevitably closer and closer until here we were, the two of us, snuggled in the entrance of the shop we'd visited so often? Just out of habit, her childish footsteps following the route we'd always followed, in a teasing game of hide-and-seek. Now, I squeezed her towards me, and she hugged me too. For a moment, an image flashed into my mind, of the derelict man we'd glimpsed from the boat that morning, in the dripping caverns beneath the city bridges, and I thought that the stab of ice between my well-padded shoulder blades would be nothing compared to the lingering death he would endure. It made me whisper to her, my mouth in her warm hair, 'Let's go home, Chloe. Come on and we'll catch the bus and we'll be back before Mummy.'

A light. We both froze. Not literally, although the surprise could almost have scared us to death.

Suddenly there was a light in the shop, and a flickering movement across it. Someone was inside.

Chloe pressed her hot little face to the window. I peered in too. The strike of a match, the flutter of a flame which caught a crumpled sheet of newspaper in the hearth. A man was kneeling there and lighting a fire. With his back to us, a bulky figure in an overcoat, he layered splinters of wood on top of the burning paper and watched while the flames licked around them. Beside him, its blade gleaming in the firelight, there lay a hatchet and the remains of a bookshelf he'd split into pieces. He applied more and more of the wood, until there was a bright, roaring blaze.

Chloe's face was lit with the excitement of it. Before I could stop her, she started patting at the window with her gloved hands.

The man turned and frowned, he raised a hand to his eyes to try and see where the sound was coming from, and then he straightened up. I tried to pull Chloe away, as if we might slip down the alley and be gone before the man came to the door. Too slow. Chloe was giggling and patting on the glass and all of a sudden the man was there.

He seemed very big. He blotted out the fire he'd just lit. He loomed at the window, a huge shadow, and he saw the two of us, a man and a child, huddling in the doorway. He turned a key in the lock. It made a dry, grating sound. The door opened.

Chapter Eighteen

EVEN IN THE half-light, there was an instant of immediate recognition. Me, I'd already had an inkling, when I'd seen him kneeling with his back to me, of the only time I'd ever seen him before. Now, as he stood in the open doorway and appraised us, especially the way he looked at Chloe, it was clear that he knew who she was.

And so we were in the shop, together. Chloe had just walked in, before either he or I had said anything. She wandered in, in the state of utter obliviousness she inhabited, as if the shop was open as usual and it was somewhere we always went on our visits to town. So the man stood aside to let me follow her. He shut the door. Still neither of us had spoken. We stood at the fire and looked at each other, and then, self-conscious, he knelt to the flames to add more fuel.

I looked around the room. The shelves were bare. It was almost completely empty, apart from a few remaining boxes of books, a litter of newspapers. Indeed, I could see from the marks on the dirty yellow walls where some of the original, old shelves had been torn down, and I realized that this man had been using them for firewood.

'I'm the oldest son,' he said into the fire. 'I've been clearing the shop. We had a clearance sale, a pity you didn't know about it, you might've found some of the kind of stuff you could've used in your place...' He angled his grey, middle-aged face up towards me, where he was kneeling in front of the flames, and I saw the weariness on it, the residual weariness of pain and bitterness. 'Oh yes, I read the local paper and I saw the piece about your bookshop and the tooth. I wondered

where it had gone. I guess you bought it, or maybe my father gave it to you, shortly before he died...'

He bent to the fire again, and his voice was vague and gruff in the crackle of the flames. '... the tooth, he always hated it, he used to mumble about how it was like that story of the monkey's paw, it was some kind of bad luck charm. He spouted a lot of mumbo-jumbo about it when the accident happened, that it was cursed and he'd dig it out and smash it up or throw it away, but then he couldn't find it. So yes, I saw your thing in the paper, Poe's Tooth Bookshop, and of course your name's a bit unusual, I'd heard it before.'

He stood up. He looked across the room at the little girl, who'd been waiting for him to move aside so she could go to the fire and stare into it. She did so now. Her face was blank, an empty canvas, it showed not a flicker of understanding of words or ideas, it showed not a hint of emotion or feeling, only the infuriating perfection of that smile. The man gazed upon her. His own face was a mask of puzzlement. He saw a lovely, apparently healthy, apparently intact child. And yet he knew she was not intact, that a part of her had been lost and might never come back.

'So,' he murmured, 'so this is Chloe Gooch. Hello, Chloe, yes, I recognise you from your photo in the newspaper. It's nine months now. It was 3rd April, wasn't it, a date your Daddy and I will always remember.'

He knelt to her, and she allowed him to take both her hands in his. He looked straight into her eyes, and when he saw the utter void in them his own eyes misted with tears. 'Chloe Gooch,' he whispered, 'are you there? What are you thinking? Can you remember anything? One day, this year or next year or in twenty years, when you wake up from your daydream, will you tell me why it happened? Will you tell me?'

'I'm so sorry,' I said, because I saw him then as I'd seen him before: a heavy, manly figure, kneeling, and his shoulders beginning to shudder with sobbing.

I helped him upright again. His face was shining with tears, he made no attempt to wipe them away. The girl stared up at him, and her smile was almost insufferable. I wanted, and I guess this man wanted, to wipe it from her mouth, or at least to turn her away and point the smile somewhere else, where it would cause no pain.

'I'm so sorry,' I was saying, 'I was there, I saw it all, not the time before or the time after, but the moment, the moment which altered Chloe. Your own daughter, I don't know, I don't know what she was thinking, why she didn't stop, what happened afterwards when they drove away...'

The man controlled his tears. He pulled himself together, he gathered strength from some secret reserve deep within him. He took out a big, white handkerchief and rubbed it over his face.

'My daughter, your daughter,' he said, 'their lives coincided for one second. One second, that's all. Your daughter is lost, but one day she'll come back to you. Mine is gone forever. Perhaps Chloe will tell us all, sooner or later, why it happened.'

Lost. His father had used the same word about Chloe. The fire was burning brightly. He'd already disposed of nearly all the curios and treasures and junk that his father had accumulated over the years, and now, to keep the place warm while he was doing the final clearance, he was stripping the very shelves from the walls and burning them. Soon, perhaps today or in another few days, the shop would be completely empty and then it might be sold or let and somebody else would try their luck – a hairdresser or a tattooist or a masseur.

'Lost,' I said to him. 'What was it your father was saying to me, the last time we were here, just before he gave me the tooth? Something about the lost, the utterly lost... I can't remember...'

Chloe and I moved outside. The alley was pitch dark. The light from the fire in the shop was barely a glow through the dusty window. Heaps. I wondered when this man, the eldest son, would try to remove those faded golden letters, his father's name which had been there for so long. And how... scrape them off? A painful, tedious, distressing task.

He loomed in the doorway. We didn't shake hands, it seemed somehow inappropriate that we might mark the solemnity of our relationship by touching. We stepped into the darkness, me and Chloe, all wrapped up against the cold, with nothing more than a clumsy wave, a hand uplifted in recognition of the strange, unexpected meeting we'd had.

But then he called something after us. I stopped to hear what he was saying. He reached for my hand and gripped it hard.

'It's Poe,' he was blurting out. 'It's from one of his stories, "even with the utterly lost, to whom life and death are equally jests, there are matters of which no jest can be made..."'

His grip was even stronger, and there was a note of pleading in his voice.

'The tooth...' he was saying. 'Forget about what I was saying, please. Forget about my father's nonsense, a bit of mischief, that's all. If it's working for you, and it seems to be so far, then all's good, all's good...'

He let go of my hand, turned abruptly and went back into the shop. Chloe was tugging me away, as though she was the one in charge and wanted to hurry me to the bus-station. My last glimpse of the man, he was standing at the fire and staring into it, exactly where I'd last seen his father.

NOT HAPPY. NOT happy at all. Rosie was waiting for us in the hallway, when I pushed open the door and we went in.

It all came out in a furious torrent. She hardly gave me a chance to say anything. Where had we been? She'd come back expecting to find us busy in the shop. Well, not busy of course, but in the shop and me writing and Chloe safe and sound, and where had we been? I tried to tell her we'd been to town, on the boat and into the shops and back on the bus, but she was upset, scared, her eyes wild and... something was wrong, more than our absence and our lateness.

'What's that?' I managed to interject, when her voice quivered so much with anger that she had to pause to control

it. 'Rosie, what's that on your face? What have you done? And I thought you'd got a meeting, you said you'd be late back...'

Wrong thing to say. It sounded like I'd been caught out, like we'd been planning to sneak back home without telling her where we'd been.

'We did have a meeting, yes,' she retorted, 'but Colonel Brooke cut it short. One of the science teachers made a remark about the creationist stuff and tried to start an argument, so the Colonel just closed the meeting and...' She shook her head, as if a hornet was buzzing in her hair and she was trying to get it off her. 'Anyway, anyway, that's got nothing to do with anything. I come home and it's all dark and empty and I come inside kind of concerned, a bit worried because you hadn't said you might've gone out and...'

'Your face, what've you done?' I tried to get close to her. I used Chloe's body, pushing her forward, to inveigle myself closer, to bring the three of us back together again. 'Have you seen it, in the mirror? You've got a cut or something...'

She backed away. She was still in her outdoor clothes, all bundled up like me and Chloe. She hadn't been upstairs yet. She must've just come in a few moments before us. She dabbed at her left cheek with the back of her glove.

'No, I haven't seen it. I know it stings, god knows what disgusting germs it's got in it. I thought you said you'd got the filthy thing out of here...'

Oh. It was dawning on me, the reason for all the panic. I felt the familiar sick plunging of my stomach, as I moved in on her, not allowing her to back away this time. I held both her hands down and away from her face. She had a cut on her left cheek, and the skin around it was reddening from the impact of whatever had made the wound.

'So I came in and felt around for the light,' she went on. 'I was freezing, fumbling around, and I don't know why, I couldn't find the switch straightaway... and then I heard something creeping around in here, like a rat or something. I even thought for a silly moment that it was you and Chloe and

you were playing a trick on me by waiting with the lights off and trying to spook me, and then it was flapping at my hands and my face and I screamed and by the time I found the switch it had...'

Her voice broke. Her anger was dissolving into hurt, into tears. I took her in my arms and held her close, and I felt her body shuddering against me. Chloe was hugging the two of us, her arms wrapped around our waists. I was saying into Rosie's ear, which was red hot on my lips despite the coldness of her cheeks, 'I'm sorry sorry sorry, my love. Let's get you upstairs. Let's all of us go upstairs and get your face washed and put something on it like some antiseptic or something. We'll all get changed and warmed up and get a drink and then I'll come downstairs, and I promise this time I'll...'

'You've been drinking already, I can smell it,' she hissed. 'You know I don't like you taking Chloe into pubs and... and then I come home and no one's here and I've been at work all day and you've been drinking in town with Chloe and...'

'Alright alright, Rosie. We just went into town, our usual thing on the boat and...'

She pulled herself away from me. She took a huge breath, held it for a long time and wiped away her tears with both gloves.

'It isn't me, Oliver, it isn't me I'm bothered about, you know that. I don't mind working while you're playing around. I don't even really mind if I come home into a silly old church and there's a bloody great bird waiting inside it and it bloody attacks me and tries to peck my eyes out. It's Chloe I care about. Don't you think she's had enough already, without this? It's dangerous. If it went for her and hurt her, I'd never...'

'You'd never what? You'd never forgive me?' I put on a bit of a huff myself. 'I said I'd get it out and I will. It's a scraggy old crow, that's all. You must've startled it in the dark and it flapped into your face. I'm sorry, I'll get it out, of course I will.'

'I'm not sure if it's still in here,' she sniffed. 'It's either gone into the vestry or it went out of the door before I turned the light on. I don't know.'

So, at last she stomped up the stairs with Chloe. Before they reached the top and disappeared into the kitchen, the girl swivelled her head back to me and – What else would she do? – she smiled.

Yes, everything was a jest for her. Other people's tears and anger, their grief and bitterness, their bereavement, their resignation to the tragedy of their lives, yes even their imminent freezing to death in a dank, dripping canal tunnel – she simply smiled at it all. And I smiled back at her. I couldn't help it. We were in cahoots. Her smile hid all kinds of secrets, truths and half truths I'd withheld from her mother. That it was Chloe who'd discovered the bird and shaken its poor frozen skeleton back to life; it was Chloe who'd teased me up into the clock-tower again and chased the terrified creature round and round until it flopped down through the trap-door and onto her Mummy's bed. And the fact that Chloe welcomed its presence in the bookshop and seemed to recognise the part it might play there. Rosie knew nothing of all this.

I turned on the lights in the vestry and went in to look for the crow. The room smelled strongly of the bird, and its mutes were splashed here and there and in one particular corner where it had made itself snug. But the bird was nowhere to be found. I was going to turn off the lights and head upstairs, but I paused for a few moments and bent to the relic.

The tooth of a boy. An old man had given it to me; a thing he'd hated, which he'd wanted to destroy and get rid of. What was it? A bad luck charm, or just a bit of mischief?

And now the crow. What was it? A starveling, sheltering from the winter, or another little piece of Poe?

Chapter Nineteen

WHICHEVER IT WAS, the bird didn't go away.

I was on the roof of the church tower. The old gent wouldn't have been pleased, if he'd seen me from his nearby house and read my thoughts: I mean, the very wizened gent who'd objected so forcefully to my opening a horror bookshop in the church. I was on the roof and wondering if it might be possible to string a washing line up there.

I'd put a wash on, against Rosie's advice. As she'd said before, how on earth was I thinking of getting the stuff dry, the sheets and pillow cases from our beds and even a great big duvet cover I'd stuffed into the machine? Put it in the airing-cupboard and the whole place would be steamed up, or take it to the hot air driers at the launderette along Breedon Street... anyway, she huffed as she busied herself and stepped out into the frosty morning, it was up to me, I was the house husband and child-minder, it was up to me to manage the domestic chores.

And then, over tea and cornflakes with Chloe, I'd had my little brainwave. Turning up the radio so she might not hear what I was doing, I'd left her in the kitchen – oh god, the keenness of the guilt I felt at leaving her alone with so many potential hazards – and I slipped into her bedroom, pulled down the silver ladder and was up into the clock-tower only a few seconds later. I closed the trapdoor behind me. I climbed a steep flight of steps, no more than a series of stone blocks protruding from the wall, and emerged through a higher trapdoor onto the very roof of the tower.

Like being on top of a castle. Massive mock battlements, with mock arrow slits, a bristling fortress of black stone. It

was a watch tower overlooking the whole of the town, across the playing fields of Derwent College and the wide expanses of the park. The sky was lightening on a clear, freezing cold morning. Faraway, on the horizon, the cooling towers of the power station were already pluming clouds of steam into a grey sky. It was lovely, a breathless, crisp, dry morning, and the forecast predicted a sunny winter's day. But, reminding myself of the reason I'd clambered up there, I realised that the temperature probably wouldn't get above two or three degrees, and even if I rigged up some kind of line the bedding would hang there limply all morning and afternoon and still be icy-damp when Chloe got back. Never mind, me and Chloe could potter along to the launderette later and get the job done. So, trying to expunge from my feckless mind an image of the trouble she might get up to alone in the kitchen, I turned slowly round and round and appraised the space up there. First of all, far from feeling bad about annoying the old man by stringing our washing from the top of his beloved church, I felt a schoolboyish tingle of mischief at the thought of it. Also, I was thinking how great it would be in the summertime, to come up with drinks and even a barbeque and enjoy our bird's eye view of all we surveyed.

I leaned over the battlements. It was a giddy height, there was a formidable drop to the pavement below. I was peering down, and my thoughts went straightaway to the fatal fall of that workman. I'd forgotten his name, the man who'd died during the construction of the church a hundred years ago. I was imagining, for some ghoulish reason, his trajectory and speed and even the sound of the wind in his clothes as he'd fallen, and guessing the spot where he'd landed... when something fell past my head.

An object, round and black like a pebble. So close that I felt the movement of it past my hair. I watched it fall. It hit the pavement exactly where I'd guessed the man's head would have struck. It didn't shatter, as a pebble might've done. It burst, with a kind of rubbery squelch.

Of course there was no one else on the roof. There was a sudden fluttering of the air around me, and there was the crow... circling above me; it folded its wings and fell to the battlements, where it settled no more than six feet away from me. It tidied its feathers with a few deft pokes and nibbles of its beak and it cocked its head at me.

'Alright,' I said, and I cocked my head curiously back at it. 'Alright. I've been reading about you. So you think you're clever, do you? And what are you up to now?'

I'd Googled carrion crow, *Corvus corone*, one of the most intelligent of birds, with an ability to use tools and tactics to scavenge food, a capacity for imitating sounds, an inclination to collect bright objects, and, unusually among almost all other birds, an ability to recognise faces. Yes, that was what it said on the websites. Unlike nearly all other species, the carrion crow might learn to feel comfortable with humans, to learn and know a particular face or a voice.

'So what brings you back up here?' I asked softly, politely. 'Me? Or were you hoping to see Chloe? Sorry, she's not...'

It dropped off the battlements and onto the roof itself. Where it hopped to the furthest corner, bent close to the base of the wall and pecked very hard into a crack in the stone, where some of the pointing had perished and fallen out. Before I could ask what it was looking for, it came away with a round, black object like the other one it had dropped to the pavement. With a couple of raggedy beats of its wings, the bird floated up and up and over the edge of the battlements, from where it dropped its prize. This time, after we'd both followed the fall and smash of the thing onto the pavement, the crow whirled down and down after it.

Snails. I bent to the cleft in the stone and found it was full of snails, dozens of them, their coiled, brown and black shells heaped together, like a cache of jewels secreted by a thief or a miser. Hibernating, were they? I pulled one out, it came away with a little resistance, a tiny kiss of suction,

and indeed the foot of it was moist, alive. Alive, at least for the time being. The snails had found a – I was going to say an impenetrable shelter for the winter, a veritable fortress where they could survive the freezing days and nights in a seemingly endless dream, a slumber, a torpor. Except that it wasn't impenetrable. The crow had found them. And its dagger beak would pick them out, one by one, drop them onto the stones far below, and float nonchalantly down to enjoy the meat from the shattered shells.

How did snails find themselves at the top of a church tower? I wasn't going to ponder that one for too long. I had one in my hand, it was real, it was alive, I could see it with my own eyes. Maybe, one day, along with the saxophone and the stars and stuffing dead animals, I might have time for the study of snails. Right now, I lobbed it over the battlements, watched it smash on the pavement below, and saw the crow springing towards its mucous remains.

Chloe, of course I hadn't forgotten about Chloe. That would be a ridiculous notion. But before I started down again to see if she'd survived my absence, I enjoyed another sweeping gaze over my domain and caught a dazzling gleam from across the park. A tantalizing, tempting dazzle.

The sun was up. The playing-fields were smoking with frost. It was a sparkling morning. And I knew straightaway what Chloe and I would be doing, once we'd finished a warming breakfast and got thoroughly wrapped up...

She was alright. But she'd been missing me. My absence hadn't gone unnoticed.

When I opened the trapdoor from the clock tower – thinking to slip down the ladder and through the bedrooms and materialise in the kitchen as though I'd been there all the time – her face was an inch below the trapdoor. Smiling, of course. Maybe it was my guilty imagination, but there was a look in her eye. That look. Where had I been? What was I doing? She'd come looking for me, climbed the ladder, and I guessed she was just about to push the trapdoor open.

'Hey Chloe, I just had to... I had to go and...' I heard myself blustering, trying to frame excuses, as though she were Rosie. 'Let's go back down, shall we? I got a great idea for a day out. But we'll need to wrap up really warm. Sorry, but I just had to...'

Me, the owner of a unique, historic property, the proprietor of an unusually intriguing bookshop... me, blustering excuses to a brain damaged seven-year-old.

Chapter Twenty

ICE. IS THERE anything as perfect as ice? Formed and hardened into an unblemished sheet. Created in a crushing, crunching silence, in the deadly darkness of night after night. Polished by a merciless wind.

Nothing more exhilarating, than to be skating outdoors, on real, natural ice.

I'd seen it from the top of the tower. Indeed, on our previous visits to the park we'd seen how the remains of the autumn flood waters, no more than an inch or two deep, were freezing hard. Now it was perfect for skating. The ice was strong enough; it only squeaked and crazed and crackled underfoot, and underneath there was nothing but grass. The ponds of residual rainwater had frozen completely.

A resourceful boy, a would-be entrepreneur, had stationed himself beneath one of the willows which lined the paths across the park. He'd mustered all the skates he could, maybe from the rink that had shut down recently in town, he had about eight pairs for hire.

What a joy. Not only the sheer perfection of the day, which was windless, brilliant. The air was so cold it nipped the nostrils and burnt the throat. I'd found some skates which were too small for me but tolerable, and I'd bound Chloe's feet into a pair which were too big but good enough for her to go wobbling and weaving across the ice. Marvellous, as we slithered and whooped and stumbled, although our skates were painful and our ankles buckled and bent and we sat down hard again and again. But also, because I couldn't help remembering the time we'd tried it at the super, world-class rink in Nottingham.

Me and Rosie and Chloe, we'd spent a fortune on the skates
and a lesson from a pro, had cokes and burgers and all the
works. And Chloe, the old Chloe, had been horrid. Oh god,
the moaning, the whingeing, the aches and pains... the number
of times we'd waddled off the rink and tried pair after pair
of lovely, new, soft leather boots with their gleaming, razor-
sharp blades, and she'd done nothing but grizzle all afternoon
in different combinations of *fucking this* and *fucking that* until
Rosie had been so pissed off we'd just bundled ourselves out of
there and home as soon as we could.

So now, in ill-fitting boots which were chafing like mad,
she was a joy. Me and Chloe, hand in hand, we managed a
few careering laps of the delicious ice. And even when we
collapsed in a bone-jarring heap, when our skates hit a tuft of
grass or we simply ran out of puff and toppled headlong, she
was smiling and giggling, her face quite pink and hot with the
fun of it all.

The new Chloe. Lost? A part of her had been lost? That was
the way dear Rosie felt about her daughter. But for me, on
that sparkling morning, it seemed that the girl had been born
again, excised of all her niggling nastiness, and delivered anew,
as pristine as the day.

It was only me and her, and of course the boy. It was a mid-
week morning. Maybe in the afternoon he'd have a few more
customers. We fumbled around the ice, and we stopped from
time to time for soup from our flask, a bit of a jam sandwich
I'd put together and chocolate. There were a few dog-walkers.
Faraway, towards the rhododendron hedges which separated
the park from the fine suburban houses of solicitors and
accountants, a retired couple were exercising themselves and
a red setter. The dog, gleaming coppery in the frosty sunshine,
was pootling beside them. They met a man with a Dalmatian,
paused to chat for a moment and then went on. At the same
time, as Chloe pointed with her chocolate bar and tried to
make me look where she was looking, we saw how the dogs
lunged on their leashes at a bench they were passing, and they

barked and recoiled in a momentary panic. There was a figure on the bench, sitting – a man or a woman, impossible to tell, because he or she was bundled so big and bulky and hunched in a coat, with a trilby tugged down. Indeed, as both the couple with the setter and the man with the Dalmatian struggled to control their dogs, as they lugged them away and then stopped and turned to stare back at the figure on the bench, it slowly leaned and toppled and lay down.

The man had tied his Dalmatian to a branch of the rhododendron. He was walking back to have a closer look. Chloe was following it all with great interest, which was good, I'd had my instructions months ago and nearly every day since then to stimulate her as much as possible. And now she was watching the distant figures and pointing and moving her mouth in silence, just making a little bubble of saliva which shone and burst and frosted her lips. The man called back to the couple, who had paused too. The woman was fumbling in the pocket of her overcoat. She found a phone and jabbed at it and pressed it to her ear.

The dogs, meanwhile, were straining at their leashes. Not to investigate the figure on the bench. But to get away from it.

Lovely, really, this tableau. Pretentious, that word. It was a picture, one of those famous oil paintings where the sky is as important as, or even more important than, the rest of the subject-matter. A Turner? A Constable? Or more modern maybe, a Barnfather? An enormous silvery-grey, mackerel sky, with the billowing steam clouds of the power-station. Bare trees, poplar and willow and then a bristle of fir. A sudden whirl of starlings from the poplar. I'd thought they were leaves, the last leaves of autumn hanging on and freezing hard on the iron-black branches – but no, they detached themselves and were birds, they were a hundred starlings which rose and swirled and shimmered this way and that and fell to the ground in perfect formation.

A picture, yes, with the inconsequential figures of people and their dogs, as though the artist had added them as an

afterthought, deliberately small, to accentuate the hugeness of the world and their paltry place in it.

The starlings had settled. They had no interest in the petty piece of drama which was unfolding nearby. The crow? Yes, it might have been a part in it. Because, as the Dalmatian man approached the figure on the bench again and made to touch it, or at least to move the turned-up collar of the coat and see the face hidden behind it, a crow burst out. It came out from beneath the coat. Difficult to see, from where we were watching. It had been doing something, between the collar of the coat and the tugged down brim of the hat, and now it struggled out.

Who might know what it had been doing there? But it burst from the body on the bench, like a bit of death, as though to announce that a death had occurred.

Chloe was galvanised into action, in a way I hadn't seen since last spring. She stood up and away from me, where we'd been snuggling down with our soup. And she made a noise, a real noise, for the first time. A crow noise. Quite distinctly, so clear and harsh in the freezing air that the three people and their dogs turned to look across the fields to see where it was coming from, she made the cawing, croaking, guttural sound of the crow.

And it beat towards us. It came fast and low, swerving with a little stutter of its wings, and it clattered into the high branches of the willow beside the frozen pond.

It perched above us. It wiped its beak on the branch, and a few crumbs of whatever dead and frozen thing it had been eating fell onto the ice.

Minutes later, while we watched and ate our sandwiches and drank the rest of the soup from our flask, an ambulance and a police car came into the park. So far away that we couldn't hear what was going on. There were a few flashes of photography and the policemen were asking questions and writing into their notebooks, and then the dead and frozen figure was lifted into the ambulance.

We skated a bit more, after they'd all gone away. But my feet were hurting. Chloe, still smiling, winced at the chafing of her ankles, the rubbing of her toes. Her lips were blue. We'd stopped for too long, and the cold was in us.

I could hardly undo her laces, my fingers were so numb, so the boy helped me to untie them. He undid mine too. We limped home. As we left the park and looked back to where we'd been skating, we could see the crow in the willow, on a branch overhanging the place where we'd been sitting. I watched Chloe's face. I thought for a moment she was going to summon it again, to make that cawing noise which signified that she was changing. She was changing, she might be coming back, as Rosie might say...

But she didn't. She opened her lips and closed them again, once and twice and three times, and she stared across the frozen fields with such a fixity of expression that I knew she was staring at the bird. But she didn't make a sound. Perhaps she knew she didn't need to.

Indeed, when we trudged painfully and wearily along the Derby Road and arrived back at our church, the bird was already there. Chloe bent to the shells of the snails which littered the pavement. The shards were like splinters of mother of pearl, they shone in the wintry light and their edges were razor sharp. She picked some of them up and wondered at them; she tested them on the ball of her thumb. And before I could tell her what they were or where they'd come from, she looked upwards, to the very top of the tower. Where the crow was sitting on the battlements. Then, only then, she made a little cawing noise, and she smiled, and I took her inside.

Chapter Twenty-One

ROSIE AND I would differ on the aesthetics of what we saw that night.

Aesthetics, tableau... sometimes these odd words come out and sound wrong, a bit jarring. Alright, so I'd only been a mobile librarian for Erewash borough council, and before that I'd got a gentleman's degree from Leicester University, done two terms' teaching history in a prep school and found out I couldn't even manage a classroom of a dozen posh little eight-year-olds. And alright, so I got out and got the job as a mobile librarian. But I read a lot of books, and so yes, I could use words like tableau and aesthetics, couldn't I?

Rosie was very frightened. For me, it was more like a sickness in my belly. Like when a doctor might say you'd got cancer, but still there'd been no pain. I got an inkling of something – how can I put it? – of some future fear. A horror which was waiting for me. Waiting.

We woke in the middle of the night. Rosie woke me. The bedroom was terribly cold. All the warmth of our central heating was somehow funnelling through and out and being replaced by the wintry air from outside. Not just cold. It was ice. The bedroom was an ice box, where dead things might be stored on hooks.

'Go and look...' Rosie was whispering to me. Although her body was hot, as she leant close and hissed at me, I could see the plume of her breath, silvery in the darkness. 'Go and look, please, I don't like it. Go and get Chloe, and bring her into our bed.'

The sick feeling, it started when I padded into Chloe's room and saw that her bed was empty. I saw, but, disbelieving what

I saw, I crossed the room and felt at the emptiness of her bedding, felt the place where she should have been lying. I was naked, Rosie and I had made love despite our falling out, or maybe because of it and the need to make up. There was a bitter draft through Chloe's bedroom, and I looked up with a dismal apprehension in every part of my shivering body when I saw that the ladder was down and the trapdoor to the clock tower was wide open.

Chloe, oh fuck, Chloe, where are you? I went up there. In all the shadows of the clock tower, where I thought I'd never felt so cold, there was no little girl. I scuffed through the dust and debris on the floor, shuffling my bare feet through the twigs and leaves and history of a hundred winters, and I whispered for Chloe, oh Chloe. But she wasn't there.

Starlight? Oh god, for a heart-stopping moment I thought that the trap-door to the roof was open. A glimmer of moonlight? A movement of a figure up there, high on the lonely battlements?

But no, it was not, it was closed and the bolt was closed. The gleam in my eye was from the broken pane in the clock face beside me, a car had swished past on the road below. The relief I felt, that wherever the girl was she had not gone up and onto the roof, was almost overwhelming. It filled my body with a gush of warmth. My knees trembling, I went down the ladder into Chloe's bedroom, pulled down the trapdoor and stowed the ladder.

So where was she? And why was the bedroom still so icy cold?

Rosie was hissing at me again as I padded past our bed. 'Is she there? Where is she? Oh god it's so cold...' And the sibilance of her words, the hiss of her breath, it seemed to add to the iciness of the room. And she followed me, swaddling herself in a dressing-gown, slinging another one at me and around my shoulders.

So cold? Yes, the door down to the kitchen was wide open. It looked like a yawning pit of darkness, so black and empty,

a void. Chloe? I called down there first, fearful of treading the stairs, fearful in my own house. Why had she done this? I knew, before I went down and down into the darkness and switched on the light in the kitchen, that I would find the other door wide open, the door going down and down again to the hallway of the church and the vestry.

There was no one in the kitchen. No Chloe. Only a black hole, from which an icy draft was seeping and swirling... the very taste and smell of the world outside, on the coldest January night on record.

Why? Chloe, where are you? She had opened the trapdoor to the clock tower, and the icy dark had crept down into our bedrooms. And then she had gone and opened the doors through the kitchen and down to the hallway. So that the winter was in the tower, from top to bottom.

There was a light in the vestry. Only a little light. Rosie and I trod towards it and we stood in the doorway.

Chloe? It's alright, Chloe. Don't be afraid. It's me. And your Mummy. I was hearing the words in my head, although I didn't say anything.

The girl was sitting at my desk. Rather lovely, really. So that the fear I felt in my stomach was a dull ache of dread, not a lancing pain. It was lodging there, it was accreting, it was a growth. It spoke of a future pain. Right now, I just stood and stared and I could see a kind of dreadful loveliness.

Chloe was sitting at my desk, at the computer I was going to write on. There was no light on the screen, she hadn't switched it on, she didn't know how to. The crow was sitting on the top of the monitor. And the girl was writing on the keyboard. Or she was pretending to. Her fingers ran deftly here and there, pausing, stopping, starting again. And she was frowning and puzzling into the darkness of the screen, as if appraising the words and phrases and sentences she was composing.

Pretending to write. Aping it. Cocking her head artfully at the screen, wincing and shaking her head, trying again, rewriting rewriting, aping the very toil and frustration of writing.

All the time, the crow hunched over her. Like the girl, it was quite unaware of us. It was too busy, preoccupied, watching her write and leaning into the screen to check what she'd written, shaking its head in disapproval and urging her on, with odd, dry, nibbly clicks of its beak. It shuddered its wings, opening and folding them like a dusty old professor adjusting his cloak. And she would pause in her writing, to glance up and into its eyes, as if it were her mentor, her inspiration, her muse.

The light in the room, it was the shrine of Edgar Allan Poe's tooth.

As Rosie moved forward with great deliberation and stealth and enfolded the child in her arms, the crow leapt away. It disappeared somewhere. It was gone. No crow. As though it had never been there and had been no more than a weird imagining – me and Rosie awakening from the strangest of naked, overheated dreams into an icy reality. Chloe was asleep. Rosie was terribly afraid. Her daughter, so soft and vulnerable in her cuddly cotton pyjamas, was asleep, and yet she'd been wandering the tower, opening the doors at top and bottom, looking for something, summoning something, entreating some dark and dangerous living thing to come indoors and be with her. And it had come. In sleep, in a world which utterly excluded her mother and her father, she had conjured a scraggy old crow.

'My darling, my darling... come on, my darling, come back to bed.'

Rosie was easing the child to her feet. Easing, yes, no struggle or objection or defiance. Even in the thrall of a dream, Chloe was easy to manage. She smiled, she caressed the keyboard as though she must leave it with great reluctance. She waved a theatrical hand into the air where the crow had been, and she consented meekly to being led out of the vestry and into the hallway.

I saw the fear in Rosie's eyes. She was hating it. The fear was a pain in her. As they paused together at the foot of the

stairs, I saw their faces in the light from the vestry and the light which fell down the stairs from the kitchen. Rosie? There was a nakedness on her. Her anxiety had erased everything else – her wisdom, her knowledge, her understanding of the real world. There was nothing on her face but fear for her child. And the mark. Where the crow had caught her with its beak, there was a livid red mark.

They went upstairs. I turned to the shrine, to switch off the lamp. I didn't care where the crow was, it could roost in any of the boxes of books it chose, on any shelf, in any corner. It was somewhere in the room and I didn't care. The shrine? There was Poe's Tooth, a poor little fragment of something or other, or maybe nothing at all. A bit of bone. An excuse for a relic.

And something more. Chloe must have put them there, on the bed of white satin. For herself, because they were pretty? Or for the crow, which would collect and display such nondescript jewels?

Diamonds of glass, from a shattered windscreen, pure and clear, except where a smear of blood despoiled their perfect beauty. And the mother-of-pearl loveliness of the snail shells. She had arranged them under the lamplight, with the tooth.

Chapter Twenty-Two

IN THE MORNING we got the crow out. It made quite a spectacular exit. Rosie insisted that she must see the bird out, she must witness it with her own eyes and know that it was gone.

She wasn't going to work. She'd called Colonel Brook and told him she had a doctor's appointment and might be in later, maybe break-time or lunch. Before going to bed she'd been dabbing the cut on her cheek with antiseptic, the whole of the bedroom and Chloe's bedroom smelled like a clinic, and she'd been up a couple more times in the night to wash out the wound with soap and water and apply more antiseptic. She'd said it was aching. So in the dark of early morning, she'd phoned the school and said she'd be late.

Spectacular, the way the crow left the tower...

The three of us had tip-toed down to the vestry, where Rosie stood in the doorway and sniffed and curled her lip and held a handkerchief tightly to her nose and mouth. Yes, it was the unmistakable pungency of a bird, quite unlike rats or mice, and the rancid whiff of its droppings. The room was ripe with it. No sound at all, at first. But then a furtive fluttering in a far corner.

I ordered Rosie and Chloe back into the hallway. I opened the church door as wide as it would go. The wintry dawn was out there; a smokey dark shadow on the pavement and a gleam of ice on the road. A few cars were already going by, on the way into town, on the way to work. And it was easy really, I strode purposefully back into the vestry, determined to show Rosie that I was totally with her in this and as wounded as she had been by the outrage the crow had committed, and sure

enough, with a few smart claps and then a few deft kicks at the cardboard boxes, I startled the bird into the open. It sprang out of hiding and past the fireplace, where I was straightaway after it and herding it towards the door, where it pottered past Rosie and Chloe, casting a grumpy glance in their direction, and the moment it got the scent of the morning in its bristly nostrils it was outside and onto the pavement.

Rosie had time to say, 'Thank God for that, now shut the door quickly and good riddance,' before the crow launched itself into the air. The rudeness of its awakening must have shocked it into action. It took off, across the road, just as a smart silvery saloon car was going by.

Whump. It hit the windscreen. Beak and claws and the negligible weight of bone, and a puff of feathers. It seemed to explode into the air with the impact, up and over the roof of the car as the driver instinctively jabbed at the brakes and swerved. And yet, when it landed a second later, it was intact again. No, not quite intact... trailing its left wing, it was a bashed and bedraggled and yet resilient creature which ran like a chicken to the further side of the road and disappeared into a privet hedge.

The car? Its nearside front wheel hit the kerb. An expensive alloy wheel, it grated horribly and threw a spray of golden sparks onto the pavement. The car kept going. A very pissed-off man – some kind of lawyer or estate agent – would be inspecting the damage in the company car park in a few minutes' time.

'Bloody thing, it can't even bugger off without causing trouble at the same time,' Rosie was muttering, although she seemed satisfied that the bird had gone.

Chloe was thrilled by the squeal of brakes, by the sparks, by the suddenness of the incident, but then, in a long lull in the traffic before a double-decker bus went groaning past, she stared after the crow. Rosie hauled her up the stairs. To reinforce what she'd already told me when we got up that morning, she called back, 'So I'll take Chloe downtown with

me, to the clinic and then the shops and maybe we'll do lunch together, me and Chloe. Alright? It'll give you some nice alone time with the shop. You'll be able to...'

I nodded emphatically at her. 'Yes yes I get it, my love, I'll have time to get it cleaned up and freshened up and everything.' Adding, as they disappeared up into the kitchen, 'and aren't you forgetting something? me as well, all freshened up too, if I have time between the coachloads of tourists etc etc.'

She didn't hear my poor attempt at matching her sarcasm. Or maybe she did and just ignored it. Before I closed the church door I took advantage of another break in the traffic to hurry into the road. I bent and picked up a long black feather. There were more, a trail of them towards the hedge where the bird had disappeared. I picked them up. Maybe the wing was broken, and the crow, not much more than a skeleton already, barely surviving the hardest of winters, would just lie in the undergrowth and freeze and die.

I shuddered at the thought of it. Eight o'clock in the morning, and minus three or four. The bird would be dead before I was sitting by the fire in the bookshop with my coffee and chocolate biscuits. By the time I'd erased every sign that it had ever been there, the room would be fragrant and warm, and the crow would be frozen stiff.

Rosie and Chloe went out. So I had *Peaches en Regalia*, Frank Zappa, my choice, not the maudlin cod-poignancy of *Year of the Cat*. I had a crackling, spitting, feisty fire. I was tidying up and wiping around, swigging a mug of coffee. And when I started to take some of the books from their cardboard boxes and thought about stacking them, temporarily, into one of the vestry cupboards, I found a half empty or half full bottle of brandy which had been tucked behind a stack of old hymn books. In the dark cupboard beside the fire, with its big brass hooks, where the minister would've kept his cassock or cloak or whatever he called it... a bottle of brandy, to have a sip or two before he strode up the aisle and mounted the pulpit to start the Sunday service, to warm his throat for the sermon, to

add strength and mellowness to his voice, to make him more eloquent. Or maybe afterwards, when he'd exhausted all his energies in the pulpit, encouraging his congregation to sing, exhorting them to put money on the collection plates, and then standing outside in the cold, and shaking hands and shaking hands and... when at last he could go back into the vestry, shut and lock the door, take off his cassock, warm his legs against the fire, take out the bottle and glug a great big slug or two.

It went very nicely into my coffee. I turned up the music. I could smell myself. No, not really myself, I could smell my favourite pullover and the big coat I'd slung over my shoulders because of the icy draft from the door. Brandy and coffee and the comforting rankness of my own clothes; the music, the spit of the fire as it tried its best to combat the cold from outside; the brandy. I had to keep the door open, of course, and yes, there'd been people pottering in and out for the past few days or a week or more, since the not-so-grand opening of Poe's Tooth Bookshop. I'd sold a few books, one or two customers had wanted their photograph taken with me and the shrine, and I'd stamped their purchases and slipped in their complimentary bookmark, with Dr Barnsby's handwritten affirmation that the tooth had indeed come from the mouth of a young, probably homesick Edgar Allan Poe.

Today, on this morning, I had two people come in, and I toasted each one with another splash of brandy into my coffee. The first was a man in blue dungarees and boots with steel toe-caps, with a pencil behind his ear. Very nice and non-confrontational, he was from the furniture warehouse next door in the body of the old church, and asking if I'd either turn down the music or put something good on. I turned it down, and he accepted a crafty slurp of the vicar's brandy. The other was Tony Heap. He loomed into the shop from the big silvery car he'd parked outside and introduced himself as Tony Heap. He didn't want to talk, he said, he'd just been passing and he'd seen the sign and he'd stopped on an impulse to take a look.

Loomed. He was even bigger now, in the daylight, than I'd thought when I'd first seen him bending to his father's plot on the crematorium and when he'd knelt to the fire in his father's shop. Then, on both occasions, he'd been nothing much more than a bulky figure in a dark, winter's overcoat, no more than a shape, a presence, a greying, middle-aged man in the grip of grief. Now, in the chilly daylight, as he strode from his car and into the shop, he was purposeful and businesslike, just taking a look, as he put it so brusquely, and his manner was slightly off-putting, overbearing, as though, because his father had given me the tooth for whatever mischievous reason, it was somehow still his, it was in his family and he had a responsibility to come in and see that it was being well looked after.

He bent over the makeshift shrine. I held my coffee mug to my face, in both hands, hunched over it and inhaled the perfume of the brandy, suddenly felt that I was hiding my face behind it and didn't need to, set it down on my desk and stood up straight. It was my shop, he was in my home and these were my books around me. It was my tooth, insofar as it could ever be someone else's tooth, other than Poe's. And so, to assert myself a little, I started forward, as he bent even closer to read the photocopied transcript of the tooth's provenance.

He was already fingering the jewels of glass which Chloe had put there. Without really looking at them, he was touching them with the fingertips of his left hand. Indeed, when he straightened up and looked around the shop, at all the books and the bright fire, he was holding one of the pieces between his thumb and forefinger and playing with it, quite absent-mindedly.

'It's alright, yes alright. I think my father might've liked what you're doing,' he murmured, as though I needed his approbation. He suddenly winced, glanced at what he was holding and put it down. He took a handkerchief from his pocket and wiped his fingers with it. He thought he'd cut himself on the glass, because the handkerchief was smeared with red when he put it back in his pocket.

And so he went out to his car and drove away. The damaged front nearside wheel... it was only a scrape, it would do as a spare, whenever he might get round to having it changed. Back in the shop I added the last of the brandy to my coffee, turned up the music again and switched on the computer. Started writing.

Chapter Twenty-Three

NOT A COACH party, but not bad, and a bit more coverage for the shop in the local newspaper – a school visit, a teacher and a group of kids doing their coursework on Edgar Allan Poe.

Rosie, bless her soul, had fixed it up. Despite her resentment about what had happened with the crow, she'd seen how hard I'd tried to make the shop nice again and she'd heard me tapping away like crazy at the keyboard, and she was still loyal to my pet project.

She'd come back later that day and told me what the doctor had done about the wound on her face. He'd cleaned it thoroughly and taped a gauze pad across her cheek, and he'd given her a tetanus jab. He'd said yes, there was a chance that it might have been infected, there was a risk from being pecked by any bird, even by a pet parrot, let alone a carrion crow which scavenged every kind of... well, carrion, in different stages of decay and decomposition. But the jab should do the trick, he'd said, so keep it clean and covered for a few days, and she should pop in again if it was sore or weeping or seeping, or whatever.

She and Chloe had had a nice morning in the lovely warm shops in the high street. They'd both had a haircut, had a pasty on the square and listened to the Salvation Army band, which was raising funds to help the homeless, especially people who might be sleeping rough at this time of the year and in the coldest temperatures in living memory. She'd let me peep behind the gauze pad, where the wound was glistening red, stained yellow with ammonia. And yes, she'd done a turn around the shop before they both went upstairs, and like Tony Heap, she'd signalled her approval.

'Nice,' she said softly. 'Cosy and nice, good job.'

It was late afternoon and getting dark outside, so the vestry looked welcoming with the firelight and the glow of the shrine and the hundreds of books on the shelves, the music I'd mellowed and turned down over the course of the day.

'And you're writing. That's marvellous.' She'd heard me hammering at the keyboard. 'No, don't tell me what you're doing. No, don't show me yet. Just keep going and then print out whenever you want to, whenever you want me to read anything.'

I got a big kiss. Another one from Chloe. All good.

And the middle of the following morning, when Chloe and I were all alone and mooching in the bookshop, I'd heard the phone ringing and ringing up in the kitchen.

Rosie's voice, calling from work. I was too breathless to say anything much at first, after hurrying upstairs, I just grunted yes and yes and yes when she asked if we were in, was everything alright, was Chloe alright... and, sorry short notice, but was I alright with Colonel Brook coming to the shop with some of his students. Yes now, yes soon, maybe lunchtime, was that alright?

I would've been alright, yes. Excited and apprehensive, I went down the stairs two at a time, thinking to get the place just perfect for our unexpected visitors. Rosie had had time to add that she'd been chatting to the Colonel at breaktime and mentioned her husband's bookshop, and he, in typically no-nonsense military fashion, had just said, there and then, that he'd like to take one of his English classes on a visit . Yes, today, at lunchtime, why not? And so I needed to hurry downstairs and straighten a few things, choose some appropriate music, cheer up the fire and station Chloe picturesquely beside it.

Except that she wasn't there.

Before I'd even crossed the hallway to the vestry, I caught a glimpse of her in the very corner of my eye. I skidded to a halt and did a double-take. There she was, she'd gone outside – and oh god – she was in the road. With a dazzling flash of

memory – the last time I'd neglected her long enough for her to wander into traffic – I dashed out of the church door.

Crash.

A thumping collision, a tumbling impact onto the ground. Me, I ran straight into my sign on the pavement and fell headlong. By the time I was on my feet again, Chloe had reached the other side of the road and was ferreting around in the privet hedge, head-first, reaching deep inside with an outstretched hand.

Oh fuck, oh god, she was safe. Winded by my fall, I had to wait for a line of cars in both directions before I could get to her and hoick her out. I stood her up and dusted her off, because her pullover and hair were prickly with twigs.

'Chloe, my love, oh Chloe...'

I was too relieved to be annoyed with her. She'd gone out of the church and through two streams of traffic, oblivious, while I'd been breathless on the phone in the kitchen.

'Chloe, please please please don't... don't just piss off on your own. I'm supposed to be looking after you, aren't I? Your Daddy's looking after you, alright? If anything happened to you, I don't know what we'd...'

All kinds of pleas and injunctions were rattling in my head, but by the time they reached my tongue they'd petered into nothing. She was pointing over my shoulder, back towards the church doorway, and in the muddle of my mind I immediately thought it was something to do with the crow she'd been rummaging for, that in some further conceit in its story it would be there, re-invented, reincarnated, born again, and...

No, not the crow. A man. He was setting up the sign I'd knocked over. He straightened it, adjusted the angle of it, re-adjusted it until it was perfectly as he wanted it, and then he dusted his hands together. He marched into the church, signalling at a group of a dozen teenage boys to follow him.

'No one here, by the look of things,' he said, as I hurried in with Chloe. 'He can't expect to do much business, if he doesn't keep an eye on the sign outside and then there's no

one around when people come in.' Louder, to his boys, he said, 'Well, gentlemen, while we're waiting for service, take a look at the books. Remember we're thinking about genre and themes. We're going to talk about artwork and concept and blurb. We're looking for the authors we've talked about, the classics of the genre, and especially Poe, for your coursework.'

I moved past him, to my desk, and still standing, pretended to check something on the computer. Without taking my eyes off the screen, I said, 'Is it Colonel Brook? Ah yes, I'm just checking the appointments in my diary, my wife phoned me to say you were coming.' And then I turned to him and held out my hand. 'I'm Oliver Gooch. You didn't give me much notice, but luckily I don't have any other visits booked for this afternoon. Welcome to Poe's Tooth Bookshop.'

He shook my hand. He was smaller than I'd imagined, and much younger, in his fifties. From Rosie's accounts of her employer's autocratic style, I'd expected a crotchety, whiskery old gent, but he had the look of a barrister or the manager of a football club. Dark suit, good shoes, not handsome, but oozing self-confidence. He had a kind of worldly swagger. He'd stared at me, flicking his eyes over my shabby shoes and my baggy old clothes to my beard and long, untidy hair. And now I found myself staring at him, as he drifted away and rejoined his boys. I wondered if he'd seen active service, had ever killed anyone with those manicured hands, and if so, what had made him a creationist and how he'd become the principal of a crammer in Long Eaton. I wanted to ask him these things. I wanted to suggest to him that he should write it all down in a book, but then I thought that, unlike me, he probably already had done.

The boys took it in turns to study the tooth. They did everything he suggested they did, they copied the transcript word by word and his translation. Without any reference to me, he briefed them about the boy Poe, who'd spent some time in England at a school in Stoke Newington, only adding at the end of account that, this evening, they should do their

homework and find out as much as they could online. He had complete control of them. They were cowed by him.

'We're doing an anthology of stories, for their English lit,' he told me, 'and one of them is Hop-Frog, by Poe, you know, the one where the court jester, a kind of hunchback or cripple, gets his revenge on the king by burning him alive. The boys have to write an appreciation of the story for their coursework, so I hope you don't mind them browsing around, it'll give them more of a feel for the genre, to see some of the authors on your shelves that we've been talking about, and of course the tooth. It's a remarkable opportunity for them, really, to contemplate the writings of Edgar Allan Poe and marvel at this little bit of him, his tooth, at the same time.'

What was truly remarkable, I was thinking, was that he, such a man of the real world, uttered not a single word of doubt about the origin of the tooth. The sign outside said Poe's Tooth Bookshop, and the blurb on the shrine said the tooth in its velvet-lined case had come from the mouth of Edgar Allan Poe. That was enough for him. Perhaps that was why he'd been a successful soldier and risen through the ranks – he'd accepted ideas and orders without question. Oh, and God created the world in seven days, it said so in Genesis, it was there in black and white, so that was a given as well. Belief, I thought. It was the belief that mattered.

All of this time Chloe had been sitting by the fire. Colonel Brook had glanced down at her and said what a lovely daughter we had, and by the way, how lucky he was to have my wife helping in the office. One or two of the boys, daring to pause in their diligent searching among the books and risk a rebuke from their teacher, had caught Chloe's eye too and elicited her angelic smile. She'd got the albino mouse out of her sleeve and was running it from hand to hand. It was a charming picture, almost literally. She was charming the boys away from their study, and even the steely colonel was watching her. She let the mouse drop off her palm and onto the floor, where it went nosing into the dust at the side of the hearth.

A rather beautiful thing happened. As the mouse nuzzled into a dense cluster of cobwebs, there was a sudden fluttering movement from deep inside it. The cobwebs themselves seemed to vibrate as something cocooned within them stirred into life.

The mouse burrowed deeper. Until, from the hole it was making in the matted cobwebs, a butterfly emerged.

The colonel and his boys couldn't help gathering around to look – at the most perfect little girl, her face reddened by the firelight and her blonde hair artfully tangled, at the white mouse and the butterfly. It was a peacock, it had been hibernating in the secret otherworldliness of the cobwebs; dormant, dreaming butterfly dreams, surviving the winter in a state of torpor. Until it had been nuzzled awake.

Chloe cupped it in her hands. It was a poor, desiccated husk of the lovely creature it had been last summer. But it was precious, and Chloe held it gently and blew between her fingers, as though she would breathe new life into it. I glanced around at the schoolboys and saw the wonder on their spotty, downy faces. Colonel Brook was gazing fondly, as though he'd seen the girl before somewhere, in a refugee camp or a ruined city on one of his tours of duty. And I thought they would all remember this moment for a long time, beyond the homework and the coursework and the relentless cramming, beyond the grotesque, gratuitous violence of Hop-Frog.

Chloe looked up at her admirers and she smiled. It was a miracle. She had breathed on the butterfly and now it was stirring bravely within her hands, as though the spring had arrived and it was alive with a new vigour. When she opened her hands, it clung to her fingertips and opened its wings. It shook off the dust of the cobwebs and was beautiful again.

And then she blew harder. As hard as she could. The butterfly was too weak to resist. She blew it off her fingers and into the fire.

In another moment it was consumed by the flames. It beat its wings, a flaring, golden, miraculous creature, like something from myth. It whirled around and around, ablaze. And then it

was gone. Disappeared in sparks up the chimney, or collapsed into dust on the fire? Impossible to tell which. It was gone.

There was an uneasy silence. The visit was over. One of the boys took a group photograph of the students and their teacher and me against the background of the books and the hearth, with the shrine of the tooth prominently displayed. The colonel said he could write up an article; he knew someone at the *Nottingham Evening Post*. It would be a bit of publicity for the shop, and of course for Brook's Academy as well.

The boys trooped outside, clutching their notebooks, armed a bit better for their exams. They cast a final, wondering look at the girl who was sitting by the fire, at the way she smiled as she picked up the mouse and kissed the top of its head. Colonel Brook bought a copy of the collected stories of Edgar Allan Poe, with its complimentary bookmark, for the school library.

Chapter Twenty-Four

'WHAT'S UP, ROSIE? Let me look at you? Maybe you should stay at home today. I'll ring Colonel Brook and tell him.'

She looked different. Yes, we'd drunk a bottle of red wine the previous evening, maybe not a good idea, after her injection and the antibiotics she'd taken. When her alarm went off in the pitch darkness, and it rang and rang and she didn't move, I fumbled for it and knocked it onto the floor, where it bumbled and buzzed like a huge fat insect, something like a cockchafer, which had crash-landed and crippled its wings. At last it stopped. I switched on the bedside lamp.

'Rosie? You alright? What's up?'

Something was wrong with her, something was different.

Although the crow had gone, it had changed us all. It had come to us, only a few hours after I'd come home with the tooth. The tooth was a dead thing. Once a part of a living human being, a piece of Poe, now it was only a discoloured fragment of bone. But the crow, in its passing through the tower, had been alive. It had touched us all with the spirit of Poe, and all three of us were changed.

Me, I'd been writing. And drinking. Whenever I looked at myself in the mirror I'd hung inside the vestry cupboard, I saw a shambling, rather disgraceful figure. A long black coat, a frayed shirt sticking untidily out of it, I was grizzly, unshaven, and my hair was longer than it had been for a decade, coiling around my ears and onto my collar. My eyes looked tired, there were dark shadows around them, but a strange spark of mischief gleamed within them, a spark which I myself found unnerving; a restlessness, an anxiety, which manifested itself more noticeably

in a tic... I would look at myself in the mirror and catch myself blinking. There was something crawling across my eyelid like an ant and making it flicker, every few seconds. No, nothing there, except a tiny spasm in the muscles of my face. When I touched the place with a dirty fingernail, I saw that my hand was trembling. I would grin at myself, see something wolfish, a leering on my mouth, then reach deeper into the cupboard for the bottle of whiskey I'd been hiding there, take a long pull and feel the heat of the liquor in my throat and in my chest. Marvellous, miraculous, it was helping me to write. And after I'd stuffed the bottle back in its secret place, winked at myself in the mirror and whirled back to my desk, I could hardly wait to get writing again.

Hop-Frog, the Masque of the Red Death, Murders in the Rue Morgue, I had the collection on my desk, beside the keyboard and the glimmering silvery screen. The little lamp was bent over the tooth and its accompanying treasures – the diamonds of glass and the snail-shells. The feather of the crow I'd stuck into a pot on my desk, stood up like a quill and adding to the perfect illusion that I was a writer: a gaunt and troubled writer with whiskey breath and dirty nails and quivering fingers. That my brain was crawling with ideas as myriad as the ants on my eyelids. An illusion? Not really, it contained a certain truth. Crouched over the keyboard, I would steal a glance at the book which was open beside me and continue to write.

Chloe was changing. She had found the crow. Briefly, she had made it hers. It had come to her across the icy fields of the park. She had summoned it with a croaking in the back of her throat, and it had beat towards her with the crumbs of a dead man's skin on its beak. In her dreaming, when she'd sat where I was sitting and caressed the keys as though she were writing, it had watched over her. She'd seen it tossed into the air and cartwheeling onto the road, and she'd tried to find the place where it had crawled away to die. Yes, it was a kind of awakening, her response to the crow, which, as far as Rosie was concerned, must be good, it must be better than her torpor of smiles.

Me, I wasn't so sure. I watched her and I waited. She was always watching me. She, more than Rosie, was aware of my weakness, my petty deceptions and the half-truths I told myself. And it made me anxious. One day she would blink herself awake and she would speak. I dreaded what she might say.

And now Rosie. Hardly discernible at first. She looked blurry and dazed, but then who didn't, waking with the shock of the alarm clock at six o'clock on a January morning, with a red wine hangover and a dry mouth and the prospect of struggling off to work in an office? Chloe was in the bed with us. I hadn't remembered how or why it had happened, but at some point in the middle of the night she must have whined or moaned and inveigled herself into the snuggly space between her Mummy and her Daddy. She too, rubbing her eyes to wake up, looked queerly at her mother.

'What? Hey, stop staring, you two.' Rosie buried her face in the pillow. 'I feel bloody terrible and I know I look terrible... you don't look so great yourselves. Leave me alone.'

Her voice was different too. Not just the wine. There was a disconnect, was that the kind of word they used these days? Something in the working of her tongue and lips which wasn't quite right. She heard it too, because I felt her body stiffen as she tried again and I could tell she was listening to a kind of dissonance in her own voice. She said, 'Yes, you could do that for me. Oliver, call the school and let them know I'm not well enough to come in.'

I got up. I guessed she would be better, sound better, when she'd wet her mouth with a nice, sweet cup of tea.

But she wasn't and she didn't. And she didn't just wet her mouth. She sat up and tried to smile, when I returned to her bedside. It was a lop-sided smile. And she cried. She cried softly at first, with a dim sense of dismay, until she was sobbing huge, uncontrollable sobs. Because she'd tried to drink the tea and found that she couldn't, without dribbling it copiously from the corners of her lips.

Unusually masterful, I had the three of us dressed and into a taxi about fifteen minutes later.

What a coincidence. It was the same Indian doctor who'd seen us at A & E at the Queen's Medical Centre in Nottingham, who'd examined Chloe after her accident all those months ago. And funnily enough, when the three of us went into his office after a rapid and expensive ride to the hospital, he seemed less interested in Rosie than in beaming foolishly at Chloe and patting her on the head as if she were a beagle puppy.

No, not funny. I said to him rather sharply, no, my daughter hadn't recovered from the blow to her head, as he'd so confidently reassured us she would, she was as distant and doolally as ever. But in the meantime, would he mind taking a look at my wife, because I was worried she might be having a stroke?

Rosie had stopped crying. She'd covered her mouth with a handkerchief all the way from home to the hospital. When the doctor asked her to remove it, she did so and started blubbing again at the same time. She caught a glimpse of herself reflected in a window, her distorted mouth, and her shoulders heaved with sobbing.

'And what's this on your face?' the doctor said. He took off the gauze pad. 'A bird? What do you mean, a bird? What kind of bird? Let me see. Is it infected?'

GUILT... A DOUBLE-edged emotion. Shakespeare did the 'sweet sorrow' of parting, and all sorts of poets and pop singers have caught the oxymoron or whatever, 'love hurts', the exquisite pain of love and all that. But has anyone done guilt?

Rosie had a scan. She wailed at the claustrophobia of being inside the narrow tube, as it clanged and banged and vibrated so hard it sounded as if the big-end had gone or something. Me and Chloe, we sat at the end of the tube. I held one of Rosie's feet and caressed it with all the love and tenderness I had within me, and Chloe gently cradled the other foot. Not

long afterwards, Rosie was sitting up in bed in a bright, breezy ward and we were sitting beside her and holding her hands. One side of her mouth had folded downwards, her eyebrow and eyelid had fallen so much she couldn't see out of that side. She was trying not to cry. And the doctor came in with a print-out from the scanner and told her that she hadn't had a stroke. So that was marvellous news, she was alright.

Well no, she wasn't quite alright. Not uncommon, but rather unfortunate. The nerves on one side of her face, the side which the crow had pecked, had suffered a trauma and caused the muscles to weaken and drop.

She didn't want me to stay. The doctor wanted to admit her and observe her for the rest of the day, to monitor the symptoms. Rosie pulled herself together, after I'd hugged her and reassured her as best I could that it was a temporary thing, that the doctor had said it would right itself with relaxation and a bit of physiotherapy after a matter of weeks... She pulled herself together and stopped crying. She took so many enormous breaths that her buxom body seemed to swell almost to bursting. She wiped her reddened eyes and swabbed at her blubbery, misshapen lips. And she managed to tell me, although her words were slurred, that she'd be alright with Chloe, that Chloe would stay with her and keep her company in the ward, and she wanted me to go out, she wanted me to go into town or something or go home and open the shop. In any case, just get out and leave her a bit of space and get out.

She started crying again, very softly, like a child. And me, feeling utterly wretched and useless and entirely to blame, I slunk out of the room.

Strange and wonderful, and really inexplicable. The guilt thing.

I'd pressed the doctor to say whether or not the wound on her face had triggered the trauma, and he'd said, with a kind of grudging reluctance, that yes, he thought it had. I stumbled out of the hospital in a blur of self-reproach and self-loathing. Into a glorious day.

All of my senses were heightened, almost to a kind of ecstasy. The sun was brighter, the cold was colder. The world was a glittering place. So, Oliver Gooch, banished from his wife's bedside because his negligence had left her with a brain-damaged daughter and a disfigured face. I would relish the beauties of this day as never before.

A taxi to the marina, a couple of tugs at the outboard motor, and I was nosing *The Gay Lady* away from her berth and the noises of the city.

A weekday morning, still only nine o'clock, and there was no one else on the canal. The surface of the water had frozen again overnight, and now the bow of the little boat crunched through it, turning the ice into a foaming, silvery slush. In minutes, we were through the new housing estates of the Meadows and into open country, gleaming with frost. Steam rose from horses and cattle, their hot breath puthered as white as the clouds from the distant power station. Lapwings lifted from the fields in languid, buoyant flight. A heron, standing so still by the weir that it might have been dead, the blood in its veins chilled into crystal. A fox, limping through a stand of derelict thistle and pausing in the sunshine, to warm its bones after a bitter night. A kestrel, hovering in a dazzle of sunlight. I thought I'd seen an otter in the wake of the boat, and I didn't mind if I had or I hadn't, because the idea itself was so delicious.

I plied the canal to Shardlow. I was alone, and relishing every moment of my solitude. The air had never tasted so good.

My wife was in hospital. She was probably crying. She would be lying in her bed, flat on her back on a mound of pillows, and she would be clutching her mirror in her right hand. She would steal a look every few minutes, she would bring the mirror to her face and frame herself in it. And she would cry, the tears would run so hot and heavy that her eyes would be swollen with them, reddened and puffy. She would see the left corner of her mouth drooping and drooping more each time she looked, until her teeth and gums were exposed and the

saliva spooled uncontrollably out. She would feel her cheek, already weeping from the wound on it, completely numb, so that, when she touched it with her fingertips it was a dead person's cheek.

Chloe would be there, but no comfort at all. Where was the comfort in a child who just smiled, who gazed at her mother's altered face and chuckled like a simpleton?

Guilt? It was a lancing pain in my chest. It gnawed at my belly. And it heightened my senses, so that every nerve in my body sang with the joy of the day.

I stilled the boat beneath the motorway bridge. I counted a minute and wondered how many vehicles had passed over my head in that time, three lanes going one way and three lanes the other, at seventy miles an hour. Hundreds of cars and trucks must have hurtled by. I saw a tiny movement on the bank, where the water was dripping from the concrete slabs of the bridge and plopping into the canal. And there was a vole, sitting and watching me, cleaning its face with its paws. When our eyes met, it stopped preening and shook itself with such vigour that the droplets flew from its fur. Just the two of us, we were alone and stationary in the dim, green place we'd found, while the rest of the world hurried by in opposite directions. Oliver Gooch, guilty, and the blameless vole.

Lunchtime. The beer in the Trip was better than ever. A pint from a brewery in Ilkeston, and a half of this and a half of that, and another half of this and that from the little breweries in Papplewick and Lenton and Eastwood, and they slipped down a treat, with the landlady's own steak and kidney pie. It was very warm in the pub. My belly was full and my head was comfortably muzzy. I sat where I always sat with Chloe, and when the landlord asked me where the little girl was today, I told him she was staying home with her Mum, who wasn't so well right now. He winced, such a negligible expression of disquiet that he wouldn't have thought I'd noticed, when I decided to finish my feast with one last pint of a guest beer from Mansfield. Perhaps it was the state of my pullover, or the

way I'd slung my big old pungent coat across the back of my seat, or the dishevelment of my beard and hair, which made him pause before pulling the beer for me.

I returned to my place by the window. The beer went down smooth and slow. When I left the pub, tugging on my coat, I was a bit unsteady, swiping at my mouth with the back of my hand.

Shit, and the cobbles were like ice. As always, in this bleakest of winters, I'd misjudged the time and it was unnervingly, loomingly dark. I slithered once, twice, the shadow of the castle seemed to bulge at me so big and black that it was a part of the sky.

Was it dusk or twilight? In January, in England, in the narrow streets of the oldest part of Nottingham, these niceties were dispensed with. Day became night, in a sudden snap of frost. One of the cobbles shifted under my foot. I sat down heavily on my backside and felt my ankle tweak. A shiver of pain, which made me sick in my stomach. I heard a muttering, a tut-tutting, and I was aware of someone standing nearby, not near enough to come and help me to my feet but watching, a spirit of disapproval. Was I a down-and-out, a drunk? No, I was Oliver Gooch, proprietor of a bookshop so famous that it had featured in the *Nottingham Evening Post*. I got up, regained my balance and a semblance of dignity and shambled forward, far enough to sit by the flower bed at the statue of Robin Hood.

Chloe? Chloe, where are you? Shit, I told you not to go running off. My stomach lurched until I remembered that I was on my own. Oh my god, I was without Chloe, such an unusual state of affairs that I'd forgotten she wasn't around. Or to put it another way, for a blissful few hours I wasn't holding my breath in case, in case... no, not blissful, because the price of this day was the disfigurement of my wife. Guilt, glorious guilt, all the sweet and positive new things in my life were tainted with it, and at the same time, enhanced.

No, of course I hadn't forgotten about Rosie. I was sorry, terribly sorry, and pained by what had happened. I had to get

back to her as soon as I could, to get her and Chloe home and safe in our tower.

Heaps? How could it be? The little shop was a glow of warm, welcoming light. Heaps? The word was still there, the golden letters on the window. I stood and blinked and re-read the name. As I trod carefully forward, feeling the pain in my ankle and sensing the nausea it might induce, I paused and stared.

Two things made me stop. First, there was a bundled figure in the doorway, nothing to do with the shop but still a typical and troubling feature of life in a big city: she was a girl, I thought, or a woman, I could see her pointy white face with a stud in her lip and her nose and her eyebrow, and her dog was growling at me. I couldn't really see the dog, they were just a bundled up body of human and animal and newspaper and a blanket, snuggled together for all the warmth they could afford one another, and they had found their place for the night. I took a breath and swept past them into the shop. The dog didn't bite me. The girl didn't reach out a quivering hand and ask me for money.

The other thing which had made me pause – the shop seemed to be full of people. I moved inside and it was surreal. The fire was the same, in the same place, of course, and blazing merrily. But the shop had been transformed into a magical world of dolls and puppets and figurines, some of them life-size or at least as big as children, which gave the whole space an illusion of crowdedness, of busyness, as if a mob of elves had swarmed in from the forest and come to toast their toes at the fireside.

A real human detached herself from the shadows. She was a woman too, but she might have been a different species, from a different planet, compared with the one shivering outside her door. At first, however, I didn't note her face, only the waft of her warm and womanly perfume and an aura of expensive blonde hair. I was too busy appraising the wonders of her shop.

A medieval world, designed for the tourists who might come in the summer; the proprietor must have opened early in the

year to get the feel of business and maybe conjure a bit of local publicity. All of the figures were 'woodland folk', from an idyllic long-ago time which had probably never happened: a merry band of men and women and children and dogs and geese and piglets, made of all kinds of materials – cotton and wool and suede – sewn and padded and costumed in extraordinary detail. Robin Hood, of course, he was the whole point, and this was a prime location, a stone's throw from the statue and the gatehouse of Nottingham Castle.

I browsed the dolls and puppets. I picked them up. Friar Tuck, Maid Marian, Little John. There was a villainous Sheriff of Nottingham and a weasly, sneering King John. Richard the Lionheart, returning from the Crusades to reclaim his throne. And knights on horses, and serfs and footsoldiers, and archers, monks, urchins and beggars and cripples. A collector, probably an American, might reach into his wallet and go home with the entire population of 13th century Sherwood Forest.

'Shall I wrap them for you? Would you like them gift-wrapped?'

Her perfume was heady. Her hair was golden in the light of the fire.

I'd chosen three figures to take back with me, already fearing I'd be late and inappropriate when I got back to the hospital. Inappropriate, a good word, the last few beers had been inappropriate. I didn't even know what time it was. My head was blurry, my ankle was hurting, I could smell the beer in my beard. I was in trouble. So I'd got a Robin Hood, that was me... a Maid Marian, for Rosie of course... and a bonny little goose-girl for Chloe.

'Yes, please,' I said. For the first time, I looked into her face. She was oddly familiar. More than that, I had, in the fug of my brain induced by the beer and my fall and now the warmth of the fire, an uncanny sensation that we'd met before, we knew each other, our lives had touched for a short but significant time.

'Heaps?' I said. 'I used to come here a lot, for books and things, when Mr Heap was...' She glanced up at me and smiled

wanly, as she cut and folded the wrapping around my chosen figures. 'I mean, I thought the shop was closed, but you still have the name on the window and...'

'My grandfather,' she said. 'Did you know him?' She smiled a rather winsome smile as she caught my expression. 'Oh dear, you don't approve? Oh I know a lot of people loved his funny old shop, well, generations of his customers. And of course we did too, me and my sister and the rest of the family, we all loved grandpa's shop and he was a local figure in the city from way back...'

She'd almost finished wrapping my presents, she was doing ribbons and stuff and going to town. She gifted me another of her smiles.

'Don't you like it, the new shop? Oh you must do, or you wouldn't have come in. Alright, so it's not everyone's cup of tea, but I thought I'd give it a whirl and see how it goes. And so yes, I've left grandpa's name on the window. I thought he'd like me to do that. Me and my sister, we loved him so much.'

She slid the beautifully wrapped parcel towards me.

'There, thank you,' she said. 'You're my one and only sale of the day, my first customer, my first customer.' Her eyes were glistening with excitement and gratitude. 'Grandpa would be pleased. Thank you.'

I took the parcel. I rummaged in my wallet for some cash and found that my taxis and beer and steak and kidney pie had left me short, so I proffered a bank card. She fumbled with it, it was all new to her, this business thing. As she was processing the card and passing me the receipt to sign, I couldn't help adding, because I was almost overcome by her sincerity, her womanliness, and the way she'd shared a confidence far beyond the usual exchange of commerce, 'Your grandfather, and your sister, can I offer my condolences?'

I was going out of the door. She called after me, quizzically, 'How did you know about my sister?' And she was looking at the receipt in her hand and her face was changing, it was a strange and terrible change, as distressing as the change I'd

seen in Rosie's face just a few hours ago. Her beautiful face became ugly. The gentle nostalgia in her voice turned into hatred and bitterness. And she cried from the shop doorway, as I avoided the snarling of the vagrant's dog and hurried down the street, 'Gooch? Gooch? Who are you? What do you mean by coming here and...?'

Bus station. A glare of lights and a stink of diesel. Hailed a taxi, tumbled in, told the driver to take me to the Queen's Medical Centre. Realised just in time, before we set off, had no cash. Bundled out again, driver swearing. Next bus to the hospital in forty-five minutes. Sensing trouble ahead, thinking fuck it anyway, sloped into an overlit bar for a horrid, fizzy pint. Eased it down with a vodka sloshed in, a poor man's cocktail called a Dog's Nose. Trouble getting into the bus, let the driver help himself to the change from the palm of my hand...

Got to the hospital, walked a mile or two through corridors before finding the ward where I'd last seen Rosie and Chloe. Got hassled, twice, by security guards on account of my unsteady gait. Rosie and Chloe weren't there. A very fat West Indian nurse told me they'd already gone home. She recoiled from my breath. Who was I? she asked, impertinent.

Chapter Twenty-Five

SUBTERFUGE. ANOTHER GOOD word. It crept into my mind, from somewhere, maybe from my writing and the research I was doing to help my writing.

Deception, musty little secrets. Like, the vicar had hidden his brandy among the hymn books, where none of his parishioners or pesky choirboys would find it. Like, I'd got a bottle of vodka tucked into the cabin of *The Gay Lady*, under the mildewy life jackets we never used. And now, over the following days and nights and weeks, I was deceiving Rosie. Chloe? Not so sure, despite her vacuous look, her ingenuous demeanour, sometimes she caught my eye with a sudden unnerving steeliness, as if she knew everything I was doing and not doing and wasn't hoodwinked at all.

Me in the vestry. In the dog-house. A madhouse? Rosie had adjourned upstairs, into our bedroom. She was no better. In fact she was worse. The laxity in the muscles of her face was a kind of dying, she said, melodramatically. She said that she felt as if her body was sagging into a morbid stupor, somewhere between atrophy and rigor mortis. At least I thought she was saying that. Her mouth had distorted so much and her dribbling was so copious that it was hard to tell what she was saying. She had taken herself upstairs to bed, to be alone with her disfigurement, as if she had the plague and was sequestered from the rest of the world. Not quite alone. She had her mirror. And I took her all the food and drink she felt like toying with and spilling onto the sheets.

And she had Chloe. Chloe stayed upstairs with her mother, not as a nurse or any kind of useful attendant, because she

was, by definition, useless. She stayed up there to provide a fuzzy feeling of company, to be a warm and genial body at her bedside and in her bed... and because, I was sure, Rosie wanted to keep the child more and more away from me.

So alright. Alright. I could be me, downstairs in the vestry. In the dog-house, since my shameful, shambolic return from town, late and foolishly drunk, when she'd been discharged from hospital. The cuddly toys hadn't done much good. Rosie and Chloe were already in bed by the time I'd got off the bus and blundered into the church and up and up through the empty kitchen and into the bedroom. Lying back on her pillows, Rosie was distraught, high on a cocktail of antibiotics and Chilean merlot, in a tangle of sheets all smudged with the wine she'd been trying to drink. She'd snarled at me, all fangs and gums and unmanageable tongue. Chloe, beaming demurely beside her, was an appalling, tragicomic touch. When Rosie had ripped open the gift wrapping, revealed the ridiculous figures and hurled them at me, Chloe straightaway retrieved them and started cuddling them on her side of our bed.

'Don't you like them, Rosie?' I'd had the audacity to ask her.

And she'd retorted, 'I don't like you.'

So I was banished. I went out of the bedroom, down through the kitchen, down to the hallway and into the vestry.

Moonlight. Lovely, through the lancet windows. I sat at my desk, still in my coat, and admired my bookshop in the wash of silver and a stripe of orange from the streetlamps on Derby Road. Now and then the headlights of a passing car played across the crowded shelves and the ceiling of the vestry.

I sat and pondered the day. Was it only a day, or was it a week or a fortnight? Waking in the darkness with a stricken Rosie, and the taxi drive to the hospital... the good news and the bad news... I could hardly believe that all of this, and then my morning in the heady perfection of wintry sunshine and the churning of ice on the canal, that it could all have happened today, on this day, this same day. Oh, and the bitter-sweetness

of the beer in the pub, my tumble on the twilit cobbles, and Heaps... Heaps?

The day had been a turbulent dream, fraught with anxiety, bright with joy, tinged with the curious, unfathomable shadows of nightmare.

The cold began to creep between my shoulder blades. I set about making myself more comfortable. The fire was soon crackling fiercely in the hearth, and all the brighter because the room was so dark. Without switching on a lamp, I turned on the computer, not to write, but simply for the gentleness of its light. It was a reassuringly unwavering glow, as still as the moon. I went to the cupboard and took out the bottle I'd hidden; not the same one that the minister had put there, which I'd finished a few days before, but the one I'd already replaced it with. I knew I could always say, if Rosie found it and brandished it accusingly at me, that I hadn't known it was there; it was a naughty secret left behind by the last occupant of the vestry. So, brandy in my mug, I sat by the fire and watched the headlamps go swishing across the ceiling. Until, by midnight, the traffic had all gone and the road outside was completely silent, and I'd seen the moon rise into the sky and disappear from view.

My head was nodding. I added more logs to the fire, moved myself back to my desk and laid my forehead on my arm. I caught the smell of beer on my sleeve, where I'd wiped my mouth and beard, and traffic and smoke and other people, the contrasting perfumes of the city. The computer screen had long ago dimmed, it was a rectangle of darkness with a pinprick of red at the corner to show that it was still switched on. I was suddenly so tired by everything that had happened, and befuddled by all the alcohol I'd consumed, that I fell into an abysmal sleep.

I didn't dream. My mind had been so crammed with the images of the day that, in sleeping, at last it blanked them out. No dream of Chloe, although when I'd been re-charging the fire before moving away from it, I'd sensed for a fleeting

moment that I was in her favourite place, that my big, untidy, smelly body was in her space and I could feel her in me. No dream of Rosie, no guilt or restless anxiety, because it was she who'd sent me away and I could almost feel, by putting a different spin on things, that I was aggrieved, that I was the wounded party. So I slept in sweet oblivion...

Until two things woke me.

A log tumbled out of the hearth. There was a clatter, a shower of sparks, a fiery avalanche which scattered across the stone flags of the floor. When I opened my eyes, I saw the flickering of flames cast onto the bookshelves. I heard the unexpected sound and caught the smell of smoke in my nostrils. The other thing – the whole room was cast in a ghostly pale light, and when I sat up and blinked around me I saw that the computer screen was glowing. Something or someone must have nudged the mouse, or maybe it was me, I'd touched it with my elbow when the fall of the fire had disturbed me.

Cold. I rubbed my eyes. My face was cold, my nose was icy. I peered across to the fire. Chloe? A small dark presence in the shadows? Or was it simply the shape of the space she had occupied? Creaky in my bones, I stood up and shuffled towards it. Chloe? I felt with my stiffening fingers at the place where she might have been. No one, of course. I kicked the fallen embers back to the edge of the hearth.

And I was bursting to piss. Too desperate to consider the possibility of hurrying up to the bathroom, I found myself struggling with the door of the church and going outside.

The world was bathed in moonlight, so white and bright it cast strong black shadows – the enormous stripe of the tower behind me, every streetlamp and tree along the side of the road, my own shadow as sharp as a silhouette. I followed it, because it seemed as desperate as I was, tugging me urgently over the road and to the privet hedge on the further side. Where I unzipped my fly, just in time, and pissed longer and hotter than I could ever remember.

The steam rose in a pungent cloud. The droplets clung to the frozen hedge and its stubbornly evergreen leaves. A shower of animal heat, they dripped into the blackened undergrowth, where everything else was dead and cold. I couldn't stop pissing. Even when I heard the creak of the church door behind me and I turned my head to look. Even when I twisted my head so hard over my shoulder that I saw sparks. Even when I thought I saw a movement in the shadow of the tower and called out, 'Chloe? Is that you, Chloe?'

There was no one. The shadow was a bar of black, anything which moved into it would be swallowed entirely. I'd left the door of the church open. I was going to hurry back. But when I zipped up my fly again and enjoyed the relief for a few moments, something in the quietness of the night made me pause.

Not just quietness. The world was utterly silent. Not a car, not a person, the town and its suburban streets were asleep. And the moonlight was lovely, a perfect full moon in a cloudless sky. Even the cold was delicious, because of the stillness. I could hear myself breathing, that was all. When I licked my lips, I could hear the clicking of my own tongue. No other sounds.

I studied my shadow. It was wonderfully obedient. It did everything I wanted it to do, unlike the posh little kids I'd tried to teach, unlike my know-all wife, unlike my truculent daughter – until a bang on the head had made her nicely compliant. Every slightest movement of my arms and hands and fingers it mirrored onto the pavement. It even caught my tousled hair and the tufts of my beard. I swayed and shimmied and made the strangest of signals with my arms, and it did my bidding.

More than that. I suddenly realised, with a lurch of fear in my belly, that I'd stopped with my hands by my side, and the shadow was still moving.

One of its hands was moving. It was making a gentle, insistent movement.

I felt the hair prickle on my scalp, I took an involuntary breath, to cry out, but then I saw it was another shadow which I hadn't noticed, smaller and less distinct, which had crawled out of the hedge and blurred into mine.

The crow. All but dead, revived by a fume of warmth. So black and misshapen, it was hard to tell if it was real or a flaw in the moonlight.

I bent and picked it up. No resistance, no need to resist, it had come to me. It felt like a dead thing. It had no weight in it, no substance beyond a rag of frozen feathers. I carried it across the road and back into the church.

COINCIDENCE? I CROUCHED over the crow, and examined it in the firelight. An absurd coincidence, that it had emerged from the hedge as I was standing there? No, I rewound it all, at rapid speed, and saw in a blur of images how everything was connected.

Why would I be pissing into the privet on Derby Road, outside the front door of my own home, except that I'd been banished downstairs? Why had I been banished? What had caused the affliction to Rosie's face? Where had the crow come from? Why had I been given the tooth? What had caused the death of the young woman? How had she happened to hit my daughter with her car? Everything was linked. This bird, a poor wreckage of a creature I placed carefully onto a sheet of newspaper in front of the fire, was a link in the chain. Back to me.

It lay very still. I had laid it on its breast, with its head on its side, in a kind of recovery position. Its beak was open, but it didn't seem to be breathing. One of its wings was open, and I'd arranged it very gently so the feathers were separated and might dry in the warmth of the fire, but the other remained tightly wrapped to the side of its body. The black, scaly legs and feet, the sharp black claws – they were cast against the white paper, like the limbs of some prehistoric raptor.

Maybe the bird was dead. It had been sleeping in the grip of ice, sipping at the air with its beak, scenting the very last moments of its existence through its bristly nostrils. And then the steam of my piss had disturbed it. I had awoken it from the brink of death, enough to drag itself out of the hedge and into the shelter of my shadow. But now it was dead.

One last chance. In a final attempt to revive it, I grabbed for the bottle to dribble some brandy onto its beak. I didn't need to. As I leaned over it and watched, in morbid fascination, the bird started to creak alive again.

It was the warmth from my own body. The droplets of my urine on its feathers, which shimmered like emeralds on a sheen of blackness, seemed to steam in the heat of the flames and soak into the body of the bird. Where the crow had been dull and matt beneath the dirt of the hedgerow, there was a new purple gloss on its plumage. It was thawing. The frozen wing clicked away from the body. It opened and spread until it was as widely splayed as the other, the long primary feathers stark against the newsprint. The legs twitched. The feet unclenched and shuddered in a spasm of wiry tendons, and the claws made a sudden scrabbling with their needle-sharp tips.

A new lease of life? Or the throes of death? The crow sneezed. It sneezed again and again, and every pathetic explosion of air seemed to wrack its chest so hard it must surely burst. I leaned to its head and breathed on it, the heat of my living breath. The next time it sneezed, the effort was so great it lifted the beak from the newspaper and touched my lips. The kiss of death.

No, the crow was alive. The sneezing fit was over. It lay calm and still, and the firelight played on its warming feathers. The ice had melted. The shimmer of green jewels had all gone.

And this time, when I sensed that someone was watching me, when I felt the prickle of the hair on my scalp and turned to stare into the blackness of the doorway, she was there.

Chloe, in her pyjamas. Barefoot on the cold stone. Her blonde hair catching the firelight.

She smiled and came forward. She was cuddling her little goose-girl. Warm and lovely, she had slipped out of her mother's bed and come downstairs, as though in a dream, drawn by some kind of miracle. She let me fold her into my arms. She gazed down at the crow and a bubble of saliva shone on her lips.

'Don't tell Mummy,' I whispered into her ear. 'Don't tell her anything.'

Chapter Twenty-Six

MUMMY STAYED UPSTAIRS. Chloe spent a lot of the time with her, and I popped in, whenever I was allowed, with necessary supplies. Sometimes I might potter in with tea and biscuits and find her sitting up in bed with Chloe, with Robin and Marian and the goose-girl arranged between them. She might ask me where I'd been sleeping, because she knew I hadn't come back and crept into Chloe's room, and I just shrugged and said downstairs, in the kitchen, it was fine, it was warm enough and I slept alright with my head on my arm, on the kitchen table. That was a little lie, not a big one, and it was meant to make her feel better, in case she was regretting what she'd said. She knew I was in and out of the bathroom, to use the toilet of course, and to shower and change my clothes. Despite my disreputable appearance in my baggy corduroy trousers and disgraceful pullover and the gothic-desperate-struggling writer's coat, I did take a shower every day. So the outfit I wore in the bookshop was part of an illusion, which Rosie saw with her own eyes. She didn't comment on it, that every time I emerged from the bathroom nice and clean and put on fresh underclothes, I then clambered back into the same old stuff I wore every day. She didn't know about the crow, it was easy to keep her uninformed as long as she stayed where she was.

Subterfuge. It was harder to cover up my drinking. I had my bottle in the vestry, tucked away behind the hymn books in the cupboard, and there was always a bottle in the boat. I might suck a mint when I went up to see Rosie, but that really didn't work. It was a dead give-away. So, if it was proving futile to try and disguise my drinking, it might be better to think of a

way to deflect her criticism of it. How? maybe by persuading Rosie to have a drink as well.

She was in a state upstairs, quarantined in her bed, in a kind of self-imposed purdah. The doctor had made encouraging noises about how quickly people recovered from this condition, and mentioned patients and indeed friends and relatives who'd made a complete recovery within a month. It was fairly common, rather distressing, but there was a very good chance that Rosie would get better and be restored in a matter of time, with care and rest and physiotherapy such as massage of the facial muscles and a regime of exercises.

But Rosie was getting worse. I went to her bedside with food and drink, many times a day, and found her weeping into her mirror. The side of her face had dropped more and she was finding it harder to speak clearly. Despite my ministrations, I would find her smudged and stained with the drinks I'd taken her – her nightdress in disarray and blotched with tea and orange juice, her sheets all rumpled and damp.

I sat with her and tried to brush her hair. She recoiled with a quivering snarl.

'God you stink... it's that pullover, for god's sake, and your breath, are you drinking down there?'

Her words were slurred into a blurry incoherence, the vowels loose and the consonants sliding this way and that off her tongue. As she heard her own voice, the tears of dismay ran hot and fast again and her eyes were red. Her anger at the state of her face ignited her resentment, fuelled her bitterness against me. She railed at me. Of course it was my fault, and, like me, she could rewind the whole thing, trace it back and back like a horribly tangled and knotted ball of knitting and, whichever way you looked at it, it was going to end up as my fault.

'What are you drinking down there? And why don't you ever change out of that stinking old pullover and those pants? Yes I know you've been in the shower, but aren't you ever

going to shave? And what's with the hair? You look like a tramp and whenever you open your mouth you smell like a tramp as well.'

'May be you could do with a drink, Rosie.' It just came out, a little stroke of genius. 'Alright, so you're upset, I can understand all the stress and you not wanting to go out and see anyone. Alright so it's cool you staying up here with Chloe and trying to get yourself better, but do you want to try a glass of wine? It might help to settle your nerves and...'

In my mind I was adding, *it might take some of the heat off me as well, get half a bottle of red inside you, get you a bit more relaxed and a bit less murderously manic...* good drinker's ploy, persuade the tut-tutter and the eyebrow-lifter to join you in a glass or two.

And it worked. Rosie liked a drink. It was one of the reasons we'd got on so well and so quickly when we'd met. Our first date: a few pints in a Yates's Wine Lodge, a bottle of wine with spaghetti Bolognese in a bistro on Weekday Cross, a cuddle in a taxi and then we were splendidly in bed in her flat by Canning Circus.

This time, she demurred, but unconvincingly. 'Don't be stupid, Oliver, with all the antibiotics I'm taking, and I'm supposed to be going back to the hospital the day after tomorrow to see the doctor again. What are you trying to do, trying to keep me up here or what?'

I ignored that one, although it was so close to the mark that I hesitated at the door and caught a knowing look on Chloe's face. And when I came back from the kitchen with a nice Algerian, a corkscrew and two glasses, she snarled at me again, 'You're a bastard, Oliver, and you're so bloody obvious,' before slurping a messy mouthful.

As long as she was drinking, and if I could keep her comfortably topped up, I could spend more of my own time in the bookshop. With the computer. With a coffee and brandy. With Chloe, whenever she came down to see what I was up to. And with the crow.

We were working well as a team, in Poe's Tooth Bookshop. Every day there would be a few customers, or visitors, or nosey-parkers, enough to make it feel worthwhile being there and open. I was selling a few books. Chloe took her customary place at the fireside. She played with the mouse, which would obligingly appear from her sleeve, run across her shoulders and in and out of her golden tresses whenever anyone came in. The fire crackled and spat and exhaled the perfume of silver birch into the room. Music and coffee. The tooth, of course the tooth, which was the centre of attention and seemed to hum with a kind of latent energy. After all, it was the tooth which held us in its sway. It was an essential link in the chain of events which had brought us all to this place, at this time.

Poe's Tooth. Dentem puer. All of the time I spent at the keyboard of my computer I had Poe's collected stories open beside me. They were my inspiration. Hop-Frog, The Masque of the Red Death – they had a resonance beyond the mere proximity of the relic in its velvet-lined box. Was it me, was I imagining it, or maybe it was the drink which conjured a tenuous connection between the things which were happening to me and my family and the macabre fantasies on the page? But when I read and re-read the last few paragraphs of Hop-Frog and sensed the relish in the description of a man in flames, I would glance over to Chloe and remember the exquisite pleasure in her eyes when she'd blown the butterfly into the fire. As for The Masque of the Red Death, was I thinking of Rosie, sequestered and disfigured in her tower?

Tenuous, yes, alright, but it wasn't just me. Colonel Brook had got his piece into the local newspaper. The main thrust of the article was a plug for the academic rigour and extra-curricular activities of Brook's Academy, but there was a good photograph of me and the schoolboys assembled around the tooth. The colonel had described the tooth and its claim to authenticity, informing readers that Poe had been a schoolboy in England in the early 1800s. And in an oddly oblique last

paragraph, he'd mentioned Hop-Frog, the story his boys were studying, and said that 'the spirit of Edgar Allan Poe is surely alive and well and at large in Poe's Tooth Bookshop'.

It was another fillip for the shop. So that was twice the shop had featured in the local press, and business was picking up. People came by and said they'd read about me and the tooth in the paper – only one or two a day, but they were customers, who bent and peered at the tooth and frowned or gasped or tutted and then bought a book, with its complimentary bookmark. They would stare at me and Chloe and the mouse. And there was the crow as well, still convalescing, which might flop from the highest shelf and crash-land onto the floor just as I was clinching another sale. All good value. It made me wonder how I might generate some more publicity.

I did, and it happened like this.

I was writing, one gloriously gloomy afternoon, I was bashing at the keys and mining from the rich seam of Poe's imagination. I'd been diligent in my attention to Rosie. To put it another way, I'd got her cosy with a nice little South African red, I'd left her the bottle and a big round glass and not forgetting a box of tissues for wiping her chin, and she was happy. No, she wasn't happy, but she was comfortably morose, so I knew I could leave her for a while and get back down to the shop. As I was slipping out of the bedroom and I glanced back at her, I saw her sinking deeper into her big soft pillows and her face askew. I felt such a surge of love for her that I almost went back and held her in my arms and rocked her gently, reassuringly, and whispered into her ear that it was going to be alright, she was going to be alright. I loved her and I would always look after her ...

Almost. But then I saw the baleful look in her eye. She glared at me over the rim of her glass, and so I started downstairs. She was calling after me, something like, 'Is there a bad smell in here? What can I smell? Is it the mouse? Can you get Chloe to clean out the mouse or...?' And I was halfway down the stairs to the kitchen and calling back, 'Yes it's the mouse, don't worry we'll do it, we'll do it, don't worry.'

So I was writing. To be more exact, I'd been sitting by the fire with Chloe and enjoying the heat on my face, the warmth of a mug of brandy. I'd been watching the flames licking around the logs I'd just put on, watching the flicker of light on the girl's hair and the mouse in her hands, when I'd heard a footfall in the hallway. A customer? In a moment I was on my feet and sat at my desk and hammering at the keyboard. I was the troubled writer, toiling at my craft.

Someone came into the vestry. I glanced up, pushing my long, tangled hair from my brow, and I frowned, as if I'd been disturbed from a moment of intense creativity.

It was the very old gent. He stood in the dark hallway. He paused there, not because he'd been impressed by my silly act, but because the place had a special significance for him and he wanted to savour it. He was such a slight, fragile figure. His clothes were too big for him. They were the same clothes he'd worn when he was a well-made man, and he had shrunk inside them. And he teetered even more than before, because this time he was carrying a heavy bag in his right hand.

'I'm so sorry to disturb you,' he said. 'But I suppose your shop is still open. Your sign is still outside.'

He came in, so gently that not a whisper of dust was raised from the flagstones. I stood up from my desk and gestured him to take my seat, but he remained standing. He looked around the vestry, as he'd done before when he'd come to express his feelings about the closure of the church and our use of it. But this time he had a softer look in his watery eyes.

With some difficulty he raised the bag he was carrying and put it onto my desk.

'I hope you don't mind,' he said. 'I've been sorting some of my things. Our things. Since my wife passed away two years ago, I've had nothing much else to do. Me, on my own, in our big old house, with all the rooms we needed when the children were little. Now they've all gone and it's empty, big and empty and... '

He peered over to Chloe, who was sitting and watching him. She seemed to be holding her breath. I found myself holding

my breath too. Despite his frailty, despite the hoarseness of his voice, as if he were only a husk who might crumble at any moment, he was impressive. He had been a man. He was still a man. I sensed, no, I knew, that he'd been more of a man than I would ever be.

He pointed a quivering finger at the bag he'd put onto my desk.

'Some books,' he said. 'I'm sorry I was rude when I came in before. What does it matter about this old place? It's just a pile of stones. Of course it has special memories for me, and these stones have special footprints on them, mine and my wife's and my children's.' He tried to smile, although the wrinkles of his face were so dry, so cold. 'But good luck to you,' he said. 'You're young, you have a life and it's up to you to make something of it. Do it here, if you want, in this building. It isn't for an old man like me to tell you otherwise.'

He turned away from me, where the tooth was illumined in its velveteen box. He glanced at it, not with contempt but with casual disinterest.

'Poe's tooth?' he said. 'Is that all it is? Let me tell you, young man, when me and my wife were newlywed, we went together on the bus into Derby and had all our teeth pulled out. A week later we went back and had our false teeth fitted. Look, that's what we did in those days,' and he clacked at me a perfect set of dentures, far too big for his shrunken chops, top and bottom clacking together like the choppers in the mouth of a ventriloquist's dummy. He grinned them at me, grotesque. 'But the books,' he said, 'you might be able to sell them or just keep them on your shelves, a few thrillers and things we've had in the house since the children were growing up... Sherlock Holmes, The Canterville Ghost, *The Turn of the Screw*, The Monkey's Paw and all that. You're welcome to have them.'

He made to go out. He paused at the door and turned back to me.

'It'll come to you one day. You'll see your babies grow up and go away, and then maybe you'll be left on your own. And what will you do then, alone in your tower?'

I tried to take his arm and steady him. He brushed me off, as he'd done before, and he leaned towards the fire and stretched out his hand to the girl. He was going to touch her hair. His long bony fingers, the fingers which had plied the organ in this church for decades, hovered over her head.

She was alright with that. She didn't flinch. But the crow launched itself from the top shelf, where it had been silent and invisible since the man came in, and flapped into his face.

'What on earth...?' The man exclaimed, and with an impatient hand he knocked the bird to the floor. He didn't seem perturbed, he could see what it was and it was only a bird which must have blown into the vestry. And as it clattered around his feet, sculling about with its wings outstretched, he eyed it with a mixture of disgust and pity and said, 'What on earth is it doing in here, the wretched thing?' His lips made a funny, writhing smile, and he added, 'Like me, I suppose, a poor old thing come in from the cold, for a bit of company.'

He was alright. Or maybe not. His bravado couldn't quite disguise the little shock he'd had, because he was quivering even more than before. His sudden movement, the instinctive swatting at the creature fluttering in his face, had left him all trembly, as brittle as a bundle of wintry twigs.

'Here, sit down... please...' I was trying again to take his arm and steer him back to my seat, or at least stand him still for a moment so he could get his breath. At the same time, I saw Chloe reach for the bird and pick it up. She held it firmly but gently in both hands, so that its wings were folded against its body, and she sat in her queenly place by the fire with the crow on her lap. It hissed. It opened its beak as wide as it would go, and it made a hoarse, gasping noise.

'Alright, alright, I'm going,' he hissed back at it. He was certainly game. He straightened up, literally pulled himself together. 'Alright,' he mouthed back at the crow, 'so this is your place by the fire, with your little princess. I wasn't going to hurt her.' And he wobbled into the hallway. There, he steadied himself. He paused and he looked around. Then, as though he

knew that he would never come back, that this would be the last time he would stand in the church he'd known so well and for so long, he marched out of the door.

Was it the cold that hit him? I went outside to watch where he went. Even me, a bluff thirty-something-year-old, heaty with firelight and brandy, I felt the cold catch in my throat. It was bitter. Freezing hard. And the old man had barely stepped a few yards from the church before his knees buckled and he went down.

He hit his head on the pavement. His teeth fell out, shattered from their plate and spilled like pearls. He was fine, he was fine, he was trying to say the words and sit up, as I ran and knelt to him. I took off my coat and folded it into a pillow for him, laid his head onto it. Blood trickled from his nose and from his left ear.

An ambulance came. The paramedics were brisk and efficient and had him on a stretcher in no time. He was a tough old bird, one of them said, deliberately loud so that he could hear her. She was sweeping up the teeth with a dustpan and brush and sliding them into a plastic bag. 'Look,' she said, pointing with her brush at a crack in the pavement. 'He's broken it with his head.' It made the old man smile. Me too. He lifted a hand and feebly waved at me, as they closed the door and drove him off.

Chapter Twenty-Seven

TOSSING SNAILS OFF the top of my tower. That was what I was doing, and when I said the words aloud, 'Tossing snails off the top of my tower,' they sounded very strange, like a clue for a cryptic crossword puzzle. I liked the assonance too, and the alliteration. All in all, I felt rather clever. I was on the roof, on probably the most beautiful morning since the dawn of time, inhaling the deliciously cold air and dropping snails onto the pavement below.

It was only nine o'clock and I'd already had a mug of coffee with a generous slosh of brandy in it. I was, of course, unshaven and tousled, and enjoying a curious mixture of emotions – joy, at the crystalline perfection of the day, smugness, as I watched the masses in their silly tin cars queuing to get into town and to their stultifying jobs, guilt and self-reproach and self-pity, of course, and sadness. I was lobbing snails over the battlements and then leaning over to see where they landed.

To get to the roof of the tower, I'd had to negotiate the bedrooms and make the right noises at Rosie. I was going to check the boiler, I told her, because it had been another freezing night and I needed to make sure the lagging on the tank was sufficient and there hadn't been any burst pipes. She was snuggling in bed with Chloe and the medieval soft toys. After her first reaction, when she'd hurled them so hard at me they'd bounced off my chest and onto the floor, she seemed to have warmed to Robin and Marian and the goose-girl. Several days of my plying her with wine, and the occasional Southern Comfort and maybe here and there a Bacardi and Coke or just a little surreptitious tipple of

brandy into her tea, and she'd only stirred from her bed as far as the bathroom and back. She couldn't speak much. She didn't move much.

I was feeding the crow. Of course it got plenty of biscuit crumbs and bits of cake when Chloe and I were ensconced in the vestry, but this morning I'd had the urge to do something a bit different with its breakfast and remembered the snails. So I'd clambered up to the tower. On the way, I'd carefully closed the trapdoor out of Chloe's bedroom, I didn't want her following me, I wanted a bit of real space of my own. And from the clock-tower or the belfry, as I'd wrongly called it when we'd first moved in, I'd gone up the funny, jutting stone steps and emerged on the roof.

The snails were in their impenetrable crevice. So they thought, if snails thought. This time, instead of a crow jabbing with its beak and prising them out, it was me. I could just about squeeze my fingers into the crack and pull them out, one by one. I loved the sweet resistance, the way the snail clenched its juicy foot on the stone inside the cave and tried to hang on, and then the lovely sucking, succulent sound: a wet kiss, as the suction-pad came away and the snail surrendered. And then, even more delicious, I would lean out from the battlements, pausing to enjoy the glittering view of fields and ice and a huge blue sky, and I would choose a mischievous moment... when a pedestrian was passing the door of the church, or when a particularly posh car was going by... and drop the snail.

Smash. Shatter it on the pavement in front of a shuffling pensioner and see him recoil from its impact. Smash it on the bonnet of a Jag or a Merc and watch the driver stop and get out and huff and puff and stare disbelievingly at the sky. But the point of the exercise, apart from my childish pranks, was to see the crow come hopping out of the church and relish its breakfast. It would spring past the feet of wondering passers-by. It dared the stop-start traffic, in and out of the cars and buses and even the cyclists who were beating the queue into work, and it picked the morsels of flesh from the broken shells.

Joe Blakesley? Was it him? I thought he might come back, or he might call me. I recognised him, even from this height and angle. He must've been having a coffee in Azri's, maybe he'd been preparing his questions and wondering how best to tease out his story, because I saw him crossing Shakespeare Street from the little cafe and heading towards my sign on the pavement.

He paused at the sign, right below me. He took out his camera, to take a photograph of it. *Crack.* I got him smack on the top of his head. The snail hit him fair and square and bounced into the road, where it was crunched by a green Suzuki. He leapt aside, as though he'd been hit by a sniper's bullet. Rubbing his scalp, he reeled and almost fell over and he swivelled his head to see what had hit him. He saw the snail, the slimy wet place where its flesh had been smeared onto the tarmac, he saw the shards of the shell. And he peered up at me. Too slow, I recoiled behind the battlements. He'd seen me.

And so I hurried downstairs.

'You alright, Rosie?' I threw the question at her as I passed the foot of our bed, not really expecting a reply. She was asleep again, after the tea and toast I'd taken her. 'You coming, Chloe?' I continued down and down, and I knew she'd be right behind me, once she'd bundled on some pants and a pullover and made sure the mouse was safely tucked away somewhere on her person.

The reporter was inside the vestry when I got down there. He was sitting at my desk and he was picking splinters of the shell from his hair. There was blood on his fingertips. Before I could finish what I was saying, he was waving away my spluttered apologies and at the same time I had a moment to reach for the computer and switch off the monitor, in case he was nosey enough to touch the mouse and see what I'd been writing.

'Yes, very funny, very funny,' he was saying. 'My first reaction, for a split-second anyway... was, you know, I'd got one of those paranormal kind of stories, like fish or frogs or whatever falling out of the sky. Until I looked up and saw you grinning from the top of the tower. Yes, very funny, and then I saw the crow in the road and yes yes very funny.'

He'd finished feeling at his scalp. Like a chimpanzee, he fetched something out of his hair and examined it minutely, and even more simian, he actually tasted it with his tongue. Grimacing, he wiped it on the edge of my desk. 'Escargots,' he muttered, 'alright if they're fried up with lots of garlic, but not so nice raw, especially when they've just been smashed on the top of your head.'

'I thought you would come,' I said.

Chloe appeared in the doorway and took her place at the fire, but it wasn't lit yet and she huddled there, shivering, straight out of a warm bed. Like a puppy, she'd followed me downstairs, ready to do whatever we were doing, having breakfast or going out on the boat or just staying in the shop. She didn't mind which, and she didn't seem to mind the dead cold ashes of the previous night's fire.

'I was kind of expecting you,' I went on. 'After what happened the other day, I guessed you might want to do a story or something or.'

'An obituary.'

In just a few weeks since I'd first met him, he'd changed from cub-reporter, wet behind the ears and deferential even to me, to a snappy, hard-nosed hack.

'I've been assigned to write an obituary. What did you think I was going to do? Another nice little plug for Poe's Tooth Bookshop?'

He softened again, bethought himself.

'But alright, I couldn't help making an excuse to slip out of the office and come out here and, I don't know, just drop in for a coffee and a chat.'

I lit the fire. We had a coffee. He'd brought a couple of croissants from Azri's. We shared them, him and me and Chloe, and we threw crumbs for the crow. The room was still very cold and would take a while to warm up, so, after he'd pretended it would be out of the question to have a brandy as well, he allowed me to rummage in the cupboard for the bottle and splash it generously into his mug.

I could see his eyes darting about. He was writing a feature in his head, if only he might persuade his boss to run it. The tower, the room, the girl, the crow... the snails landing on his head as if they'd been whirled up in the vortex of an alien space craft and dropped onto Long Eaton, of all places. As the fire crackled and I saw his face flush with the alcohol in his coffee, I had a real surge of affection for him, almost love, for this young man who was so like the urgently inquisitive writer I might have been, I could've been, I should've been. His hungry eyes flitted across the display of Edgar Allan Poe's tooth, they puzzled at the jewels of glass which lay scattered about it and they saw how a litter of snail shells had already been left there, like offerings at a pagan shrine.

'He died, you know,' he said rather hoarsely, after he'd tried and failed to refuse a second and a third little splash of brandy. 'Mr Leonard Vaughan, who would have celebrated his 91st birthday later this week, passed away after a fall etc etc. The organist and choirmaster at Shakespeare Street Anglican Church since 1948, much loved, a stalwart of harvest festivals and carol services for more than fifty years etc etc. It's going to be a nice simple, respectful obituary, about him and his family and his life. Did you know he'd been in North Africa during the war, the desert rats and all that? and then a successful local businessman and a magistrate and... extraordinary, when you look at a feeble old man and think of all the things he's done.'

Sad. That was why I'd been sad on the top of the tower. Mixed into my silly mischief with the snails, my self-pity and general shittiness, not to mention the exhilaration I still felt at watching other people going to work while I was in my scruff, I was thinking about the old gent. Yes, even me, feckless and lightweight and glaringly obvious Oliver Gooch, I wasn't impervious to sadness. I knew he'd died – an hour after he'd been taken in the ambulance, I'd called the hospital to ask how he was getting on and they'd told me. The books he'd brought me were still in their bag, on the desk. I hadn't even looked at them yet. While the young man quaffed his

coffee, while Chloe warmed her smile at the fire, I reached
for the books and had a look.

Nothing special in themselves. As he'd implied, they were the
kind of classics you might find in comfy suburban homes all
over the country. But some of them had been stamped inside
them, or had beautifully embossed plates pasted onto the flyleaf,
to mark them as gifts and prizes from long-ago christenings,
Sunday school, confirmation, communion, the rites of passage
of the old man himself and his children. So yes, they were
special. They'd been special to Mr Leonard Vaughan and his
family, whose voices had rung in these very walls, whose music
had celebrated dozens of happy and sad events in this church.

'But then I was thinking,' the young man said, 'I was thinking
I might write a kind of feature and show it to the editor, a bit
more about your shop and the tooth, and the angle would be...'
He hesitated, as though he was about to divulge something
inappropriate. 'Something about a kind of curse. It doesn't
have to be true, I can just make it up, something along the
lines of the tooth bringing bad luck, you know like the curse
of the mummy's tomb or the monkey's paw or whatever...'
He raised his eyebrows at me, over the rim of his mug. 'What
do you think? Of course, if you don't like the idea I'll drop it
straightaway.'

'I think it would be in very bad taste,' I said, 'and if you don't
mind me saying, a bit presumptuous.'

I felt a bristling of annoyance, it was like a rash or a flush of
blood in my chest and into my neck.

'You've no idea, have you?' I went on. 'So, why do you think
you can just go making things up? If you'd asked me first of all
if you could write about how me and my wife came to be here,
in this tower, about what happened to us and our daughter to
bring us here and how I came by the tooth, I might've thought
about it for a few seconds. And then I would've said no, because
the whole thing's so odd and disturbing and yes, tragic, that
first of all you wouldn't have believed it and secondly I'm going
to write it all myself one day.'

I could feel the heat rising into my throat and colouring my cheeks.

'So no, thank you but no,' I finished off. 'Do your obituary for the nice old gentleman. Just because there's a crow hopping about in here, and the tooth of Edgar Allan Poe, and the old guy happened to keel over and bang his head outside his own church, it doesn't mean there's a curse.'

He shrugged, he got up and did a final sweeping appraisal of the room before he moved towards the door. He was not at all fazed by my blustering. He was young, and I remembered the time in my own late teens and twenties when I couldn't give a shit and couldn't be rattled by other people's testiness or ill humour, when I didn't care whether I'd caused offence or not.

'The crow, yes,' he murmured, amused by my reaction, 'yes, I was going to ask about the crow. And your lovely daughter too, why she just sits there smiling and silent and she doesn't go to school? But no need, it didn't take me five minutes to look through our files and find out what happened to her. Oh, and the people in the car which hit her. And your wife, I asked around and I found out she works at Brook's Academy, and when I phoned them they said she was off work right now, had a kind of stroke or something?'

He was going outside, swaddling himself in his coat and deliberately eccentric scarf.

'So, Mr Gooch, I'm sorry if I riled you a bit, with my ridiculous idea about the curse. But funnily enough, your denial of any such thing is kind of more revealing than if you'd agreed with it. You know what I mean?'

I followed him outside. He was smug. He had a tiny triumphant smile on his mouth, as if he'd baited me and I'd swallowed the bait and he'd pulled me in. He'd already done a bit of homework. He knew more than I'd thought he did.

'Don't worry,' he was saying, as he turned away, 'I'll just do the obituary.' His feet crunched on the shells shattered onto the road, he rubbed the top of his head. 'If I do get another story out of this, it won't be anything about a curse or whatever.

You can do that yourself. You're living it, you're living in it. But I might do a little spooky thing about snails dropping out of the sky, you know, *X-Files* or *Twilight Zone* or whatever...'

He'd gone. His words were ringing in my head.

I was living the curse? I was living in it? Who was cursed? Me, Oliver Gooch, or my daughter Chloe Gooch? No, it was nothing like the monkey's paw. Long before I'd been given the tooth, I'd got the things I'd wished for: the money and leisure I'd craved, an angelic daughter. If I was living in the curse, I was very comfy too, in my swaddle of guilt. I was the lord of my tower, and my lady wife was miserably numb in her chamber, I was imprisoning her up there, keeping her pickled...

So fuck off, Joe Blakesley. You think you know stuff, but you don't. You think you're a super-investigative journalist, but there are things you'll never find out, things you'll never dig out of your files. The curse I'm living in is real, you don't need to make it up. I've been walling myself up inside it, like in another of Poe's stories, with alcohol and deception and duplicity and the compliance of my daughter. And one day she'll blink and we'll get out. But is that what I want? And the tooth? Get rid of it, old man Heap got rid of it, he gave it to me. The bird, the tooth, they've got to go...

In a blur of indignation, I went back towards the door of the church. I paused to move the sign. Annoyingly, the reporter had turned it a little bit, when he was going to take a photo, so I put it back exactly where I wanted it. And then I saw something in a crack in the pavement. The paramedic had joked that the old man had broken the stone with his head, and I'd wondered for a moment if this was the spot where that workman had landed when he'd fallen and died during the building of the church. Whichever it was, or whoever it was whose skull had left its mark, there was a small white object stuck there.

It was a tooth. I picked it out and held it to the sunlight.

The paramedic with her busy dustpan and brush must have missed it, after all it had been dark in the late afternoon,

confused by the flashing lights of the ambulance and its puthering exhaust fumes. As I moved back to the doorway, I marvelled at the whiteness of the tooth, how purely perfect it had remained after more than forty years in the organist's mouth. I supposed it was made of porcelain or something, and every night it had been cleaned in a solution and left to soak in a glass on the marital bedside table. I could picture the two of them, Mr and Mrs. Vaughan in the bedroom of their semi-detached house in Trowell Grove, snuggling up and exchanging gummy kisses. The tooth was pristine. It could've been new.

Where to put it? When I went back into the vestry to make sure Chloe was alright, I was thinking I should call the hospital and tell them, maybe it was a legal requirement, maybe it was illegal to knowingly retain a piece of a recently deceased person. Chloe stood up from the fire, which was blazing brightly and warming the room. She'd been holding the crow on her lap, and the mouse was peering from her sleeve and disappearing again, instinctively wary of the bird and its heavy black beak. Just then, it seemed the obvious thing for me to do, to place the tooth onto the display, another gift at the shrine of Edgar Allan Poe, with the blood-stained glass and the fragments of snail-shell.

Chloe, curious, came to look. She picked up the tooth and smiled at it. She put it to her mouth, as if she would taste it, and I said quickly, 'No no, don't, that's not nice,' and tried to take it from her.

But she stepped back and withheld it from me. She held it close to her smile. Its whiteness matched hers. Of course, I suddenly realised, because the tooth was hers.

'So that's where it went to. Was it the crow who took it out there? What do you want to do with it, Chloe? Do you want to show it to Mummy, and then we'll put it under your pillow for the tooth fairy to come? No?'

She didn't answer, of course, not in words. She put it where I was going to put it. By Poe's tooth.

Chapter Twenty-Eight

I WAS WOKEN by screaming.

I lay on my back with my eyes wide open and I thought the screams were a part of my dream. The room had been very dark when I'd slipped into bed, so dark and silent that I'd done everything in my powers to keep it so – by tiptoeing, by holding my breath, by slipping between the sheets so softly that not a sigh or a whisper of my nakedness on the cool white cotton would be heard.

But now the room was not so dark. And not silent. I leapt out of the bed and tumbled across the room to see what on earth was going on.

A scene of gothic madness. Bedlam would have been like this.

I called out, 'Rosie! Rosie! What are you doing, Rosie?' But she couldn't have heard my voice. Because she was writhing on the bed and screaming.

I'd been in Chloe's bedroom, I'd sneaked in when I knew Rosie was unconscious after a nightcap of tawny port. After my banishment to the kitchen and the nether world of the moonlit vestry, I needed a bed. Now, naked, I'd blundered into our bedroom, where Rosie was in the throes of a terrible nightmare.

Chloe was crouching beside her. If it weren't for the inane fixity of her smile, I would've said she was paralysed with fear. She was clutching her goose-girl. The Robin Hood figure as well, he was sprawled across her pillow.

Rosie... in the dim light of the bedside lamp, she was writhing on the bed. No words, at least no words I could recognise. Her

mouth was wide open and red. It was a dribble of port and... a kind of sangria, fermented in the coils of her gut and bubbling back, a bitter bile in her throat and on her tongue and spewing past her traitorous lips.

'Rosie!' I was stumbling forward and trying to take hold of her, but her flanks were slippery with sweat.

I fell on top of her. She was writhing underneath me, and it was extraordinary and disturbing for me, and no doubt for the onlooking Chloe, to see how I was aroused, my nakedness erect on her hot, pneumatic body. She couldn't really speak. Even when I'd quietened her and she lay heaving and her eyes rolling like a mare stuck in a ditch, she was muttering and cursing and rubbing at her face. She was a mess. And the bed too. I thought maybe she'd woken in a fit or a seizure, or she was having the stroke we'd suspected before.

My mind was racing. I knew she'd fallen asleep drunk, of course I knew, because it was me who'd helped her to slurp down the port in a considerable quantity to make her comfortable, and I knew I'd had my share too. So, if and when she ever calmed enough to be manageable, it would still be quite a feat to get the befuddled two of us, and the bemused Chloe, dressed and into a taxi to hospital again.

'Rosie! Rosie, my lovely Rosie. Be calm, be calm, relax and breathe and breathe and breathe...'

She wasn't lovely. She looked terrible. Her hair was a Medusa mess.

I reached for Chloe and felt her little body trembling. The smile was nothing, of course we'd known this for a long time. Beneath the blissful calm of her face, who knew what torture she was enduring? I laid my hands on her and tried to soothe her, and at the same time I saw the madness in her mother's eyes and felt her reaching for the mirror, that wretched mirror which was always there, somewhere in the tousled sweat of her sheets and she would rummage for it and press it to her face so she could see how her youth and beauty had collapsed so utterly.

Cruel, truthful mirror. She was squashing it hard to her face. She was pressing it to her cheek with all her strength, as if she was trying to crush something, to erase, to annihilate some unwanted part of herself.

'Rosie, Rosie, let me see, please...' and I prised the mirror from her hands.

The wound that the crow had made. Yes, it was worse. In my ministrations, as I'd plied her with the numbing wine and spirit and helped her to the bathroom, I hadn't really looked at the wound. I looked at it now. After all, it was that impact, beak into flesh, which had started it all, which had triggered Rosie's calamity. I peered close. It was raw and wet. I caught a smell from it. Something off, something past its best. A dead thing. Worse, it wasn't dead. When I pinned her down and grabbed the mirror away from her, when I gazed so close that my breath made her eyelids flutter, I could see something moving.

A worm? Worms? They were tiny and white. They had no faces. They didn't need faces. They only needed mouths and stomachs, so they could burrow blindly into living flesh and feed on it.

I almost retched. I felt a squirming in my belly, I felt my gorge rise. In a moment I was off the bed and in and out of the bathroom and back again, and I stung the wound with antiseptic. Rosie writhed beneath me. Despite the dereliction of her face and the ugly sounds she was making, I felt the ridiculous, inappropriate arousal which must have been so bewildering to Chloe. Again and again, I dabbed the wound and its inhabitants with ammonia. It dribbled down her face and onto her sheets, with the stains of wine. I peered again, using her infernal mirror to angle the light and see the effect of my clumsy attempts at nursing. I saw an ugly place, a piece of my wife which had been fragrant and kissable, and I smelled a deadliness inside it, which the ammonia could not disguise.

As though in a nightmare, she was shoving me away with an unnatural strength. Something else, other than the discomfort of the wound, had woken her in distress. She turned her

attentions to Chloe. Smearing at her mouth with her forearm, she managed to form some barely coherent words, as she sprawled across the bed and seized the girl by the wrists. Something like, 'Where is she? Where she gone? I want her back I want her back. Who took her?'

Chloe was afraid, I could see the fear in her eyes, although she gleamed her smile back into her mother's face. As gently as I could, I tried to prise Rosie's grip from Chloe.

'Rosie, Rosie, you're frightening her, you're frightening me. We'll get her back, we'll get her back. One day Chloe will come back and everything will be alright...'

'No, no, not...' Rosie was muttering, and she was suddenly more compliant in my arms, as though exhausted by her hysteria. She lay back, her hot naked body quite flaccid, only staring over the rumpled bedding and around the room for something lost, something which had been taken from her. 'No no, where is she? I want her back again...'

I realised she didn't mean Chloe. After all these months of yearning for the return of her daughter, that the girl might wake from the dream she was locked into, Rosie was looking for something else. I almost laughed out loud with relief.

'Oh god, you mean your doll? Your Maid Marian? Don't worry, we'll find it... hey Chloe, let's look shall we?'

Yes, Chloe had her goose-girl, which I'd meant to be her, and the manly Robin Hood, supposed to be me, was lying beside her. But Rosie's winsome Marian wasn't there. Not a problem, it must be hidden in the tumbled bedding. Chloe helped me to look, although she had a mysterious twinkle in her eye, and it was a good reason to get the bed stripped and remade. While I'd got Rosie into the bathroom and under the shower, we tugged everything off the double bed and bundled it up for washing, found clean linen from the cupboard, and when Rosie reappeared, wrapped in a big towel, her bed was crisp and cool and all in order. She was a bit better, she was calm. But her face was puffy, the wound was raw; and in her demeanour, in her very being, she looked beaten.

I held her very close, I folded her in my arms. So this was the strong, brave woman I'd married, this was bossy, controlling, wearing-the-pants Rosie. She was utterly disconsolate. I unrolled her from the towel and sprinkled her all over with talcum powder, put her back into our bed.

'We'll find her, Rosie,' I whispered to her, although Maid Marian had disappeared.

A mystery... I'd searched under the bed, shaken out all the soiled bedding, I'd even pulled the bed away from the wall to see if the doll had slipped down.

'I'll find her, she's got to be somewhere in this room. But more important, tomorrow we can either get you down to the clinic for some stronger antibiotics, or I'll go the pharmacy, and hey, I think your mouth is a bit better, isn't it?'

'It might be, yes, a bit...' she mumbled. She inhaled a huge breath, controlled the quivering of her lips and framed the words as clearly as she could. 'Yes, it might be. Thank you, my darling, thank you for looking after me, and for looking after Chloe.' She gazed up at me, and the love in her eyes was almost unbearable. 'Where have you been?' She was trying to say, 'What've you been doing? I don't want to lose you as well. I've lost Chloe, and me, I feel like I'm losing myself... and you too... what's happening to us?'

I slipped into the bed with her. Chloe had moved to the door of her own room. She was standing there, with the two other figures in her arms. For a moment she just stood there and stared at us, her father and mother together again, and then she turned and disappeared. I heard the rustle and creak of her getting into bed.

BIG WET MOUTHS. *laughing, big wet mouths. library van, hot and full of people.*

too many people. can't read can't think, all pressing around me, got books open on my table and the words and the pictures are swimming in front of my eyes.

saxophones, constellations. maps, telescopes and taxidermy.

impossible to read them, people pushing and braying. so many people, the van swaying, and the noise.

can't breathe. get up and push to the open door. a village square, a church and a pub and a shop. a few cars parked. nice little sports-car right outside, with the top down. nice, with wire wheels and shiny mirrors on stalks.

they're all talking and laughing inside the van, i turn back inside and into their wet mouths, wet lips and tongues, loosened by drinking. a young couple, she's blonde and he's dark, type-cast in a soap. old heap, throwing his head back and laughing. his son, big man, braying too.

they're laughing at chloe. i don't like it. something she said. she's naked, no, not naked, but her pudgy little body is mottled and reddened, her baby tits are striped as if she's been nubbing them with her fingers, clawing them with her nails. something she said. she flails her arms around her head and she's crying, her face is distorted with distress and pain and the unfairness of everything, everyone is braying with laughter and their wet big mouths are shouting fuck you dad it fucking stung me that's why...

on the roof. on the roof of the tower. at last i can breathe. barbeque? was it my idea? big sky i can breathe. all on my own at the top of my tower and smouldering a smokey barbeque. and they're coming up, one by one, oh fuck they keep on coming up and up through the little trapdoor, they're coming up through the clock tower the belfry whatever and up and up to the roof of my tower...

look over the battlements, see that little nice car stopping at the kerb, far far below. they look up at me and get out and they wave. old heap, he pushes his head through the trapdoor and he's wheezing. and his son, helping him, pushing his aged father up and onto the roof and then reaching down to help his daughter... and the other sister whoever she is with her medieval dolls there's three fucking generations of heaps, elbowing and shouldering through the trapdoor and up and up onto my roof, onto the roof of my tower.

and blakesley? fucking cheeky, got that clever little know-it-all smile on his face and he's reaching into a crevice in the battlements and pulling out snails and popping them onto the barbeque, and he's murmuring about escargots and he's turning them on the grill until the shells pop and the flesh oozes out and he's...

colonel brook, in a waft of after-shave. old gent, mr vaughan, war hero and sunday-school teacher how fucking perfect can you get, he claws himself up and glances around as though it's his tower, his church, he's acquired it by all his years of being there. me and chloe and rosie, of course, oh, and the mouse, nibbling out of chloe's sleeve and dropping out and great hilarity as it scurries and...

and the crow. it's whirling overhead. lovely, criss-crossing the sun. no, not lovely, it's a blot. the sun is lovely and cold and crisp and the crow is a blot. sick in my stomach, me, when i see the shadow crossing, criss-crossing.

at last we're all gathered for our barbeque on the roof. trapdoor shut.

crowded and laughing. a lot of teeth. why are they all so perfect, the soap-opera teeth and the colonel and the organists's dentures, and the youthful blakesley? rosie, as toothsome as only a dentist's assistant can be, and chloe with her smile that smile that permanent smile? so crowded on the roof, i'm crushed to the battlements and leaning out. i'm standing on the trapdoor. i shut it and stand on it and everyone's laughing...

and then they stop.

they all stop, as if they're listening for something. holding their breath. the mouths are still. even the swoop of the crow is still.

something moving under my feet. i can feel it. i'm standing on the trapdoor and something is trying to push it open.

my weight is too much for it. but i can feel it pressing against my weight, trying to push me off the door, trying to lift me up and off it. i'm sick with fear. my stomach is sick.

help me, please help me. the fear is sick in me. i'm crying out, in a suffocating dream, for people to help me, to help me,

oh please to help me stop whatever it is which is crawling out of the blackness of the tower... i'm calling for help fuck to try and stop the trapdoor from creaking up and bursting open ...

they don't help me. they're watching, and listening but they don't help me. they are silent. their perfect smiles and laughter have been quenched.

someone is coming up. i step off the trapdoor. it opens slowly. a boy. he looks up and he smiles. a mouth full of blood.

Chapter Twenty-Nine

I WOKE WITH a start, stared into the darkness for a few seconds and then reached over Rosie to try and turn on the lamp.

But I stopped myself just in time. I didn't want to wake her. A ray of orange light from the street was falling into the room, and I could see her face, so still and quiet and perfectly peaceful. She was lying on her back, snoring so softly that her lips barely moved. Her mouth was slightly open, drooping to one side, and a trickle of saliva shone on her chin.

I was afraid. The dream had shaken me. And I was cold. As I'd struggled, in my nightmare, to maintain my balance on the trapdoor and keep it shut with all my weight, I must have kicked the duvet off my side of the bed. I was naked and uncovered. I sat up and reached for the duvet to pull it on top of me again.

And I heard a sound.

Not a dream. Cold reality. The kind of reality which is so dreadful, literally full of dread, at two o'clock in the dead of night.

Footsteps. Not in the room. For a bewildering second I thought they were overhead, that someone was moving in the dusty darkness of the clock tower. Footsteps, very slow and soft. But no, they were not in the room and not above me.

Below me, somewhere. I turned my head on the pillow, as afraid as if I were a child, filled with the terror that children feel in their worst and most terrible dreams. I stared at the door of the bedroom. It was shut. But the fear I felt, like ice in every part of my body, was behind that door. And it was coming up the stairs.

I forced myself off the bed. I crossed the room and put my ear to the door, and I could hear the footsteps. More than that, I could feel them, their rhythm was palpable in the air around me. The footsteps grew louder. Not heavy, indeed they were as gentle as a child's footsteps, but then, when I saw the handle turning, the fear was so great in me that I leaned with all my weight to try and stop the door from opening.

Nevertheless, it opened. I must have stood back and allowed it. I must have known, in my grown-up's mind, that I was awake this time and there wouldn't be, there couldn't be a boy, with blood spilling from his lips...

Chloe. She stepped into the bedroom.

She brought with her a mist of ice, as though she had been so deep in the darkness of the stairs, down into the hallway and the vestry, that she'd gathered a cloak of the freezing night around her. She even smelled of the night. The smell of ice was in her hair.

'Chloe?' I think I said, although my voice was no more than a plume of frost. 'Chloe, where have you been?'

She stepped past me. As she passed through the orange light from the road, I saw that her face and hands were smudged with something. Ashes? Soot? She had smudged her face with it.

When she saw the empty half of our bed, she crept onto it. Before I could reach her – I was standing naked and paralysed by the door – she tugged the duvet over herself and snuggled against the soft, warm flank of her mother.

I stood at the open door, a yawning, icy-black hole. I should have gone down, I was the man of the house and I should have gone to see what on earth Chloe had been doing and if she'd left the kitchen door open or even the doorway of the church for the night and all its whispering spirits to come in...

But I didn't. I closed the door and I crept into Chloe's room and into her bed. I lay awake for a long time. Like a child who'd had a nightmare, I was afraid to go back to sleep, in case the nightmare was waiting for me. If I closed my eyes,

it was lurking in the shadows. My eyes open, I could see the trapdoor above me and imagine the boy pressing against it with his head and his shoulders and clenching his teeth so hard that the blood welled from the place where his tooth had been... and if I turned my head I could see across to the other bedroom door, the door I'd tried to hold shut until a sooty, smiling Chloe had somehow stepped through.

Where do you go, if both dreams and reality are too frightening? Where else is there?

I tiptoed to Rosie's bedside. She and Chloe were breathing easily, in the bliss of each other's body. I found a bottle on the floor. The remains of red wine? Was it rum or the last cloudy swirls of the port? Whatever, it was a friend in the night. I took it to bed with me.

QUARANTINE. I DIDN'T open the shop the following day. All morning and all afternoon, I didn't go downstairs. The three of us, we stayed in our tower, locked in, closed in from the outside world.

We didn't need to go out, we didn't need anything. All that morning and afternoon, we neither went up nor down. Rosie had awoken better and calmer and more herself, and said we might put off a visit to the hospital another day or so. She'd be alright, she said.

So the limits of our world were the bedroom and the kitchen just below it. Sometimes we heard the scrabblings of a rat or the flutter of a bird in the clock tower above our heads, but there was no reason to go up and look. And we heard the traffic in the road, far below, the movement of other people, but they could have been some kind of aliens going about their business, because they didn't touch us at all.

A few times I heard the rattle of the church doorway, someone trying the door and maybe wondering if the shop was open, but I ignored it. Once, there was a persistent knocking; it became an exasperated hammering, one of those

members of the public who thought a shop must always be open and available and the proprietor amenable and servile and obsequious and fawning and... anyway, it was so loud that Rosie and I looked at each other with eyebrows raised, and Chloe froze her smile in anticipation of my getting up and going downstairs. But after a while the hammering stopped.

All day we stayed in the bedroom. Me and Chloe, we went down to the kitchen now and then, to make coffee and toast and honey for a breakfast which we carried back upstairs so we could all three of us eat it in bed, and then at lunchtime we did scrambled eggs with mushrooms and bacon and brought it upstairs again. Rosie didn't have to move from the sprawl of her bed. Her sheets were clean and fragrant, she had slept in the cuddle of her daughter and all would be well. Apart from eating, apart from waiting on Rosie and keeping her as cool and comfortable as possible, what did we do? We did Radio 4. We dozed, we read through a slippery heap of glossy magazines we found under the bed, until we could've been experts on the glitz and glamour of last year's celebrities and footballers and eligible young royals. Chloe played with the mouse. She improvised a run for it. She made mountains and caverns and deserts through our bedclothes, so that Mouse could embark on his quests for adventure.

Mid-afternoon. We were still aloft in our tower. Whatever might be happening in the shadows of the clock tower or on the battlements of our roof, we didn't care. And far below us, in the hallway or the vestry and in the scurrying, myriad world outside, there was nothing to touch us, nothing we needed, nothing we even needed to think about.

I blocked it all out of my mind. In my fanciful daydreams, whenever I thought of the shop downstairs and the relic which had come to define it, we were like the revellers in The Masque of the Red Death: we had deliberately and defiantly incarcerated ourselves in our great stone castle, we had everything we needed and the outside world could go hoot. I tried to block it all out, because I sensed, with a feeling of

dread in my belly, that with sleep there would come dreams – crowded, baleful dreams which might bring back to me the reproachful reality of my life.

Aloft we were, but not unassailable.

The night was crawling around our walls. Where there had been a silvery daylight at our windows, it faded to grey. I had a feeling that the shadows of dusk were slithering up the tower. It was coming from the frosty fields across the road, from the dark dead trees, it was hissing along the road with the tyres of the homebound traffic. In a matter of moments, the windows were black. I felt a panic of claustrophobia. No, not as dramatic as that, but the cabin-fever of being in our bedroom all morning and afternoon. Suddenly, the cosiness of our little nest was stifling me. I needed something to shock me alive again.

While Rosie was snoozing again, with a magazine lying on her face so that her lips blubbered softly against it, and while Chloe was lost in another epic journey with the mouse, I got off the bed and went down to the kitchen. Found rum, and ice.

Ice. I could feel an icy darkness pressing around the tower. And I carried a jug of ice upstairs. And when I got there, finding that Chloe was burrowing somewhere in the bedding and fantastically removed from us, I lifted the magazine from Rosie's face and did two mischievous things – I plopped a cube of the ice onto the dip in her throat, and, as she moaned and squirmed and tried to sit up, it slipped down between her breasts. At the same time, having swallowed a slug of the rum and kept a residue in my mouth, I met her gasping mouth with mine.

The rum and the ice, hot and cold, it worked for both of us. It had done before, long ago when we'd been courting, if it was appropriate to use that genteel word for the boozy foreplay of our earliest dates. Alcohol-fuelled sex – a few months of it before we'd got engaged, another six months of it until our wedding. And then Rosie had remarked, after we'd been married more than a year, that we'd never made love sober,

that maybe we should try it one day. We did try it, and it was ok. But now we let the rum into our heads and enflame us, and our love-making was better than nice, it was hot, slippery sex.

Where was Chloe? She was somewhere down there, and maybe the urgent tumbling of the bedclothes around her and her mouse was a part of their quest, it was the rumbling of an earthquake or an avalanche or the eruption of a volcano. Me, I took more rum into my mouth and we shared it on our tongues, and then I kissed it onto her wound, so that she winced and panted as it stung into the tiny white worms which were writhing there.

Alcohol and ice. Hot and cold, positive and negative. They jump-started us, like they were the red-and-black crocodile clips from a buzzing battery. Whatever, we made healing love.

It made us drunk. The alcohol went straight to our loins. Chloe surfaced from the bedding. She was like us, red-faced and panting, and indeed I'd felt her bare skin against me as I'd lost myself in Rosie's ample body. The girl was naked too. She must have slipped out of her pyjamas as part of her game with the mouse, maybe because of the heat of the bed as she'd been submerged inside it, or maybe in some precocious imitation of her mother and father and the proximity of our nakedness.

The three of us lay together. Rosie and I must have slept again, and we made love an hour or two or three hours later, our bodies moving in a delicious slow-motion. We were buried in the bedding, we'd somehow pulled it over us so completely that our heads and faces were covered and we were suffocating sweetly in a fug of our own heat.

And Chloe? In the fume of alcohol, in the stupefying darkness, there was a strange and giddying sense that she was there as well, somewhere, that her presence was on us and somehow between us and a part of us. In a blur between waking and sleeping.

Chapter Thirty

WHEN AT LAST I truly awoke, I found myself in a kind of limbo.

The room was very dark, someone had switched off the bedside lamp. I knew I was awake because, beside me, Rosie was so fast asleep that she could have been dead. She was so still, she hardly seemed to be breathing. I leaned to her to feel for a flutter of breath from her lips, from her nostrils, and yes she was alive. The waft of rum from her body was strong, and I knew it was in the sweat of my skin as well. Rosie was drunk, and she had found peace in sleep, exhausted and spent.

I turned and sat up. No sign of Chloe. I went unsteadily to the bathroom. I looked into her room and she wasn't there either. Not for the first time, I shuddered with apprehension at the thought of her going up to the clock tower or even onto the roof, but the ladder above her bed was still stowed, up there on the ceiling, by the trapdoor. Our bedroom door was open. She had gone down.

I hurried down to the kitchen, drunker than I'd thought. The darkness of the stairs was like a heavy black blanket hung in front of me, something I had to push through and past while it tangled in clinging folds around my face and my shoulders. Even before I'd started down and down towards the hallway, from where such a blast of icy air was coming that I was sure she'd opened the church door and left it open, I could see a glow of silvery-grey light from the vestry. And I could hear a sound, a pattering, a tip-tapping, and I was glad, because I knew that Chloe was in there. In a moment I was in the hallway, relieved to see that the door was shut – the draft was only from underneath it, a scalpel of cold, slicing into the body

of the church as if it were unresisting flesh – and I could see Chloe in the vestry.

She had switched on my computer. She was sitting, naked, at the keyboard. It was the only light in the room. She was rapt. Even when I walked behind and stopped, and she must have heard me and felt the warmth of my body close to hers, she seemed oblivious. She didn't turn to glance at me. When I touched her shoulder, and I was surprised to feel how hot she was in the freezing room, she didn't move. I was naked too, and shivering. The room had been empty and neglected all the previous night and all day, without a fire. When I squeezed her shoulder a bit, and whispered, 'Chloe? Aren't you cold? shall we get you upstairs and back into bed?' my breath was as silvery as the screen.

She didn't respond in any way. She was pattering on the keyboard. With both hands and all eight fingers, with occasional bumps onto the space bar with her thumbs, she was randomly hammering at the keys. *dckjfapis klkxcj alaflertiojfmamcositf ucklzerjlffopl ingpjkpaaaaaws tungmedspomrtha tsojoswhy oklkmlm*

She kept on hammering. Hammering is the wrong word, because she was rather delicately composing what she was writing, she was copying the way I did it with pauses and flurries and pretend hesitations and marvellous flourishes. Copying what her Daddy would do whenever a customer came into the shop and he was suddenly the great and gothic writer in his beard and oily hair and his pungent coat, when he was Poe. I bent over her shoulder and I could smell the soap on her body, the shampoo in her hair, the natural little girl fragrance of her skin. And just as I was leaning closer and about to plant a paternal kiss on the back of her neck, there was a different kind of flurry in the room... and the crow dropped off its top shelf and fluttered to the floor.

It always did that. Normally I appreciated its timing, a kind of shock tactic, whenever there was a customer in the shop who was browsing the books and then ogling the tooth, it would reveal itself, a phantasm of Poe, and clinch a sale with a few

miraculous beats of its wings. It was an embodiment of Poe, or, as Colonel Brook had written in his article, the spirit of Poe was alive and well and haunting the bookshop. Me, in my Edgar Allan scruff, all gaunt and haggard and sunken-eyed etc. I was just a ham, like one of those out-of-work actors doing ghost tours of York or hamming Heathcliff at Haworth. But the crow was phantasmal. And now it detached itself from the highest shelf and beat into my face and I knocked it away from me with an impatient hand.

It shuffled itself back into shape. Like a pack of cards, its feathers shivered into shape again. *Bastard fuck,* I was thinking and hearing inside my head, and all the rum seemed to surge between my ears like an alcoholic tsunami, banging and crashing all its debris of fragmented memory and half-remembered dreams. *Fuck you bastard,* as it clawed itself onto the desk and onto the top of the monitor and adjusted its whole crow-like demeanour as though it was posing for a publicity shot. The crow, not quite a raven, but as near as dammit; Poe's crow posing in Poe's Tooth Bookshop, with the tooth itself framed carefully behind it.

Poe's crow, posing in Poe's Tooth Bookshop. I tried to say it. Couldn't.

It stood on the top of the computer screen. I leaned closer again to Chloe, and again I read what she had written. Yes, she was still writing, more of the same, and although it was a whole lot of random gobbledegook I was kind of jealous, because, unlike me, at least she was writing something and it looked original and it had probably never been written before. This permutation of letters and words and phrases had probably never, never in the history of literature, been written before. She'd composed another deliciously original sentence.   *;xlknf;lkj;lkexffu als ckyouzpok[p daddkoopoi cososknmit fucppokuing 0ookstun -gme tha ts [ijokwh okjlpky*

I suddenly thought that I had never felt so cold. Not just the cold. But alone. And separate from... from everything and everyone.

I was naked, nearly forty years old and just as naked as the moment I'd been born. My own daughter was sitting in front of me and I was touching her, but she responded not at all. It was as though, for her, I did not exist. I couldn't make her hear me or feel me. And even when I lowered my mouth to her skin to kiss her, to kiss my own flesh and blood, there was a bird which came down and battered into my face to prevent me. My wife? She was somewhere upstairs, in a ridiculous tower, separated from me by walls of stone and a trauma which I had caused. Could you be more alone, Oliver Gooch, than to be naked and drunk and middle-aged, in the vestry of a mock-medieval church, with your alienated daughter and a crow?

What to do? Drink more? I did so. The bottle was in the cupboard, in its place where I had left it; at last there was something certain and reliable in my shivering world. And fire. While Chloe was tooling at the keyboard and putting me to shame with the fecundity of her imagination, I could at least make fire.

I did so. I tried to do so. Why was it so difficult? Because I was so cold and naked and it felt ridiculous to be sitting naked in a bookshop in the middle of the night with my naked daughter? I tried again. Twists of newspaper on top of yesterday's ashes... splinters of wood... applying a match and instant satisfaction as it all bloomed into a brilliant yellow chrysanthemum flame. But then, as I started to lay a few of the logs I always used, the smoke from my incipient fire just coiled and confused and puthered, and instead of streaming up the chimney, it blew back at me, into my face, and back into the room.

Chloe – she was still writing, but slowing and pausing and stopping. Whenever I turned to glance at her, I caught her watching me and smiling. And then she would bend again to the keyboard and resume her hammering on it. She was watching me trying to light the fire. Oblivious... not any more, she had pretended to be oblivious of me when I'd first come into the room, but now, although she was working on her next piece of purple prose, her next deathless phrase, she was alert to what I was doing,

'So what's up with the fire, Chloe? What do you think?'

She threw me such a knowing glance, it was hard to imagine that she'd been so lost, so utterly lost for the past months.

'Shall I not bother? Shall I leave it and we'll do it tomorrow, together? Hey, it's so cold in here, wouldn't the sensible thing be for the both of us to go back upstairs and into bed?'

She bent to her writing again. It was as though she was testing me. If she'd just smiled and sat there and done nothing, we could have turned off the screen and watched it fade into darkness and gone back to bed. But she did a little frown, something she'd learned from her father, and pattered at the keyboard again. She did another flurry, tossing her hair. She was goading me, she was making it look easy, just sitting there and thinking and then committing her thoughts to paper, as it were, as if to say what was so hard about that? Of course, she had the crow. Perched at eye-level, on a level with her thoughts, it was her muse.

So I tried once more with the fire. I shoved more screwed-up balls of newspaper among the smouldering tinder and lit them with a match. Again, the gratification was instant, but short lived. There was a glorious blaze of light, which brightened the whole room and gave an illusion of warmth. The tinder caught, the logs caught, and their smoke was dense and blue and it swarmed to the chimney.

But then it writhed back again. The fireplace coughed and belched and a great sooty-black cloud spewed into the room. I sprang away from it, choking. At the same time, I saw Chloe stand up abruptly from the desk and stare towards the door of the vestry.

It was Rosie. For the first time in days, she'd come downstairs.

'Are you there?' she blurted. 'What on earth are you doing down here?' And she pushed through the smoke and into the room. She saw me spluttering by the fireplace, she saw Chloe in the light of the computer screen. 'God, Oliver. What are you trying to do?'

She pushed me aside, just as a mess of soot collapsed out of the chimney, totally quenched my feeble attempt to make fire and scattered all over the floor.

'What is that? Can't you see, Oliver? There's something blocking...'

Before I could stop her or try to see what she was doing, she was kneeling in all the soot and reaching her right arm up and up into the chimney. She grabbed something which was dangling there. Something stuck there. She pulled and pulled, and suddenly, with a tremendous whoosh, an even greater avalanche of soot came down.

I helped her up and away from it, lifting her to her feet. She was covered in soot. I was covered in soot. Chloe came forward and the soot was all over her too. Rosie squirmed away from me, bent to the mess on the floor and lifted something out of it, the thing she'd tugged out of the chimney.

It had arms and legs and a head, it was like a charred skeleton of a human figure.

Rosie stared at it, aghast. She whispered, 'So there you are, I've been looking for you everywhere,' and carried it away from the fireplace and across the room.

I switched on the lamp which shone on the tooth. The smoke blew through and around the beam, a fume of blue mist. The crow was nowhere to be seen, fortunately. It must have flopped onto the floor and found a discreet place to keep out of the way, as Rosie sat at the desk where Chloe had been writing.

Chloe and I stood beside her. There was a surreal calm. It could have been shouting and madness and a hellish nightmare, but Rosie somehow settled a motherly order on the strangeness of the situation. She didn't rail and rant about her Maid Marian, who'd gone missing and been found stuck up the chimney. She examined the figure, which was so thickly caked with soot that it could have been a ghastly human relic, the body of a child recovered from a terrible fire. She glanced up at me. For a moment, as I shivered like a

lunatic in my filthy nakedness, with my hair and beard awry, she might have thought that I had jammed the doll up there.

But no, I could tell from the deep anxiety in her eyes that she knew I hadn't. Who else could have done it?

She looked sideways at Chloe.

'Oh my poor darling,' she murmured. 'My poor baby, what have you been up to? Where do you get such silly ideas from? From your Daddy? From his silly books?'

She looked across to the lamp, its circle of smoke filled light. To the tooth. It nestled on its bed of velvet and assumed the focus of the room, of the tower, of the moment. It drew all our eyes to it.

'What do you think it is, Chloe?' she whispered. 'Is it just an old bit of bone? Or is it the tooth of a little boy, a boy who grew up strange and sad and had lots of mad ideas? I suppose your Daddy is right... it doesn't matter what it really is, it's the belief, it's what you believe that matters.'

She stood up. 'Why don't we go upstairs and get under the shower? Daddy can clean up his mess tomorrow. He'll have plenty of time.'

Her calmness was uncanny. It frightened me in a way I couldn't fathom. It made my stomach sick with apprehension. As she manouevred Chloe away from the desk, she tossed the horrid rag of the doll into a corner of the room. It landed, and there was a scuttling movement in the shadows.

Rosie heard it. She knew what it was. With a big breath, she managed to control her fear and anger. At the same time, she must have nudged the desk enough to bring Chloe's writing back onto the screen.

'And what's this?' she asked. 'Has Daddy been doing a bit of writing? Anything original? Or is it like the beard and the hair and the smelly old coat and the getting pissed and... just a lot of copying?'

She leaned to the screen and squinted at it. I put in quickly, 'It wasn't me, it was Chloe, she was playing, that's all.' And as usual, trying to counter her sarcasm, 'It's all her own work.'

'She wrote this?' Rosie leaned even closer. 'What does it mean?'

She peered at the screen. She was reading it. I was about to laugh out loud. Couldn't she see it was nothing but random letters and spaces? But when she recoiled from it and turned to look at me, her face, already distorted by the wound on her cheek, was a mask of contempt.

'You tell me, Oliver, what the hell do you think it means? Did she write this, or is it one of your sick ideas? Where did this stuff come from?'

'It doesn't mean anything,' I retorted. 'For heaven's sake, it's just her bashing on the keys. What do you mean what does it mean?'

Rosie was dragging the girl across the room. She was hissing under her breath. It was sick and I was sick and she was getting out of here and taking Chloe and...

They were gone, up the stairs.

I DIDN'T STAY a lot longer in the vestry. I was naked and covered in soot. There was nothing in the room I could improvise as a blanket or a rug, otherwise I would have thought about swallowing the rest of the bottle, lighting the fire as big and blazing as possible – now that the chimney had been unblocked – and trying to sleep in front of it. But still, two out of three ain't bad, as someone had once said, so before I dared to tiptoe up to the bedroom and negotiate a snarling Rosie, I opted for the bottle and the fire... kindling a tremendous crackle of flames and crouching over it like a caveman, and swigging the rum until my throat was burning too.

No, I didn't stay long. Even with the fire and the alcohol, I knew I couldn't bear a night down there, sitting and toasting my face and my chest while my back was freezing.

I heard the crow fluttering somewhere, not so much a flutter as a rustle and bristle of its wings as it settled into a dark corner of the room. For an ugly moment I felt a surge of such hatred

for the bird that I jumped up to grab something big and heavy to throw at it, and there I was, with a copy of the collected works of Edgar Allan Poe poised high above my head. But when I found the crow snuggling in the arms of Maid Marian, I lowered the book slowly, ashamed, and resumed my maudlin contemplation of the fire.

jsdpkjdpjs cmvnow eritcdkwohjedlfu ckyou;s]a dadcos llklqitfuc kin g okdkcmvmstung mep kthat swh y [kl per neekmg[pwcmm axsjpmfk fkppkkp

With a last look at the screen I switched off the computer.

And I switched off the lamp, deliberately averting my eyes from the tooth in case it set my mind whirling with doubts and curses. Upstairs, the kitchen was in darkness. Our bedroom was in darkness. I could smell from the fragrant steam in the bathroom that Rosie and Chloe had showered, although I didn't turn on the light to see their sooty towels or the rime in the bath. I could make out their mounded bodies in the double bed, and I knew from the unnatural silence that they weren't sleeping, they were holding their breath in a pretence of sleeping while I shuffled past them. Without so much as splashing my face or rinsing my teeth, I moved into Chloe's room and slipped into her bed. In my sweat. In a state of naked filthiness.

Doubts and curses. Burrowed under the bedclothes, I kissed my own shoulder. I tasted myself, smelled myself, and I could taste Rosie on my skin as well. I could smell Chloe too.

I whispered, 'Goodnight, Oliver Gooch. Goodnight, Rosie. Goodnight, Chloe.' And just as I closed my eyes and plummeted into an abyss of sleep, I had a flash of the computer screen again. *fuck you dad cos it fucking stung me that's why.*

Chapter Thirty-One

'YOU'LL NEED THE 7B,' I said to Rosie, pretending to study the timetable posted on the bus-stop.

We all knew it was the 7B. It was the Nottingham bus, it went through Long Eaton and Toton, on to Chilwell, past the army depot and Chilwell Manor Golf Club, through the middle of Beeston and past the university and the Queen's Medical Centre, along Lenton Boulevard and into the city centre. Stopping at Broadmarsh, very convenient for the shopping or sight-seeing in the middle of town.

I was going to recite the whole thing for Rosie. Just stopped myself. We were all three of us standing at the top of Shakespeare Street, and I was so sick with unhappiness that I just wanted to say anything, anything to fill the bitter silence which hung around us, even a blithering recital of the 7B's route into Nottingham.

'Yes, I know,' she said. 'It goes through Long Eaton and Toton, on to Chilwell, past the depot and the golf course, through Beeston and past the university and the hospital and into the city centre. Stopping at Broadmarsh. Yes, I know. But we're getting off at Chilwell, we're going to stay with Auntie Cissy. Aren't we, Chloe? You used to love Auntie Cissy, didn't you, and her nice old house? Didn't you, Chloe?'

So Rosie filled the silence. We stared at each other, terribly distanced by our anxiety and bewilderment, and yet realising, through some weird telepathy of local bus routes, that we were still on the same wavelength. This morning, taking advantage of the extra time I needed in the shower and the kerfuffle I made of stripping Chloe's bed, she had got herself and Chloe

packed and ready to go by the time I came down to the kitchen. The two of them were wrapped up warm. They'd already had porridge and toast and tea, they had a little suitcase each. They looked so perfectly prepared and snug in their coats and gloves and novelty bobble-hats that it was inconceivable they were leaving me in such turmoil. They looked so nice. As though they were going on holiday. They were going to sit upstairs and at the front of a splendid double-decker bus as it swayed along and swished through the overhanging branches of the wintry trees, they were going to be happy together.

I knew they weren't. But Rosie was determined they were going. She'd said – in the kitchen, before we all trooped downstairs and out into the bright, frosty morning – that they would stay with Auntie Cissy for a week or so, and I would have time to get sorted. Get the vestry cleaned up. Get myself straightened out. Decide if the bookshop and all its theatrical-gothic nonsense was more important than my family. Stop drinking. Get rid of the bird. As for the tooth... well, decide if it was just a bit of bone and throw it into the hedge, or, if I was really such a sucker to believe in stuff like that, take it to Bramcote crematorium and dispose of it decently.

The bus was coming. The 7B. We all hugged each other. I could tell in the strength and warmth of Rosie's arms that she could almost have changed her mind at the last moment, and we could've gone back into the tower together for more toast and tea.

But she didn't. She blinked at me through teary eyelashes. I felt my eyes stinging too. Her voice was hoarse as she undid herself from me and said, 'Me, I'm going to get my face checked up again. I'm going to call into the clinic at Chilwell. When I come back I'll be as beautiful as ever.' She tried to smile. 'I'm so sorry, Oliver, you're weak and lazy, but it isn't really your fault, is it? Is it?'

They clambered on board with their cases and up the steep, narrow stairs. I had a moment to move to the front of the bus and see them high up there. Rosie was looking down at

me, although she didn't respond when I waved. And Chloe, she had her face pressed hard against the glass, she was quite oblivious of me and was staring up and up into the sky, up to the top of our tower. She was pointing at something, she was grabbing her mother's arm and trying to make her see, pointing and staring and...

The bus moved off. I stood there, alone. Instinctively I glanced up to see what the child might've been looking at. I narrowed my eyes into the cold, clear sunlight, but it was too bright, the sun was too low and I could see nothing.

WHO WAS IT who said, where there's muck, there's money?

I brought a mug of coffee downstairs and lit the biggest, crackliest fire of all time. It roiled sweetly up the chimney, just what I wanted to draw away as much of the soot as possible. I put on *Led Zeppelin*, full volume. To clear the decks and make myself some space, I threw open the church doors as wide as possible, shoved the sign outside and all the untidy boxes of books I hadn't sorted yet. And I rolled up my sleeves to clean the vestry.

It was a horrible, stinking mess, like some prehistoric cave. The blaze of the fire was great, but the pall of smoke, the shelves of gloomy books and the doomy, relentless music made the place feel like a pantomime set, some kind of dungeon or the lair of an ogre. It reeked of the rum I'd swigged and spilled last night. I started sweeping and dusting, with a handkerchief tied across my mouth and nose. I lost myself in my toils, trying to forget myself in the effort of cleaning. The place wasn't fit to open for business, no way. I reckoned it would take a day or two before it might be ready for customers.

Wrong.

When I staggered outside for air, with my mug of coffee in one hand and my brush in the other, so blinded by soot that I blundered into the sign and knocked it over, there were people. They were rummaging in the boxes of books. They

were standing in the sunlight, wrapped in their thickest winter clothes, rapt in the tatty paperbacks they'd picked out. Not a lot of people, but three or four. No, maybe eight or ten. As I blinked around me and tugged the handkerchief off my face, as I set the sign up again, I saw how the soot was fuming out of the church door. And the music, Communication Breakdown, such a peal of pure and untrammelled desperation that the fusty old church had never heard before.

Someone said, 'Are you open? Or are you just clearing out?' And I was about to reply, no, sorry I'm not open, I'm doing a bit of stock-taking, or something like that... but they were starting to move inside.

I followed them in. For a few moments I just stood at the door and watched, as they felt their way around. The fire had sucked some of the smoke away, and I'd billowed a lot of the soot outside. Still, every inch of every surface was covered with black dust, and the sweet, stale smell of yesterday's alcohol lingered in the air. But no matter, I had people in the shop. The flames were licking hungrily up the chimney. The music, too loud for talking, was perfect for losing oneself in an underworld of dangerous and uncompromising books. When I realised what was happening, that I was well and truly open for business, I switched on the lamp and pointed it onto the display, and everyone looked around to see where the beam of light was coming from and where it was shining.

Poe's Tooth. It was powdered with soot. Soot swirled in the lamplight. I bent to blow it away, but then I stepped back. One by one, the people in the room came forward to see the tooth and read the slip of paper which said what it was.

Puer dentem. The tooth of a boy. The tooth of a sad little boy in a dismal boarding school, a long long way from home. No wonder he grew up so strange and full of mad, unhappy ideas. The people stared at the relic. With a dreadful cry, the crow emerged from the shadows and flapped onto its usual perch, on top of the computer. I bent to the floor and picked up the ghastly figure of the doll, blackened and charred from

its murder in the chimney, and I sat it beside the hearth. And when at last the people continued their browsing through the filthy shelves, they would return to my desk, I would stamp their chosen books and give them a bookmark, and I would take the money they proffered.

AND SO I stayed in my lair, my dungeon, at the bottom of the tower. Me and the crow.

Oh, and the mouse. The mouse, forgotten, abandoned, running like a lunatic on its wheel. White mouse, in a beam of silvery moonlight.

I suffered a curious reaction to Rosie's leaving me. Childish, maybe, like a sulky boy. I decided to leave her. And since she was already gone and had taken my daughter with her, the only way I could leave her was to sequester myself in my own place and eschew the home we'd made together.

In other words, it came upon me to inhabit my own little world in the bookshop. The neat, newly converted kitchen and the bedrooms above it were the places we'd shared, as man and wife and father and mother, with our darling child. Alright, if they wanted to clear out, then so did I.

It only occurred to me when it was already dark, by the evening of that day in the sooty bookshop. There'd been people, not crowds of course, but odd-bods throughout the morning and the afternoon, enough to keep me downstairs and not wanting to miss anyone by nipping up for lunch or anything. At noon I'd run across to Azri's for a coffee and a burger, ostentatiously unfolding the notes from my pocket and pretending to fidget while I waited and told him I had to hurry back to the shop because I had customers waiting. By the time it was dusk and twilight and the frost seemed to clang onto the pavement outside the church door, a harder and steelier frost than ever before, I'd already had a few invigorating mouthfuls of the rum in the vestry cupboard and slipped out for another bottle. Next to Azri's there was a convenience store, only a

nook of a shop but bright and neat and filled to the ceiling with everything one might possibly need; the sort of treasure-trove of food and drink and comfort that a survivalist might stash in case of apocalypse. I got rum. On impulse, although I knew there was bread upstairs in the kitchen of the tower, I got bread. And milk, and coffee, and chocolate. And I came out with a bulging bag of stuff, as though I'd heard there might be a bomb tonight and I needed to hibernate.

Yes, by the time I'd crossed the road and was back into the vestry, where the fire was the best it had ever been after a long day of diligent refuelling, I'd decided to sulk it out. Rosie and Chloe had gone away. They'd quit the marital home and right now, at this very moment, they would be snuggling in Auntie Cissy's living room with cups of tea and glasses of sherry and *Countdown* or *Deal or No Deal* or some other afternoon quiz-show. So me, I'd get out too.

I only made one foray upstairs to get what else I needed. And that was when I heard something...

I was in the kitchen. On the table I'd got kettle, toilet paper, towel, toothpaste. And I was about to go up to the bedroom and bathroom and I heard... the swish of the traffic on the icy road? The bubble of hot water in the immersion heater? I was halfway up the stairs to the bedroom and I stopped, to try and work out what it was.

It couldn't be the crow. It was down in the vestry, it was dozing in front of the fire with its breath wheezing through bristly nostrils, its wings outstretched, like a cormorant drying itself in the wind after a dizzy, dashing, submarine hunt. No, above my head there was a rhythmic, scratching sound. Relentless. Indefatigable. Mad.

Chloe had forgotten the mouse.

Poor, abandoned, orphan rodent. Maybe Rosie had rushed her too much, while I was showering off all my soot and stripping the bed and Rosie had been hurrying Chloe to get ready and packed so that Daddy wouldn't emerge and try to dissuade them or stop them or. Whatever, Rosie must've

bundled Chloe out of the bedroom and down to the kitchen so quickly that the mouse, or Mouse, as it had been rather unoriginally named, had been left behind.

In a beam of silvery moonlight. I stepped into the bedroom and there it was. It was running so hard its little heart might burst.

I looked around the room. Our bed, carefully made-up, but empty. Robin Hood and the goose-girl naughtily entwined, as though they were taking advantage of Maid Marian's mysterious absence. Chloe's room, empty, the bed stripped. I didn't switch on any lights, I didn't need to, because a shaft of moonlight fell through the window and onto the mouse. Silvery – a sliver of silver. Was it running after the girl? Was it chasing a moonlit horizon? Would it run until it reached the end of the world and simply dropped off the edge?

Empty. Just me and the mouse. 'Alright, so it's just you and me,' I was whispering, but I might've been talking to myself because it just kept on running. 'Just me and you, alright? Rosie left me, I thought she loved me through thick and thin, for better or for worse etc etc, but she left me. And Chloe left you. When it came to the crunch and they were off to Auntie Cissy's cuddly cosy living room, she forgot all about you, didn't she? So it's just me and you, alright?'

I couldn't persuade it to stop. I had to reach into the cage and lift it off the wheel and slip it into my shirt.

I went down the stairs with Chloe's mattress and duvet. Shut the bedroom door behind me. The marital, family bedroom: closed until further notice.

Went down to the kitchen. Somehow, with great care and slightly drunken sleight of hand, down and down to the hallway of the church with mattress and duvet and kettle and towel and whatever, without falling headlong and breaking my poor silly neck on the flagstones.

Run away from home. I was somehow further away from home than Rose and Chloe were. Me and the crow and the mouse, by the fire. I felt like I'd run away, like some kind of

hobo, I'd gone feral, I was on the road with my crow and my mouse and my bottle of rum and we'd lit a fire... under a motorway bridge or in a derelict building or a barn or the tower of an old church or...

Cheers. I'd put down the mattress and the duvet. I had a marvellous blaze. A masterpiece of ruddy and amber flames, blue as well, as the bark crisped and curled from the fragrant silver birch. I didn't know when my wife and my daughter might come back. I didn't know when I might go home. In the meantime, I didn't need to. I was smugly and snugly self-sufficient, with money in my pocket and the prospect of another day's business tomorrow, and my post-apocalyptic store just across the road.

Chapter Thirty-Two

THE BOY. I saw him.

Puer. I did some Latin at school. I could decline the word puer, boy. Puer puer puerum, pueri pueri puerum... by, with, or from a boy. So they gave me a Latin class when I thought I might try to be a teacher. Boys. And a few girls. They did their Latin exercises from a crummy little text book, and then they came up to my desk and I marked them as they stood close to me. The smell of small boys, unmistakable and uniquely sweaty and... and a girl, a girl called... can't remember her name, but she leaned very close with a different smell as I marked her horrid, blotted book and her ridiculous sentences. I never touched her. I swear. But she would swing her skinny little legs against my leg, fiddle her foot onto mine, and then one day when I made to push her away she squealed and pouted and accused me.

So I didn't stay long. Couldn't. I protested, but realised fast and full of futile indignation that protesting my innocence was taken as guilt. My word against hers. They believed her.

The boy. I'd seen him in a dream, when he'd come up through the trapdoor onto the roof of the tower and his mouth was full of blood. And I saw him again. Skating.

It was a glorious day, perhaps the most glorious day since the last most glorious day a few weeks ago. I'd woken in my fireside bed, stretched magnificently under my duvet and realised I'd slept like a king. The embers were still glowing, it took only a moment to rekindle them with a log or two and there was a breakfast blaze. While the kettle was boiling for coffee, I was stripped naked for an icy top-and-tail in the

tiny wash-room, and dressed again. How joyful, to be out on the pavement, a wintry dawn at eight o'clock, holding my steaming mug in both hands, inhaling the delicious, smokey, suburban air and watching the slaves go by. They sat fuming in their traffic jam, crawling to their offices and workshops in town. They stared at me from inside their cars, and I grinned back at them.

I sold a few books. I had a customer or two before I'd even rolled up the duvet and leaned the mattress into the corner. I got croissants from Azri. It was a blissful morning of utter selfishness and loneliness and I listened to *Abbey Road*, hadn't heard it for such a long time and it made me cry and I switched it off in the end – *and in the end the love you take is equal to the love you make* – because it made me think of Rosie and Chloe and our home I'd so perversely left and locked up, upstairs, just above my stubborn, sulky head.

Blinking tears, I thrust the mouse into my shirt, threw on my coat, herded the crow outside and brought in the sign. Closed the shop.

Skating. The fields of the park were sheeted with ice. It was a dazzling world, huge and empty and perfectly flat. I marched along the footpath, between the tall black poplars and the frosted rhododendron, and then the emptiness of the park was breathtaking. Acres of ice and a vast blue sky. In the further distance, the town was a blurry dark line on the horizon, the cooling towers billowing steam. Lovely, the way the ice creaked and squeaked under my feet as I crossed towards the distant figure of the boy. He was sitting where he'd been sitting before, and I thought, yes, although just then there was no one else about. It must have been worth his while because I could see how the ice was scored with lines and curves and scratches and gouges, freshly made.

Magpies went churring through the bare branches. Gulls, hundreds of gulls, whirling so high in the blue that they might have been wisps of steam from the power-station. And my crow. It was the only crow in the whole of that enormous sky,

it beat through air as I crossed the field and it settled in the branches above the boy's head.

I chose some skates. The boy took my money, without looking at me, without even looking up. There was something furtive about him, he ducked his head and pretended to be busy with the money he'd made from his business initiative. I guessed that he was playing truant, he should have been in school, and so he didn't want to engage in any small talk or even show his face in case some busybody queried what he was doing. I sat on the roots of the tree and put on my skates and didn't say a word. I only saw an anonymous boy, wrapped in a coat, jingling a few coins in his mottled fingers.

And then I was skating.

For the first few minutes, it was an almost delirious pleasure. The purity and clarity of the air, the taste of it in my mouth and the fizz of it in my nostrils, as I found a rhythm and eased myself this way and that. The clean, cold sound of my blades, and, as I looked down, the myriad bubbles and the grasses crushed and frozen beneath the ice. Gaining confidence, I looked up and around me and even into the sky, and the world whirled about my head. At first it was good, so good it replaced every other notion or memory which had been troubling me. It wiped everything clear.

But then... I heard the crow beating closely above me. I saw the shadow of its wings on the ice.

And I was aware of someone else, another skater, somewhere behind me and following me. Mine were not the only blades scoring the frozen flood-waters on the park. I turned and nearly fell, and there was the boy.

He sped past me. I could smell his coat and the fusty, unwashed-boy smell of his hair. Head down, face averted, he went by in a rush of curious odour. The crow followed him. It seemed to detach itself from me and became one with him. Its shadow blurred into his. He weaved around me, so close I could feel the flurry of wind he created. And with the flurry of wind, he created an inexplicable feeling of unease. More than

that. It grew in my belly like a physical sickness. It was dread, utterly alien in the loveliness of the morning and my childish abandon.

I stumbled. One of my skates caught on a tussock of grass protruding from the ice. And as I windmilled my arms and tried to keep my balance, I fell headlong and heavily flat on my face.

Winded, I lay still for a moment. I could hear the swish and the crackle as the boy continued to skate around me, my cheek was on the ice and my lips could taste it, I could see his blades cutting close to me – closer, closer, throwing a powder of ice into the air, so fine it fell on my lashes like spray. And I felt something moving inside my shirt. Before I could stop it, the mouse came creeping out of the collar of my shirt.

It scampered away from me. It paused and sniffed the air. It snuffled at the ice and seemed to wonder at the strangeness of it. Just as the boy came hurtling past. I cried out, but my voice was hoarse and I was still out of breath. Maybe the mouse was invisible to him, and in its perfect whiteness it was just another bubble trapped beneath the surface. So fast and so deadly true, one of his blades cut straight across it.

Before I could get up or pull myself close enough to see what had happened, the boy was there. Maybe he'd felt an impact. He skidded to a halt and dropped to his knees, and with his head down so that his face was almost touching the ice, he was examining the mouse.

'Get off it,' I was saying. 'Just get out of the way and let me have a look, will you?'

When he kneeled up and aside, I saw the mouse. It was lying in a pool of blood which was spreading around it.

Appalled, I touched it with one fingertip. So warm, and it seemed unmarked. There was blood, and I'd been expecting to find it gruesomely decapitated or even cut in half. But the body of the mouse was intact. Indeed, reacting to the tiniest pressure of my finger on its belly, it suddenly wriggled away and ran. No longer a pure white albino, but splashed with pink, it ran across the ice.

I turned to the boy. He was still kneeling. He turned and grinned at me. Blood welled from his mouth. It dribbled from his lips and down his chin and splashed onto the ice.

I recoiled from him. The crow was beating around his head. And then, seeing the mouse exposed and defenceless on the expanse of ice, it feinted in mid-air and dived towards it.

For a second the crow had the mouse. It lifted it into the air. The mouse wriggled and fell back to the ice. The bird tried again, it landed with a clatter of its horny black claws and lunged forward with half open wings. I skidded forward on my belly and grabbed the mouse, just as the crow stabbed at it and banged its beak hard on the back of my hand.

In doing so I'd rolled away from the boy. And by the time I'd sat up and cradled the mouse for a moment before slipping it back inside my shirt, I looked around and saw that he was already sitting under his tree, hunched over his coins as though nothing had happened. The crow, calmly oblivious, was perched in the branches above his head, nibbling its feathers back into place.

I got to my feet and hobbled across the ice towards him. Out of breath, I leaned heavily on the tree and fumbled to undo the laces of my skates. My hands were shaking. I was staring at him, at the fall of his lank blond hair, and I heard my own voice inside my own head before I actually uttered a sound – *Who are you? What do you want? What are you doing?* – although the only sound I really made was the rasping of the breath in my throat.

He turned his face up and towards me.

A pasty, shivery boy. No blood. I must have been staring at his mouth, because he swiped at his lips with the back of his hand and said, 'What you looking at? Just fuck off and mind your own business...'

In a daze, I stepped back into my own shoes and stumbled away without bothering to tie my laces. He followed me with his eyes, with that defiant look of any disaffected teenager playing truant from a school he hated. When he sneered at

me and showed his teeth, there was no blood in his mouth or on his cold, thin lips, no blood on his chin. And when I slithered across the ice where I'd been skating, and I could see the scratches I'd inexpertly made and the place where I'd fallen and banged my face and lost the mouse. There was no blood at all. Not a drop.

I couldn't remember getting back to the church. Only that the crow was moving around me. There was an unsettling duality in its presence, as unnerving as the vision of the boy. I mean, a blurring of dream and reality. As it whirled around my head and I could feel the movement of the air on my face, it was a real bird, it was the wretched starveling that Chloe and I had found in the clock tower. But then, as the wintry sunlight threw shadows around my feet and I wandered home in a state of fuddled distraction, it was a flicker of darkness, a fragment of nightmare. Not real.

I got home, somehow.

No, not home. I didn't go upstairs. I was a vagrant, crouching over my fire, seeking the comfort of my blankets on the floor, cuddling my bottle. The mouse emerged from my shirt. And I wondered at its purity, for not a smear or a smudge spoiled its pristine whiteness.

Chapter Thirty-Three

FROM THEN – FOR who knows how long? Because my days and nights seemed to blur into the timelessness of dream – the boy would come to me.

Was it days and nights, or a week? How long was it, since Rosie and Chloe had left me and gone away? Was it last week, or only yesterday? Would they ever come back? In the bottom of my tower, locked away from the reality of the rooms above my head, I felt as though the normal parameters of time and space and routine had slipped away from me.

The boy. Puer. Puer eapoe. I thought at first he was a dream. But then I thought he was not, because I could smell him and I could feel the touch of his hand on mine, and I could see every detail of his hair and lashes and eyebrows and the down on his cheeks and lip.

I awoke in the night, I was lying by the fire. The flames had died down and I was cold, and was going to get up and put more logs on the embers as I'd done every night since I'd moved down into the vestry. I lay for a moment and I stared around me, and I could feel the buzz in my head and the dryness of my mouth which I'd got used to more and more since I'd been drinking more and more and falling asleep more or less drunk. And I sensed a someone in the room.

I blinked and the boy was standing beside me. He knelt to the hearth and reached to the logs and rebuilt the fire until the flames were licking and crackling and I could feel their warmth on my face.

If it was a dream, it was the clearest and most natural dream I'd ever been in. He gestured at me to get up, and I did so. I

was in my clothes – I always slept in my clothes since I'd been sleeping with the bottle – and I followed him away from the brightness of the fire and to my desk. And I wrote, yes I wrote. He showed me how to write, he guided my brain and my mind and my hands.

My muse. The boy. No need for a light, because the glow of my computer screen was enough. He brought me my glass and filled it. He threw my coat around my shoulders. With a snap of his fingers he summoned the crow, and it appeared from the shadows of its corner on the floor where it customarily cuddled with the corpse of the doll, and it beat once and then twice and three times and landed on the top of the screen. But, what to write? The screen was blank. I felt the fear in my belly, confronted by my own mediocrity, the dearth of ideas. Everything was in place, except for the very thoughts and words which I might tap out with my clumsy, lazy, drunken fingers. I had fire, I had alcohol. I had the crow in front of me and cocking its beady eyes at me like an irritable schoolmaster. I had the boy, the very warmth and scent of him as real as the flesh and blood of the boy whose tooth had been saved and kept since it loosened and fell out nearly two hundred years ago. But what to write? How to begin?

The tooth, yes. The boy opened his mouth and smiled at me. His mouth was young and clean, but there was a gap where the tooth had been. And so, because I'd been its diligent guardian, and, more importantly, because I'd believed in it and deserved the reward of its inspiration, he reached for the tooth from its velvet box. He lodged it back into his mouth. And then, his smile complete, he reached for a book and opened it and laid it on the desk to the left of the keyboard. With a nod of encouragement, he signalled that I should write. To start me off, he ran his fingertip beneath the words as I slowly, hesitantly, began to tap the same words and phrases and sentences onto the screen, and once I had achieved a momentum only interrupted now and then as I took more and more fiery mouthfuls from the glass he kept refilling, he simply

stood at my side and was there, a presence, my muse, as I wrote and wrote and wrote.

How long did I write? For an hour? All night? How long is a dream? Is it merely the fluttering of eyelids, a few seconds of restless sleep, or is it real time?

The fire dimmed and died and the boy rebuilt it. My glass emptied and the boy refilled it. The coat slipped from my shoulders and the boy lifted it back again, so that I might not feel between my shoulder blades the icy draft from beneath the door of the church. However long it was that I wrote, that night, he was there and it was a joy, an effortless flow of writing.

Until the dream dimmed. I felt the flow of my writing falter.

A strange thing – as the presence of the boy seemed to fade and he was less of reality and more of a shadow, the only piece of him which remained strong was his smell. Indeed, it grew stronger. It was a stale boy smell, the smell of the little boys who'd crowded me with their inky, blotted Latin books and pressed their fusty bodies against me. Even the crow cringed from it. It shivered its feathers, a kind of shudder of disgust, and it fell away, onto the floor, and I heard it scuttling into the darkness. The boy's face swam in front of me. He was signalling me to slow down my writing and stop, he reached across me and his smell was strong and he closed the book from which I'd been writing. And at last – to switch off the power he'd bestowed on me, the power of his ideas and the torrent of his original thoughts – he smiled a horrid crooked smile and reached his fingers into his mouth. He pulled out the tooth.

There was a gush of blood from the hole it left. It filled his mouth and overflowed his lips and down his chin. With bloody fingers he dabbed at the keyboard – delete delete delete. In a moment he'd deleted everything I'd written.

A blank black screen. And I was asleep again.

It was a recurring dream, a dream of great exhilaration, and then a horror which dashed everything. In the mornings, when

I woke and crawled wretchedly out of my pit beside a cold dead fire, I would limp to the desk with the shreds of the dream clinging to the inside of my poor, addled, hung over brain like dirty old cobwebs, and I would search for any evidence that what I'd dreamed might have some connection to reality. Yes, the book was there, closed, beside the computer, but when I riffled through its pages I could never find the ones from which I'd been writing. When I switched on the computer, it was blank, there was nothing of the myriad, miraculous words I'd written. My glass was there, of course, and an empty, overturned bottle, but they were such a constant piece of my world that it didn't matter if they inhabited my sleep or my waking or both. There was no evidence that the boy had been there. When I sniffed at the space where he'd been standing and tried to recapture that whiff of unwashed clothes and rancid hair, I only caught the smell of myself.

I examined the tooth for a smear of blood. There was none. It was a bit of yellowy bone, nothing more, defying any rational or educated person to believe it was anything else.

And the days?

I had only a dim perception of them, the daylit hours between my nights with the boy. They were an unwanted interruption in my craving for his return.

I think I washed from time to time, but maybe I didn't. I drank coffee. Of course I lit the fire, a great spitting turbulent blaze which coiled and writhed up the chimney. I think I crossed the road for pies or pizza or whatever instant gratification I might get from Azri, and I got rum and vodka and similar solace from the shop next door. Customers? People? There were some. I would throw open the doors of the church, first of all to clear the stink of the air: the brew of alcohol and soot and crow and mouse and me. And then, with the first slurps of coffee and a deafening blast of *Revolver* or *Rubber Soul* to blow the dust of dreams from inside my head, they would wander in. And sniff around. And marvel at the dirt, at the crow, at me. And they might sneer at the tooth, or shrug, or

frown, or gape in wonderment bordering on tears. And they might buy a book.

The days... they were grey and cold and mercifully short.

By mid-afternoon, when the light was fading at four o'clock and the fire was roaring and puthering great plumes of smoke into the room to tell me it was time to close the doors and shut out the gathering night and shut out the stream of lights of the hoipolloi in their traffic jam, I was glad to do so. I would clang the doors shut. Another day had passed in a dim, grey blur.

So it was closer to dream time.

Alcohol. Flames. The skittering of the mouse in the firelight, through my fingers and into my sleeves and inside my shirt and its little hot body wriggling on the skin of my belly and chest. The crow, the very embodiment in flesh, yes the incarnation of the boy I was waiting for. With the closing of the church doors, it would creak and shuffle out of its corner, sooty from its canoodling with the doll. It might spring onto the top of the computer screen, as though taking up its position in readiness for the coming of the night, or flap to the lamplight and peck at the tooth of the boy. And then pick up a piece of glass and hold it to the light, so, that the blood would shine like ruby. It might pick up a different tooth, which was Chloe's. When I clapped my hands, it would drop the tooth and return to its vigil on the desk.

Waiting. I wanted him back. So I could woo him with rum and fire. The bigger my blaze, the more I drank, the more I stared hopelessly into the my empty unforgiving accusing screen and couldn't write a word. I was willing him to come and inspire me, until I would tumble like a useless, sozzled soul in my soiled clothes into my bed by the fire and snore myself asleep.

Soiled, yes, poe poo pee. What difference did a few vowels make? A loosening of the vowels. Edgar allan poe poo pee oh shit.

One night I awoke on the boat.

I opened my eyes and I knew where I was straightaway, my eyes on the wooden ceiling of the cabin and the smell of paint

and the unmistakable fragrance of the canal. I hauled myself off the narrow bunk and crept out of the cabin, careful not to knock my head on the top of the tiny doorway, and there we were, cruising silently and beautifully along the canal on the frostiest iciest night of all creation.

Ice. Moon. Stars. The boy was there, he was at the helm of my little boat, and we were slipping along the canal in utter silence. No engine, no chugging motor, the boat was crisping through the ice on the surface of the water. Only a hiss and a crunch as the prow of the boat cut through the ice and sliced it aside. I smiled at the boy and he smiled back. I leaned over and saw how the ice curled from the boat in a spangle of foam. I saw how the moon shone into the blackness of the water we had created, and then I looked up and saw the moon itself, and the stars.

Ice. Moon. Stars. To left and right the fields were a smouldering of frost. White... no, they were silvery grey, and there were horses standing like statues, frozen and monumental, huge shuddering figures cast in steel, and cattle, steaming. My breath, the boy's breath, every breath was a word, a wonderful word which took shape and then was lost in a whisper of ice. I blew a cloud into the air and for a moment it was an owl, quartering over the fields, white and holy and deadly pale... but then it was the crow. Me and the boy and the crow. We were gliding through a silent, shivering world.

And then I was home.

Home? No. I still couldn't think of it as home. But I was back in the firelit shadows of the vestry and I was writing. The boy, he had his finger on the page and was prompting me to write, I could smell him, I could see the black rime under his nail as he pointed at the words he wanted me to write. The crow was there, on top of the screen. With its quizzical, impatient look, it was watching me write.

Until the inspiration dried up, or the muse was tired of me. Delete. Delete. Delete. I tried to stop him, but he was uncannily strong. His fingers were thin and white, he was only a waif,

he was a homesick, undernourished boy from a horrid little boarding-school, but he was too strong for me. Once he had done with me, he would pluck out the tooth and put it back in its box, he would lick around his mouth to suck and swallow the blood, and despite all my efforts to stop him he would click delete delete delete until everything I'd written was gone.

One night I awoke on the top of the tower.

Always the moon and the stars, and ice. I was on the battlements and overlooking the sleeping town and the frozen white fields of the park. Me and the boy, we were picking the snails out of their crevice in the wall. I could feel his fingers against mine as we reached into the hole together, his fingers were so cold and bony and strangely prehensile, and I heard a tiny kiss of suction as I pulled a snail out, only the slightest, sweetest resistance of its moist rubbery foot. Me and the boy, giggling like kids on the roof of the tower, our breath pluming into the air, while the rest of the world was fast asleep. Taking it in turns, we would toss the snails over the battlements and watch them fall and smash on the pavement below. For the crow, of course. The bird was whirling around our heads in excited anticipation. And then it would plummet past us, tumbling in the air like a falcon, open its wings just in time and float to the ground as light as thistledown. To peck at the silvery spatters of juice and flesh.

And then writing. The book open on the desk beside. The boy and the crow. My coat around my shoulders, a blazing fire, a glass by my hand, filled and refilled until my throat and chest were burning and my head was in a giddying turmoil.

So giddy that I was never aware of what I was writing.

I was an automaton, writing what the boy guided me to write. I had an exhilarating sense of it, that it was a torrent of feverish and dangerous ideas which miraculously took shape as words. But each time, at the end of the dream, when the boy's smile became a sneer of exasperation and contempt and he would feel into his mouth with his fingers... then me, yes even before he could loosen the tooth and pull it out, I would feel such self-

reproach and disappointment that I would press delete delete delete until I'd erased everything I'd written. Because I knew it wasn't me, it wasn't mine, it couldn't have been mine but only the thoughts and ideas the boy had lent me.

'WHO IS THAT? Is that you, Rosie?'

I was in the tiny washroom, stark naked. I'd woken to a dim grey light in the vestry, a light I hadn't seen for weeks. Something was different, something had changed.

I rolled out of my blankets and sat up. The fire had died completely, but somehow the air in the room was warmer, it didn't snap at me as it had done every morning since I'd been living downstairs. I listened, I held my breath, I blinked around me, and I knew straightaway what was happening.

It was raining. The tyres of the commuter cars were swishing through rain. It was pattering against the windows and streaming down the glass.

Thaw. The crackling frosts and bitter cold of the past month had gone.

I'd creaked off my bed and stood up. Warmer, yes, and a stale fug of air in the room. I'd made for the washroom, fuddled by such a hangover that I couldn't wait to strip off my clothes completely and splash my face and all my body with as much chilly water as I could from the little wash basin.

And then, through the splutter I was making and the water in my ears and dripping through my hair, I heard something... or someone.

I stood as still as possible, stopped breathing. Listened. I called out, 'Who is that? Is that you, Rosie?'

Rosie and Chloe? I could hear another pattering sound, not the rain on the windows. Unmistakably, it was sound of the keys of the computer.

'Rosie, are you back? Hang on, I'm in here...'

And I'd burst out of the wash room, with just a hand towel pressed against me. My head, my belly, was churning with

a mixture of feelings – a rush of joy that they were back, unannounced, sooner than I'd expected, and a nausea of anxiety, an unaccountable sensation of dread.

But there was no one. The door was closed. The hiss of the traffic was loud and rhythmic. It was gloomy, the rain on the windows gave the room a dim, submarine look. The pattering of the computer – as I stared towards it, I saw a shadowy movement and the silvery glow of the screen.

The crow. It was fidgeting across the top of the desk, fluttering to the display and back again, and every time it skittered over the keyboard it rattled its claws on the keys.

The joy faded from me. The anxiety too. Replaced by a wave of guilty relief which made me shiver in my bare, wet skin. A shiver of anger.

'Bloody filthy thing!' I dropped the towel and strode across the room, almost tripping headlong on the bedding in front of the fire. 'Bloody get off there.'

It had been onto the display table and pecking at the relics. When I regained my footing and glanced at what it had been doing, I saw that the iconic tooth was missing, the fragments of windscreen glass were scattered about, and just then, as though to taunt me with the absence of my daughter when for a split-second I'd thought she was back again, it had Chloe's tooth in its beak.

'Bastard, get off there, will you?' I went huffing towards it, waving my arms. And when it rattled the keys of the computer again and I saw a screenfull of jumbled letters, my outrage and jealousy were ridiculous. 'Fuck off there, will you? What the fuck do you think you're doing?'

A crow was writing on my computer. A crow had my daughter's tooth in its beak. I clapped my hands at it, and a shower of water flew from my hair. As the bird flopped away and onto the floor, it dropped the tooth onto the keyboard. And I could see that the boy's tooth was there too, and some of the pieces of glass. I sat heavily at the desk. Naked, dripping wet, I fumbled at the keyboard to try and pick out the teeth

and the glass from among the keys, but it was difficult. My fingers were cold and clumsy, and the silly little things were stuck into the cracks between the letters.

I tried to catch the yellowy old tooth between thumb and finger, with a blaze of irritation at the irony of Edgar Allan Poe losing one of his teeth between the o and p of my keyboard, and as I fumbled and inadvertently pressed, a flurry of letters ran across the screen, adding to the nonsense the crow had left there.

opopoppopopo opppppppppop

And my daughter's tooth, white and fresh, I tried to pick it out from the crevice of c and d and f but it was stuck and...

ffcddcfcfcfccccfccccc

I scrolled up. Nothing of mine, of course, except a few of the pretentious ramblings I'd committed to posterity when I'd been posing at my desk for the customers. Not a word of the tumultuous stuff I'd written with the boy. All deleted. But there, on the screen, the collected works of Chloe Gooch, my brain-damaged daughter, and the crow.

It was just a blur in front of my eyes.

Chloe had written *gjpeojwopeifms efu ckyo udad w[eio cos prjqo it ffu ckingjd [pj[pkj[p stu ngme th ats [qpdjj whyj jdpklq pk pioscvnmp...*

The crow had added *pispejkf dfbn qutt erly feklost pdpkfg lif e pandt s [gdea th are hjjkequ ally rwiojidnb,x ckjest smp[...*

My contribution was *oppoppoopopop poopoopppp* and *fdccccccdfffcffdccccdccdscfccc.*

That was the sum of our literary collaboration.

The book lay open beside me. It mocked my laziness, my inadequacy, my pretention. The boy had opened the pages and pointed at the words with his skinny fingers, his dirty nails, and I'd simply copied. Like an ape. Like an automaton. Like a silly drunk. I stared at the pages and flipped forwards and backwards through them, and I remembered now, with a flaring of light across my brain as bright and searing as magnesium, what the boy had had me write. I'd copied whole paragraphs, whole stories, word by word.

Hop-Frog. Murders in the Rue Morgue. Masque of the Red Death. Berenice. Yes, Berenice. I'd written it out verbatim, and thrilled at the exhilaration of writing it, as though it were mine, as though the ideas and the words were mine! Now, blinking at the pages, it all came back to me, that I'd spent hours and hours of nights and nights in a giddy helter-skelter of plagiarism, and I'd loved it. Through the agency of the tooth, in the dream-time I'd spent with the boy, I'd been Poe. I'd written his stories. With the same kind of despair and loneliness in my heart that he might have felt, with the same ache of cold between my shoulder blades that he might have endured, with the same miserable abuse of alcohol that he'd inflicted on himself, I'd been him.

Word after word after word. And then, delete delete delete.

I stared at the screen long enough for it to go blank again. Then I stared at my own dim reflection. A naked, shivering, middle-aged man, utterly lost, for whom life and death were equally jests.

The door of the church opened. A draft of windy, wet weather blew into the hallway. And with it, Rosie and Chloe.

Chapter Thirty-Four

'ROSIE... WOW, YOU look great.'

I managed to get the words out before she could say anything. In fact, she was speechless for a few seconds, as she stared aghast at me and at the state of the room. Chloe came tottering towards me and unselfconsciously hugged my chilly nakedness.

'Really, Rosie, you look good,' I went on. 'And you're back. And how was it, with Auntie Cissy? And did you see the doctor? And...'

She crossed the room towards me. 'Oliver? Oh Oliver, what on earth...?'

Yes, her face was better. She still wasn't herself, she wasn't the Rosie I'd met and wooed and married. With her slightly drooping, disgruntled mouth, she could've been Rosie's older sister, gazing at me in disbelief and disapproval. But the rain on her cheeks and lashes was lovely. I wanted to take her and hold her close, because I was genuinely thrilled to have her home again. But when she hurried towards me, hissing with disappointment, it was only to pull her daughter away, as if I were a rabid dog. But then her expression softened, when she remembered that I was only a man, the man who'd wooed her and married her, and she stared at me with great puzzlement.

'Oh Oliver, you hopeless, careless, thoughtless man. You've had time, haven't you? I gave you time, so what have you been doing? Look at you, look at this place. It's just the same. No, it's worse, the stink and the soot and everything. And you... you've been sleeping on the floor and you stink of drink and...' And as I stood away from the

desk and swung the overcoat off the back of the chair and around my shoulders, she went on, 'And so I come back and find you sitting naked in a room with no lights and no fire, like a caveman or something... and empty bottles and rubbish and... and what's this? What's your excuse? You've been writing or something or...'

She shoved past me and nudged the computer. The screen lit up. She bent and peered at it.

'What is it? What does it mean? It's just a lot of rubbish.' And then something, some combination of letters must have caught her eye, because she leaned so close to the screen that her nose was touching it and then she recoiled as if she'd been burnt. 'For heaven's sake, Oliver, did you write this? Are you mad? Have you gone mad?'

And she was back into the hallway, with Chloe, and halfway up the stairs to the kitchen before I could hardly blink. She paused long enough to call to me, her voice hoarse with breathlessness, 'I don't like you, Oliver, I really don't like you. But I love you and I want to help you, to help us. Get some clothes on, light the fire, and I'm coming back down...'

Then she was gone, banging upstairs into the kitchen and the living room and bedrooms I'd abandoned not long after she'd abandoned me.

Calm, I tried to stay calm. I took a few long, deep breaths. I knew Rosie well enough, after eight years of marriage, to understand that her anger was manageable, that she herself knew how to manage it. She was a mother-hen, she was a busybody, she got things done, that had always been her forte; now, she was fed up with the whole situation, but she was shortly going to tumble back downstairs and focus her resentment onto the job in hand, not directly onto her feckless husband. Which was good. I was ready to go along with it, meek and repentant. So, before she reappeared, I did the two things she'd instructed me to do, I threw on some clothes (and the big old overcoat, as usual), I built a blaze in the fireplace, and I did a third essential thing too.

'Right, you filthy bastard, I don't care if you're a reincarnation of Edgar Allan Poe or the fucking Dalai Lama, you're going out... out, out, out!'

But it wouldn't go. I flapped it round and round the vestry, flicking the wet towel at it, herding it with my feet as though it was a farmyard goose, but the crow evaded me time and again and swerved away from the door. The wind gusted in, I'd thrown open the big front doors of the church, and a spattering of warm rain fell onto the flagstones. Outside, the road was gleaming in the headlamps of the passing traffic. I could see the lights of Azri's cafe, the raindrops streaming on the cosy, steamed-up windows. I drove the crow closer and closer to the doorway, but it blinked and baulked at the fumey commotion of the real world and sprang past me again, back into the vestry.

Calm, stay calm. I was determined we were going to have a lull, not a manic melodramatic climax. Rosie was furious with me, but she was going to vent her anger on soot and empty rum bottles and discarded pizza boxes and my dirty clothes, and I thought I knew how to handle her like that, to help her and keep things calm. The crow wasn't helping. It simply shouldn't be there. It had been top of my list of things to tackle, when Rosie went away. Now, I felt a bubble of panic rising in my chest as I heard the kitchen door opening and Rosie starting to come downstairs again.

Oh fuck, the crow leapt away from me, towards its favourite, revolting corner of the room, and as it skidded on the top of an open cardboard box and fell inside it, I grabbed the charred Maid Marian doll and stuffed it on top of the bird and folded the box shut.

I was carrying it outside, as Rosie stepped into the hallway.

'What's in there?' she said. 'If it's old books, don't put them outside, it's raining and they'll get all soggy.'

Yes, her face had recovered somewhat, not completely; she had a trickle of saliva, like the trail of a snail, from the corner of her mouth. She'd had her hair trimmed into a sleek,

swinging bob. She'd taken off her outdoor clothes, and now she was fragrant, her lips shining, she was shapely and plump in blue jeans and a red pullover. We stood and appraised one another. She looked warm and smelled lovely, but I was holding a cardboard box with a carrion crow inside it, so I couldn't take her in my arms as I dearly wanted to do.

Witless, I turned back into the vestry. Too late the words came to me. No they aren't books, they're bottles, I'll put them out – but too late, by then I'd already bent to the floor and set the box down again.

Briefly, she allowed me to take her hands and pull her towards me, so that I could feel her body against mine. She squeezed me so hard that I gasped. She whispered that Chloe was good and she'd be alright upstairs in the bedroom with her colouring books for an hour or so... and then she perfunctorily pushed me off and strode past me into the vestry.

Rosie dusted and swept a storm. She told me to do the same. I carried out the empty bottles and my other rubbish and left them for the dustbin men to collect. Not all the bottles were empty, there was one with a good few slugs of rum still inside it – a work in progress, I might have joked to Rosie if joking had been in order. It wasn't, so I said nothing and just put the bottle discreetly behind the computer. No jokes, no music. I didn't put on any music, as we'd done in the first days of getting the shop ready for business. It would've seemed frivolous, too sudden a return to normality, a premature assumption that I was forgiven and all might be well. No, far too soon. Right now, I was well and truly in the doghouse.

So we toiled in a formidable silence. I thought, more than once, as she moved things and swept out the darkest corners of the room, that when she glanced at me she was about to ask me to confirm that the crow was gone. She didn't ask. But I guessed that sometimes, when she shifted a box or pushed her brush tentatively behind a pile of old magazines, she was half expecting to flush it horribly into the open. And so I tried a stealthy move to carry the box with the crow outside, while

Rosie's back was turned. I was going to take it around the corner into Shakespeare Street and tip it onto the pavement, where it could either hop into the traffic and get run over or scuttle off into the hedgerow.

But Rose spotted me. She was too much an eagle-eyed supervisor to miss a trick like that.

'No, Oliver, no I told you, it's still raining, they'll just get spoiled.' And forever the goody-two-shoes, she added sanctimoniously, 'Books are precious, you should know that as a librarian and the owner of a bookshop. Even if they're raggedy old paperbacks you don't want, I can always find a home for them at school or in one of the charity shops in town.'

To make sure I didn't try again, she made me put the box down and she lifted another one on top of it. 'You can sort through the old books tomorrow or another day, a nice clean job once we've done all the dirty work.' She must have caught a forlorn look on my face, because she gave a sigh of mock exasperation as if she was dealing with a reluctant teenager, and said, 'Alright then, maybe it's time for a break. Why don't you go upstairs and make us both a cup of tea? Say a proper hello to Chloe, and bring her down with you. It's clean enough now, I didn't want her in here when it was so disgusting with soot and dust.'

'You go up,' I suggested. 'Tell you what, you go up and make tea and I'll run across the road for a bit of cake or something?'

She smiled the softest, sweetest smile. But in her eyes there was a gleam of something, some female intuition. Suspicion.

'No,' she said. 'You make the tea. I'll do a bit more down here.'

'You look good, Rosie,' I said, thinking to distract her, and I moved to take her hands again. 'What did they say at the clinic, about your face?'

'I was going to call into the local surgery,' she answered, 'near Auntie Cissy's house, but we were on the bus into Nottingham one afternoon and I decided on impulse to jump off at the

Queen's Medical Centre. Yes, me and Chloe were on the bus, enjoying the ride upstairs on the top deck, and I suddenly decided to maybe kill two birds with one stone.' She hesitated and smiled enigmatically, as if her turn of phrase might jog a guilty little memory in me. 'And we were lucky, because I had five minutes with the doctor, you know the same one who treated Chloe last year and who treated me. I told him I'd been doing a bit of physio with Auntie Cissy, exercising the muscles and drinking lots of water, and he reckoned I was making a steady recovery.'

'Good,' I said. I tried to peck her on the cheek, but the phrase, the very connotation of the words made me stop in mid-air. 'And what did he say about Chloe? Hey, why don't you tell me when you've made a cup of tea? I'll build up the fire, I'll nip over to Azri's for a couple of croissants and...'

No good. I went upstairs.

Chloe was at the kitchen table. She was colouring a picture of a cat. Not colouring, she was blocking the whole of it in black, pressing so hard that the stick of charcoal she was using kept snapping and splintering and she had to reach for more from the box. She was so intent that she hardly moved, she hardly glanced up at me when I bent to kiss her. When I did so, she writhed away and snapped another stick of charcoal.

'That's pretty,' I said, trying not to sound sarcastic, as I stood away from her and put the kettle on. 'That's pretty, a beautiful pussy cat, all black and... well, all black.'

As if to challenge the very blackness of Chloe's vision, the mouse jumped out of the pocket of my coat and onto the table. I hadn't known it was there, it must have been burrowing asleep in a handful of used tissues. It was a fortuitous moment, or at least I thought it was just then. It scampered across the colouring book, superbly white against the ugliness of the child's cat, and, with a chuckle of pleasure, she snatched it up.

Good timing. The kettle boiled. I quickly made two mugs of tea – opening a tin of condensed milk I found in a cupboard

because all the real milk had gone off while I'd been a vagrant downstairs – and it was easy to usher Chloe out of the kitchen and downstairs. She had Mouse. She obviously loved Mouse more than she loved her Daddy. Holding the creature to her face and cooing at it as though she'd missed it terribly, she pottered down the stairs in front of me and into the hallway.

Into the vestry. Rosie was crouched by the fire. Her face was reddened, from her proximity to the flames which she'd built to such a roaring blaze that the back of the chimney was alive with sparks. Reddened, but her eyes were bright and somehow cold. Cold, despite the heat of the fire.

'Rosie? Are you alright? Here's tea. And here's Chloe. And we found Mouse, he was in my pocket.'

Something had been lost from Rosie. In the few minutes I'd been upstairs. The warmth I'd seen in her, which I'd thought I might rekindle with judicious meekness and many mumbling apologies, was gone. Odd, and disquieting. Just as the thaw had come, and the chill of ice had changed into a swishing of warm rain and blustery wind, Rosie had a breath of frost upon her.

When she spoke, despite the fire, there was a mist of ice on her lips.

'What does it mean, Oliver?' – *fuck you dad. cos it fucking stung me thats why... and the utterly lost ... life and death are equally jests* – 'What does it mean?'

I stared at her, not understanding what she was saying. The child was kneeling beside me, running the mouse through her fingers. The fire was unusually bright. At the very core of it there was a dazzling whiteness, as though it might burn my eyes if I stared too long.

She saw me wincing from the brightness, and when she spoke it was barely a whisper.

'It's the tooth. I put it into the fire. And don't worry your poor foolish head about the stuff you wrote. I've deleted it all. And the tooth, it's all gone.'

*   *   *

I STARED AT her, disbelieving, and not really comprehending the words she'd said. I took three steps across the room to the display table and the desk beside it.

'What are you saying, Rosie? I don't get it.' And I was staring into the empty velvet box and poking through the few bits of broken glass, and then peering among the keys of the keyboard, where the bright white tooth from Chloe's mouth was still lodged between the c and the d and the f and there were other diamond-bright fragments of the shattered windscreen.

'Where is it, Rosie? It was here, I tried to get it out but I couldn't it. It fell into the keyboard and got stuck and...'

'I saw it,' she said. 'I was re-reading what you'd written and deleting it, and I saw the tooth. My fingers are smaller than yours, I got it out easily. And I've thrown it into the fire.'

'The fire? What? The tooth? You mean the boy's tooth?'

I pushed past her. My mind was blank. No anger. Just a blank of not understanding.

In my clumsiness, I knocked over one of the mugs of tea I'd just delivered, and it sizzled onto the heat of the hearth. My legs brushed against Chloe, so she rolled away backwards and the mouse escaped from her fingers. I seized the poker and started jabbing it into the heart of the flames, where the brightness was so intense it flared onto my retina, and I was half protesting and half laughing.

'So why did you do that, Rosie? What were you thinking about? and anyway, what's the point? I can always find it when the fire goes out. It isn't going to burn, you must know that, surely, I mean about teeth and stuff and...'

I stood away from the heat, which she had stoked like a furnace. We were still almost sane. Melodrama and madness, they were still avoidable. I stood away, trembling, holding the poker like a sword, took an enormous breath and fixed a big, clumsy smile on my mouth.

'So why, Rosie? I never said I believed in it, did I? But you must've done, or you wouldn't be making such a theatre of trying to destroy it. Am I right?'

I tried to laugh, but it was a dry, ugly sound.

'Of course it won't burn entirely,' she said, and the smile on her mouth was as fragile as mine. 'The enamel is almost indestructible, of course I know that. But when it's degraded it becomes friable, and so it can be ground into powder, it can be crushed and ground into dust. And that's what we're going to do, me and you and Chloe watching, when the fire goes out.'

I tried another laugh. I was looming over her, holding the poker.

'So what do you think, Rosie? Is it cursed? I thought I was supposed to be the gullible one, but you're making a drama out of destroying a little bit of bone like it's the monkey's paw or something.'

We stared at one another. There was a kind of madness in her eyes, or perhaps it was reflected from mine. But there was love and hope as well, it could go either way. It seemed that our whole life together was in the balance. We were close to madness, we were near the brink, but there was still a chance we could step away from it. We could've have burst out laughing, the two of us, and then hugged and kissed and laughed and wept. I had a flash of a great idea, yes, that in less than a minute we could be upstairs and in bed together and making hot, healing love.

I took another big quivering breath. I fixed my smile ever more firmly. I set down the poker. I put out my hand to touch her face, in a gesture of abject submission and reconciliation.

'I'm so sorry, Rosie,' I was saying. 'I love you and I love you and I love you and I'm so sorry.' And when she lifted her hand to my face, I thought for a miraculous moment she might reciprocate with a tender touch and everything would be alright.

But then...

MOUSE SKITTERED ACROSS the floor.

Chloe jumped up and tried to catch it. The mouse quailed under her outstretched hand. It tried to escape her, by scrambling up the side of a cardboard box and on top of it.

The only sound in the room, apart from the crackle of the cremating fire, was the mouse's claws on the cardboard.

But then there was an answering commotion from inside the box.

Such a violent commotion that the boxes on top of it - the boxes Rosie had put there to thwart my attempts at sidling outside - wobbled and shook.

Something mad and manic was trying to get out.

Chloe reached for the mouse. The boxes toppled onto the floor. The box at the bottom fell open.

Chapter Thirty-Five

AND SO OUR lives were changed. By a mouse. By a crow.

The crow came out of the box like a maddened thing. The doll fell out. It looked like a dead child. It was charred, like the body of a child recovered from a terrible fire.

And the room, which had almost achieved a semblance of normality, with a father and a mother and their child sipping tea by a beautiful fire, was thrown into madness.

The child was chasing the mouse. Rosie sprang to her feet, yelling, 'You bastard, Oliver! You lying lazy bastard!' Mad with anger, mad with me and the bird. And me too, I lost the calmness I'd tried so hard to hold onto, and the three of us were thrown into a sudden chaotic motion.

It was only a minute. But it felt like an hour. Or a lifetime. In less than a minute, the destruction of the lifetime we might have had together.

The crow flapped across the floor and into the air, thrashing its wings so hard that soot billowed and clouded the whole room. Rosie was shouting, I was shouting, Chloe was laughing, utterly blithe, utterly lost in the blurring of joy and tragedy and quite oblivious of the difference.

'Out! Out! Out! I'll bloody kill you!' Rosie was shouting, the words distorted by the panic in her voice and the enfeeblement of her lips.

I had picked up the poker again and I was waving it. I was jabbing it furiously into the fire, I was jabbing for the tooth and then reeling away from the heat and joining Rosie in her pursuit of the crow, in a kind of reaction to my being unmanned and feeling hopelessly, horribly, that my life was

being torn away from me and out of my control and the things I loved were flying away, and I needed to grab something, some weapon, some thing, some manly dangerous thing to wave and threaten and strike with, like a man like a man...

The crow was on the table. As it beat across it, knocking over the lamp with a crash and an explosion of the bulb, it picked up a glitter of glass and tossed it aside, it caught a corner of the velvet box and threw it onto the floor, and then it was on the keyboard again, skittering its claws across the keys this way and that, as though it wanted to add some more of its literary gems to the nonsense it had already written.

Rosie had a book in her hands, the biggest and heaviest she could find – the collected works of Edgar Allan Poe. She raised it and smashed it down.

Where the bird had been. Like a wraith, it was there and then it was gone.

The book crashed onto the keyboard. The bird was already in mid-air, a filthy black shadow. Not real. A piece of imagination, a fragment of nightmare. A figment of bad dreams and horrid ideas fomented in the mind of a frightened and lonely little boy.

The boy? We all stared at him.

Me and Rosie and Chloe, we all saw him and stared at him, because he was standing beside the desk, where the collection of his monstrous, poisonous stories had been hurled at the bird. I could smell him. I could smell the cold stale smell of his breath, the stale smell of his unwashed body and his hair. He stood where he'd been my teasing, mocking muse for all the nights of my nightmares.

His breath was a cloud of ice. The crow reappeared in it. The boy exhaled and conjured the bird from within himself, as though he'd created it with the breath of his inspiration. And the bird was on the keyboard where he had urged me to write, where the bird had written more and more meaningfully than I had ever done.

Mocking. Yes, mocking me and taunting us...

The crow pecked into the cracks in the keyboard. For a moment it stood there, gleaming purple and black in the breath of the boy. It had Chloe's tooth in its beak. It tossed it into the air and caught it again and swallowed it down.

Rosie stepped forward.

'No!' she yelled. 'No! Not that! I don't care what you are or what you do, but not that!'

She'd already lost a part of her Chloe, she would not relinquish anymore. Not even an unwanted tooth. She reached for the bottle of rum I'd put beside the computer. With a steely look of death in her eye, she set herself to swing at the bird and smash it, destroy it, kill it forever.

Chloe was right behind her. She seemed to blur into the body of the boy. Just as he faded and disappeared, just as Chloe assumed the very shape of him and the space in which he'd been standing, Rosie swung the bottle up and over her shoulder.

Bang. It hit Chloe right between the eyes.

Chapter Thirty-Six

SHE DIDN'T CRY out. She didn't fall over. She stood very still for a moment, her eyes wide open and very puzzled. Then she teetered slightly, and before either of us could catch hold of her, she sat down heavily on her bottom.

We were both of us there, kneeling to her. Rosie was mewing over her, with her arms around her body. I bent close and peered at her forehead where a bump was already growing.

'Oh Chloe, I'm so sorry, so sorry my darling, my darling so sorry...' Rosie was cooing into her hair.

She'd put the bottle onto the floor, and I saw it rolling slowly and beautifully in front of the fire, the rum inside it glowing golden in the light of the flames. I was muttering nothings into her ear as well, as she sat there and stared into a space between us, as she blinked and frowned and licked her lips.

And then she did a strange and unexpected thing. She shook her head, like a child awakening from a bewildering dream. She felt into her hair – no, not at the place where the bottle had struck her – she felt at the back of her head, as though it was the wounded place. She stared suddenly up at me, and her eyes were cold. She blinked again, recognising me. She started to get up...

'Chloe? What are you doing?' Rosie was quick to say. 'Just stay still, stay where you are, don't start jumping up and...'

Not quick enough. Chloe was on her feet.

She sprang away from me. With a snarl of contempt, she recoiled and started yanking at her clothes.

In a moment she'd torn off her pullover and was wriggling her t-shirt up and over her head and hurling it aside, and she

was standing in the firelight, naked from the waist up. She clawed at her body, nubbing her little tits and scoring welts on her belly with long raking strokes of her nails. And she hissed at me, the first words she'd uttered for nine months.

'*Cos it fucking stung me, that's why! And fuck you Dad! Keep your hands out of my pants. I'll tell Mum, I'll tell her...*'

CHLOE WAS BACK. I thought she was coming for me, like a wild cat. No, she went for the bird.

It had flopped onto the floor as Rosie raised the bottle above it. It must have skulked into a corner as we were tending to the girl. Now it rose from the shadows of the floor, blacker and sootier than ever before, bigger and more threatening, as though it had gathered strength from the compliant limbs of the doll. It writhed up and out of the darkness and into the light of the grey wet morning as though it had a purpose. It confronted Chloe.

She sprang at it, reaching for it with both her hands and uttering a half-hissing half-screeching guttural cry, as though she knew it had her tooth in its craw and was working it into the toxic juice of its gut.

The crow – it avoided her with a clumsy feint, it tumbled from the desk where it had gathered itself and spread its wings in a defiant, mock-heraldic pose, and it thrashed past her, and past us, and plunged to the heat of the hearth in a raggedy confusion of feathers. It landed there, sudden and swift as a hawk, and just as terrible. Its claws were onto the mouse, it stamped and stamped and then it stabbed with its beak and tossed the creature into the fire.

The mouse ignited. No smouldering and smoking and blooming into flame. No, the heat was so intense that the mouse simply burst into a stink of fire and was gone, consumed in a second and crinkling into a ribbon of black stuff.

Me and Rosie, appalled, we cringed from the horridness of the spectacle.

Not Chloe. Half-naked, painted by the flames like a storybook savage, she flung herself forward. For her tooth? To avenge the mouse? To exact some retribution from the spirit of the crow?

Before we could intervene, she was so close to the fire that I could smell the heat of it on her skin, and she was grasping for the bird, her little hands and chubby childish fingers closing again and again on thin air as it fluttered and flapped in the smoke which puthered from the cremation of the mouse. And then, perversely, because I knew with a horrible certainty that if Chloe had closed on the bird she would have torn it into pieces and fed it into the fire, it poised for a daring moment in front of the flames and deliberately thrust itself in.

Even Chloe stood back. The brightness and the heat, too intense. The bird dived into the fire and was a living, burning part of it.

The fumes, the stench of it; a crow on fire.

Its blackness was a coat of gold. It was some kind of medieval monstrosity, a folk-memory of witches burning, of martyrs burning, a memory of images blazed onto our brains by legend and lore and the reality of human atrocity. When at last it recoiled from the flames, or rather the flames spat it out and onto the hearth, it was still alive, a creature born of the fire. And in its beak it had the tooth.

It had plucked it out. For the tooth of the boy, it had endured immolation.

We all three stared at it, as it beat and shuddered and rowed on the flagstones in front of us. Chloe was reaching for it, she too was reborn and shuddering with a new life, the invigoration of her awakening.

'No, Chloe!' I heard myself shouting, and I was holding her back with one hand while instinctively reaching for something, anything, with which I could quench the burning bird. Fool, utterly foolish and without a glimmer of sense in my brain, I grabbed for the bottle of rum and twisted it open and splashed the precious, golden liquid all over it. It exploded into a billow

of blue and green and orange flames, the most repulsive dish a gourmet had ever created, with such an acrid pungency that it sent us all sputtering and choking backwards.

But it had the tooth. And when the alcohol was consumed, and the crow – like a changeling from an arcane book of fantasy – was no longer a nightmarish vision of smoke and fire but a raggedy bird again, it held the tooth tightly in the tip of its beak and sprang away. Towards the door of the vestry.

Chloe sprang after it.

Was it Chloe? Or the boy?

They were one, at least in my eyes, in my tortured imagination. I could see both of them blurred into one, as she or he or the two of them went after the bird. They were a folding of blonde hair and limber young limbs, a boy and a girl from two hundred years apart fused into one.

And with a single purpose, to get the crow. For the girl, it had her tooth, it had a piece of her deep in the coils of its gut. For the boy too, it had his tooth, a piece of him.

By now, all but consumed by the fire, the bird was an appalling, smouldering thing. Could anything be more black than a burnt crow? A crow, black in itself and to the depth of its ravening soul, from the tips of its claws and satanic feathers to the tip of its beak – and now, blackened by burning – was there anything blacker?

It couldn't fly, its wings were all but destroyed by the fire. A pall of stinking blue smoke arose from it. Alive, infused by a seemingly unquenchable life, it avoided Chloe's attempts to catch it. She, part girl and part phantasmal boy, chased it across the vestry and into the hallway.

Rosie and I? We stumbled behind them in a strange somnambulant slow-motion.

As we lumbered to our feet, from where we'd been crouched and cowed by the fire, it was a chaos of jumbled sensations, a dissolution of our senses. Belief, disbelief, what did it matter?

Believing or disbelieving what we saw or felt or smelled or tasted in the whirling, fumey, sooty air, what difference did it make? It didn't hinge on belief. It was all unhinged. Belief? the very word implied a process of thought and a rational conclusion. Didn't it? Now it was smoke, it was a stink of burning feathers, it was our child, half-naked and filthy and yelling fuck this and fuck that and blurring with the sweat and breath of a boy whose tooth had come to me, into my life, coincidental with the damage and death I'd caused.

Rosie was blurred by the dream too. My real-life Rosie, pragmatic and practical and untroubled by nonsense – she was consumed by the nightmare, I could see it in her eyes and the curl of her lip and the flaring of her nostrils. She'd seen the boy, she was seeing him still, she'd signalled her belief in him the split-second she'd thrown his tooth into the fire. There was no turning back from that, no room for doubt. The two of us, we blundered behind the girl, the boy, we were in their thrall.

And in our dream, we were on the roof of the tower.

How did we get there? How, in dreams, do you shift from moment to moment and place to place and world to world?

Somehow, in pursuit of the crow – such a horrid apparition that only Poe himself could have imagined it – we were up and up the stairs and through the kitchen and the bedrooms, never mind the silvery ladder and the clock tower and the trapdoors... all of those real places were subsumed by the unreality of dream. We were on the roof, where a lowering mist of thaw and drizzle fell around us like a cloak.

Nothing but mist. No town, no park, no clouds of steam on the horizon. No horizon.

The charred remains of the crow summoned one last reserve of strength. A prehistoric half-bird, half-reptile, using its beak and claws and the exposed bone of its wings, it grappled itself up the stone face of the battlements and perched on top.

Chloe stretched up to it, and her pudgy little body was disconcertingly taut for a second or two. She or he, Chloe or

the boy, gleamed in the sheeting rain, wet hair darkened from blonde to gold.

The crow juggled the tooth of the boy, tried to swallow but couldn't. It rowed its pathetic stumps so furiously that it rose from the battlements and into the mist.

Chloe clambered after it. She slipped, she grazed her belly on the stone, but still she climbed, pulling herself up with sinewy, long fingers, with a boy's strength, with the lithe, lean muscle of a boy. She was there, high on the brink, when the bird fell back. And with a strange crowing of triumph that she might seize the bird and tear it apart for the relics it withheld, she lunged for it.

It fell away. In a swoon of weariness, an acceptance of death, the crow slipped off the edge of the tower.

Chloe too. She stretched so far into the mist that her fingertips were lost in it. She lost her grip on the stone and toppled forward. She seemed to swim into space, into a netherworld of cloud and rain and nothingness.

She fell away, gleaming, slippery, so that, when I shook off the thrall of nightmare which had been so suffocating, when I hurled myself up and out and caught her wrist, I felt it slithering through my grasp.

She was dangling somewhere below me. I had her fingers, but she was invisible. The dead-weight of a little girl, the wiry, prehensile strength of a boy.

I saw the crow falling and falling, no more than a smudge of black in the grey cloud. And then it was gone.

I pulled with all my weight and strength. The mist parted. Chloe reappeared.

Epilogue

BELIEF IS ONE thing. Disbelief is another. When the whiff of suspicion hangs about you, you protest too much and it starts to stink.

It happened before, when I was finding out I couldn't teach. Something happened; it was my word against another's, and they believed a snotty little eight-year-old girl, not me. Actually, nothing happened, but when she sniffed and snivelled and whispered her dirty story, they believed her. Not me.

Rosie believed Chloe. And so they went away again. Ironic, I might say, after nine months of grieving and praying and beseeching her beloved Chloe to come back from wherever she'd been despatched by the bang on her head... within an hour of her return to normality, Rosie had spirited my beloved daughter away again.

Normality? Chloe woke up and yes she was normal again, she was her normal, sneering, foul-mouthed self.

She recounted what had happened. She blurted a torrent of ugly words, as though they'd been pent up for all those months and couldn't wait to come spewing out, as vivid as though it was yesterday, right up to the moment of her sudden loss of consciousness. The library van on a bright April afternoon, Daddy ignoring her, too busy with his silly old books. Her running to the pub for crisps and lemonade... the wasp... Daddy laughing and teasing, spilling the fizzy stuff all over her and trying to tug off her clothes, Daddy's fingers, groping into her pants all hot and sticky and... and Daddy laughing as she ran out of the van and into the road.

No good. The more I protested my innocence – that yes, I was teasing but I never touched Chloe like that, I never oh god I never for the tiniest millisecond touched her like that – the more I could see the doubt in Rosie's eyes. The disbelief. I could hear myself wheedling, feel myself wriggling, and I caught in my own nostrils the first whiff of it, the unmistakable suspicion of my guilt. I protested louder, more forcefully. It started to stink. She believed Chloe, not me.

It's March. Springtime. I'm on the roof of the tower. It's a warm afternoon. I can see far across the fields of the park and there's a haze of green in the blackened winter hedges. There are daffodils, splashes of yellow in the fringes of the woodland.

Away to my left, the town is a shimmer of blues and greens, the houses and workshops and factories where thousands of people are busying their complicated lives. Ahead of me and on the horizon, the cooling towers of the power station are vast and yet strangely elegant, somehow at rest, not a wisp of steam emerging from them. Gulls in an empty sky – silent, soaring, silver and grey in the sunlight.

I peer over the battlements and down to the world below me. The traffic on Derby Road, a few pedestrians, a customer emerging from Azri's dabbing his lips with a paper tissue... My sign is down there, but I know I can leave the shop and come up for some air because there's been no customers all morning, hardly a one for the past days and weeks. Why would there be? I don't have any books which can't be bought in the high street, either in the mainstream outlets or the charity shops. Poe's Tooth? It's just the name of the shop, it doesn't mean anything.

What's become of the tooth?

I lean out and over the battlements and remember how the crow fell into the mist. I see a darker mark on the pavement, not far from the door of the church, and I figure fantastically what it might be – a ghastly vestigial stain where the head of a workman hit, when he'd fallen from high on the scaffolding; the spot where the gentleman organist cracked his skull and

joked about it, scattering his dentures like the confetti of his own long-ago wedding; the place where the crow might have landed, unseen, unnoticed, on a drizzly January morning, and was swept up by a council workman.

The tooth?

Dentem puer. Trodden into a crack in the pavement, just outside my doorway, until a mooching schoolboy or an eagle-eyed investigator like Joe Blakesley prises it out and slips it into his pocket? Pressed into the tread of a tyre, Anthony Heap or his daughter passing the shop and carrying it with them, unseen, unnoticed, until a curious traffic warden or mechanic teases it out and wonders what it is? Or is it lying in the hedgerow, bedding harmlessly into the earth, among the bones of the crow?

A tooth of Edgar Allan Poe. Extraordinary that it's somewhere here, in England, a few yards or miles away. A little, indestructible piece of him.

And it was mine. I believed in it. So did Rosie and Chloe. No one else ever will. How can they? It's just a tooth – no mischief or malice or sinister intent – an anonymous bit of bone. Without belief, it's nothing.

I'm about to go downstairs. Close the shop, have a drink. I watch the traffic for another minute and breathe in the smell of it, the fume of the road and the unmistakable fragrance of spring. From my left, a bus is coming. It's the 7B from the Broadmarsh Centre in the middle of Nottingham, it's come through Beeston and Chilwell and now into Long Eaton and it'll go all the way through Breaston and on to Derby. It goes past the top of Shakespeare Street and I can see the great red slab of its roof beneath me. Next stop Derwent College, just another hundred yards, where I used to get off with Chloe after a day out on the boat and into town.

The bus stops, away to my right. When it pulls away again, it leaves two figures on the pavement.

A woman and a child. They stand for a moment, unsteady after negotiating the steep narrow steps from the top deck.

Rosie leans down and fiddles with Chloe's coat, straightening the collar and doing up the buttons. Chloe, fidgety as ever, squirms away from her. When Rosie reaches out to try and make her stand still a little longer, the girl avoids her outstretched fingers. She moves to one of the great pillars of the entrance to the school and her fingers feel at the smooth stone. She bends into the hedgerow, where the twigs are prickling with green shoots, and she makes to pick something up.

Not for long. Rosie is quick and firm and uncompromising, not at all a soft touch like me. Whatever the little girl has caught up in her inquisitive fingers, Rosie shakes it all out. Jewels of light, they drop back into the hedgerow.

Hand in hand, they walk along the pavement. When they pause and wait for a gap in the traffic so they can cross the road to the church, they both look up.

They see me. I wave at them. I see the gleam of their mouths as they smile up at me. I hear Chloe's voice as she calls out, 'Daddy, Daddy, I'm back!' And then, when Rosie bends close as if to prompt her what to say, Chloe is calling, 'I'm sorry, Daddy, I'm sorry.'